I0663859

Shadow by the Bridge

Suzanne Zewan

NFB
Buffalo, New York

Copyright © 2017 Suzanne Zewan
Printed in the United States of America

Shadow by the Bridge/ Zewan —1st Edition

ISBN: 978-0-9988811-8-8

1. Shadow by the Bridge 2. Mystery 3. Murder 4. True Crime
 5. Based on Real Events 6. Zewan

Cover designed © by Douglas Russo
Author photo by Zoë Thayer

Although based on real events this is a work of fiction. Events
have been changed and altered, characters have been invented.
Any resemblance to actual events or locations, or persons,
living or dead, unless specified, is entirely coincidental.

No part of this book may be reproduced or transmitted in any
form by any means, electronic or mechanical, including photo-
copying, recording, or by any information storage and retrieval
system without permission in writing by the author.

NFB Publishing
<<<>>>
No Frills Buffalo/Amelia Press
119 Dorchester Road
Buffalo, New York 14213

For more information visit

nfbpublishing.com

For my husband, son, family, and friends who have supported me through this journey.

"The oldest and strongest emotion of mankind is fear."
~H. P. Lovecraft

One

Linden, New York—November 12, 1917

I held my fox trap in my hand, remembering when my father told me that man is the only creature who can find amusement in killing. But he wasn't one of those men. He killed only by necessity; he believed that God put plants and animals on this earth so that we could eat and stay warm. Plus, I needed pelts to make my mother a coat for Christmas.

The neigh of a horse in the distance caught my attention. *Who's coming?* I set my trap on a small boulder that was the size of a carriage wheel. Then I peeked through the naked branches, past the decaying cornstalks, and settled my eyes on the road.

The Indian sun hit my cool cheeks as the scent of burning birch swept me into a memory of my father— not long before he died—placing a frayed white log on the fire. I remember watching him as he stood by our fireplace. He took a deep breath, turned to me and said, "I love the scent of burning birch; don't you, Fritz?" I inhaled deeply and nodded before I finally exhaled.

"I do, Dad, I really do."

I stopped my thoughts from wandering as the far-off neigh signaled the approach of Frank Harlow and his horse pulling an empty cart, probably coming from Batavia after selling his goods. When I saw him pass by our house in Linden the day before as he headed to Morgan's General Store with his goods, he told me that I could trap on his farm anytime I wanted to. He hoped that I'd catch the pesky red fox he saw around his chicken coop. I carried on with setting my trap to kill the fox so I could make my mom a coat.

I heard a woman yelling.

Who's coming? I thought. I peered through the trees again and saw a woman lagging behind a man; they were walking down the road next to the cornfield. The man was now yelling back at her. I continued with the more important task—setting my trap in the perfect spot—and then drove the stake into the ground with a rock. The voices were getting closer.

Now that the trap was set, I crouched down behind a piney bush and watched them. They were traipsing through the dry stalks of corn, coming toward me. I crept further, until I was behind the large rock, and kept my eyes on them. The man had tanned skin—maybe he was French or Italian?—and was wearing a colorful plaid cap and a long tan coat that flapped in the wind. He was standing at the edge of the trees and waving the lady into the woods. She was holding up her ankle-length dark blue skirt and took each step with trouble. Her waist-length brown hair blew across her face as she finally made her way through the trees. It was strange to see a lady with her hair down. I thought it was a rule that women had to wear their hair in a pile on their heads, like my mother did.

The two looked too dressed up to be having any business in some trees. I pressed my cheek against the cold rock as I waited, not making a sound. My father taught me a lot of things, and one of them was to mind my own concerns. But Leon Chapman, one of my friends who lived not too far from me, told me that men and women like to neck, undress, and touch each other from time to time. Suddenly, I became interest-ed in the couple's business. I found a way to watch them around the side of the rock.

"In here." The man turned and pushed a sway-ing branch away from his face as he cracked his way through the brush as the lady followed him. He stepped over a mound of dirt that stood in his way. The belt of the man's coat hung close to the ground. If I crawled a few feet, I could have yanked it. He shoved his hand in his coat pocket and pulled something out, but I couldn't tell what it was. The man stood there with his back toward me. I couldn't see his face.

The lady was facing him. She brushed the hair away from her dark eyes, then adjusted her small purple velvet hat that had fallen to one side. Finally, I was able to see her face. I didn't recognize her. She had lovely small features and a warm, soft face. She looked old enough to be my mother, maybe thirty or so. In other ways, though, this woman was very different from my mother. I had noticed recently that my mother's previously chestnut-brown hair was starting to look like pumpkin mold.

"I don't understand what this is all about! And what we're doing out here?" she said with a huff, and then she crossed her arms and coldly stared at him.

"I think you do understand," he replied with a heavy foreign accent. He then hit her across the face. Blood started dripping down her jaw as she started kicking him with her black boot. Then, she broke free from his grip and tripped, snapping branches as she fell to the ground. Her coat was ripped, and the collar of her ivory blouse was sliced and bloody. The lady touched the side of her face and stared at her bloody hand.

"You bastard!" she cried, and then she stood up. She ran toward him. With her bloody fists, she pounded his chest and face. He shoved her back. The dust rose as she stumbled over a pile of dirt onto the dried leaves. Then he slowly bent down and picked up a thick broken branch lying near the dirt pile.

I watched in disbelief; my heart pounded and felt as if it was going to break my chest open and run, pulling my fear-laden body with it. I trembled. I wanted to help her. But the man had to be at least six feet tall and solid as the rock that I was hiding behind.

I shook and stared. The man's back was still to

me. She was lying on the ground face down, shaking as she sobbed. He turned around and glanced over toward Harlow's farm as if he heard a noise. Quickly, I moved back behind the rock and stared at its solid-ness, wishing I could find a crack in the rock to seep into. My fear kept me still as if I was being held with sharp claws. I was left with only a prayer.

"You're nothing but a whore," he yelled.

Again, I peeked around the rock.

She sat up and wiped her watery eyes. "I—I—"

The man stood over her and pounded the branch into her face, again and again. The sound of her moist flesh breaking weakened my bones. He then set the bloody branch down next to the rock and next to me. Pieces of bloody flesh were dangling off the jagged wood. *He killed her! God, no, no, he killed her!* I felt my blood drain from my face.

The branches rustling above seemed louder than ever as a huge gust of wind sent the dead leaves spi-raling around me. My sweat was cold. I could hardly breathe. I heard what sounded like him dragging her across the ground, and wanted to look, but I was fro-zen. If he caught me, I'd be dead too.

Minutes passed. I didn't hear anything but a crow's squawk and the wind whipping its way through the bare branches. I knelt down and stared through the bush. I looked around; I didn't see him, but I wait-ed to be sure. I listened, and listened, still shaking. I crept over to her lifeless body. He had moved her over to what seemed to be a shallow grave. Tears poured out of my eyes, as if I were a girl.

Trembling uncontrollably, I stared at her, watching the blood pour down her neck and onto the leaves and dirt. There was so much blood; blood was everywhere. Her lovely face was a broken crater of flesh, blood, and bone. As I stared, I started to see black and broke into a cold sweat.

I leaned against the cool rock to keep from passing out. My forehead, neck, and back were wet, which sent a chill over my skin and into my bones. I brushed my hand across my sweaty forehead, and then felt my stomach clench. Bile shot up the back of my throat. I heaved what was left in my stomach. The yellowish liquid dripped from my tongue onto the ground. My throat burned as I heaved and heaved. I couldn't look at her again.

A few minutes passed before my light-headedness cleared and my shaky legs were able to move. Finally, I stood, set my hand on the rock for a moment, and gathered my strength. Then I broke through the trees and began to run toward the road. Out of breath, I stopped dead in the middle of the dry and lifeless stalks of corn.

There he was, standing at the edge of the road, staring right at me.

Two

Istared back at him, shaking. He took a couple of steps toward me. Then he began running. *I was about to die.* I ran and I ran, like a wind storm that would carry me into tomorrow. The soles of my boots turned the lifeless cornstalks to dust with each step.

"What did you see?" he yelled in a foreign accent.

I kept running. *You know what I saw!*

"Come here," he shouted.

I looked over my shoulder. He was getting closer to me. Then I saw a small farm house with a barn beyond some scattered trees. Suddenly, I heard dogs barking. I saw two large, black dogs standing on the back porch of the house. I ran through the scattered trees and past a tractor sitting next to the barn. To keep out of sight, I ran up a small hill behind the barn and into another patch of woods. I stumbled over the tree's tangled roots, and then landed on the ground. I crawled over to a small bush at the edge of the woods. The man stopped at the edge of the scattered trees. He peered through the wooded area looking for me.

"What's going on out here?" a man said as he stepped out the back door of the farm house and began to look around.

Staring through the trees, I watched the man who

was chasing me turn around and run toward the road. With my hand pressing against my chest, I tried to stop the pounding of my heart against my lungs as I caught my breath. I wiped my tears and sat there for a few moments in thankful silence. *I was alive.*

"It's just a damn rabbit," the man said gruffly. "Come on inside, you two. I've had enough of this noise." I rolled my gaze through the trees and over the fields, but saw no one. I moved and stood behind a small group of trees wide enough to hide my scrawny body. Then I saw the man running down Ellicott Street Road toward Batavia.

"Thank you, Dad," I whispered, staring up into the blue sky as a bird circled above me. A sense of warmth held me like a set of wings for a moment, and then it drifted away with the cool breeze. I knew my dad was with me. "I'll get the trap back too, don't you worry," I whispered.

I pulled my dad's tarnished, brass pocket watch out of my front pocket, the watch that held the moments of the past between its hands. The past I carried with me, always.

I thought back to the night of my father's funeral, after everyone had left our house; my mother walked into the parlor and sat down next to me on our sofa. She gently grasped my hand and placed my father's pocket watch into my palm and closed it. The watch was warm from her holding it.

"Your father would want you to have this," my mom said to me. Her eyes were swollen with tears.

I nodded with tears pooling.

"Are you sure?" I asked softly.

"Yes, he always carried it with him," she replied as she held my hand. "Did you know there are a couple of reasons why a watch has hands?"

I shook my head. "No."

"It's a magical piece," she said. "It holds the owner's memories." She assembled a partial smile. "So when you find yourself missing him, hold his watch and remember a happier time. And the other reason: this watch can be a way for you to reach for his hand when you need it or just want to hold it."

From that day on, I had carried my dad's pocket watch with me.

My watch read 12:15. As I looked down, I noticed the blood and dirt on the knees of my trousers, the stains which told the tale of my morning. The dirt was nothing new to my mother, not that she appreciated the mud one bit. The blood was going to be a little harder to explain, especially since I wasn't dragging a dead animal behind me. I dropped my watch back into my pocket and rolled around in the moist dirt to make sure all the blood was covered up with mud.

If I didn't leave then, I was going to be really, really late. My mother told me to be back by noon. She hated it when I was late. She liked everything in its proper place, even time.

My trousers now had several layers of mud to hide the truth of my morning. It was the best that I could do, but just to be sure, I dug my hand into the ground and grabbed another fistful of the cold dirt and rubbed it into the blood. The sight of the woman's broken face flashed in my head like a lighting strike as I stared at the knees of my pants. I stood up and left the woods for home.

My mouth watered as the aroma of chicken and gravy welcomed me into my kitchen.

"Ma," I called.

"Where've you been, Fritzelle Reynolds? I've had your dinner ready for almost an hour," she yelled up from the cellar.

The lies swirled inside my mouth. The most believable one tumbled off my tongue. "I got busy looking for places to set my trap." I grabbed a bowl from the cupboard, and I dished a few forkfuls of juicy chicken over three biscuits. Then, I reached for the ladle and poured a heaping amount of gravy over the mound on my plate and sat down at the table. I didn't know which lie was coming next.

I saw something I shouldn't have. And the man knows I saw something I shouldn't have. What if the news spread from town to town that I was the boy in the woods... with him?

"What happened to you?" my mother asked, staring down at me with a basket of folded clothes on her hip. "You look as if you spent the morning in a hog's pen."

I gazed at my plate as I spread the chicken and gravy over the biscuits. I felt the heat from her eyes on my head. I slowly looked up at her. "What're you talking about?" I asked as I continued to move my chicken and gravy around the biscuits with my fork.

She set the basket of clothes on the chair next to me. "Are you all right? You don't seem like yourself." An icy chill landed in my gut. Sweat beaded on my forehead as my mother stood there watching me for what seemed like a million years.

"I'm not feeling so well. I'm going upstairs to lie down." I set my fork next to my plate and pushed my chair out.

My mother's eyes softened. She removed her hand off her hip, gently grabbed me by the arm, and pulled me away from the table. Her eyes widened. "What did you get into?" she asked, wavering between concern and anger. "You're covered in mud!" She looked down at the kitchen floor. "And it's all over the floor!" Her face reddened. "Don't make another move; you'd better undress right here! And take those clothes upstairs and soak them in the tub. I want all the dirt out of them before I wash them."

I nodded, then pulled off my shirt and dropped my trousers on the floor. The sound of dried mud hitting the wooden floor seemed to echo. I stood there in my skivvies, trembling with goose bumps.

"Here, let me help you with them." She wrapped them up as more chunks of dirt fell. She looked down in disgust, shaking her head, and pulled a pillowcase out of her laundry basket to stuff my clothes inside. "Here, put them in here. I'll just rewash it. Put all of these in the tub to soak." She handed me the slipcover.

"All right," I whispered.

Her gaze gently rested on mine. "Let me feel your head." She brushed my hair out of my eyes. "You don't feel warm."

I shrugged.

"What's this on your forehead? Whatever it is, it's in your hair too."

"I don't know." I began to tremble, and it wasn't because I was cold. "I don't know. It could be anything." My voice shriveled like a dried leaf.

"It looks like dried blood," she said, holding my hair off my forehead. "Did you cut yourself?"

I shrugged. "Maybe... I could've." I answered her without looking up; I could feel her eyes crawl up and down my body like a spider.

"Well, I don't see any scratches." She shook her head with her lips pressed together. "Now, what's bothering you? You're not acting like your normal self."

"My stomach hurts. I feel like I'm going to be

sick," I replied in an achy voice, gripping my stomach.

"Well, you do look a bit pale, I suppose." She opened up the bottom cupboard and pulled out one of her tin mixing bowls. "Here: keep this with you in case you can't make it to the bathroom. And don't forget to put your clothes in the tub and fill it."

I ran up the stairs, and set the bowl on my night-stand. Then I headed into the bathroom. The hardwood floor was cool beneath my bare feet. I reached into the clean smelling pillowcase and found my trousers. I pulled my pocket watch out of the pocket and set it on the sink. Then I dumped my clothes and all the dirt into the cast iron tub, and I dropped the pillowcase in with them. I grabbed the long, cold iron handle and began to pump the water from the cistern. For some reason, pumping the water seemed harder than normal. My muscles felt weak and ached with every push of the handle. With the mud covering most of my clothes, no one would be able to tell what the stains really were. I kept pumping as I watched the clothes slowly disappear under the muddy water.

I grabbed my pocket watch off the sink and stared into the mirror. A frightened face stared back at me. I remember Leon calling me "Fearless Fritz" once. That name hardly fit the person in the mirror. I pushed my brown hair out of my eyes. There was dirt on my face, dried blood in my hair, and more blood on my fore-head. I gazed into my dark blue eyes, the eyes that had seen the black hand of evil.

For the first time, I saw how much I resembled my mother. People always said I looked like her. I had her blue eyes and long lashes, but my nose was definitely my father's nose because it sloped up a bit at the end. I touched the scar on my forehead, then tilted my head to see the one under my chin. I had earned both scars within days of each other, the first one from jumping off our barn roof into a small pile of hay and the second one a few days later, after falling out of my Uncle John's red maple tree and hitting my chin on the way down.

I turned back to the tub and pumped more cold water onto my clothes. Once the water was flowing, I switched to pumping with only one hand so that I could splash some fresh water on my face with the other. I needed to rub the dirt and blood off. The blood and dirt were dry and itchy—pulling my skin taut and reminding me of all that I had witnessed. After I was done rinsing my face, the dirt had come out of the trousers and the blood stains were starting to fade but needed to soak more. So I headed to my bedroom and lay down on my bed.

How was I going to get my fox trap back? My father gave it to me for my tenth birthday, three weeks before he died. On our way to check his traps, my father would always say to me, "Ya know, Fritzy, it's important to know how to live off the land." He would run his hands lovingly through my hair as he spoke, going on to tell me about how he could count on a red fox or a rabbit being there the next day same as he could count on the sun coming up.

For the past year, I'd been setting my trap in every patch of woods I could find... but all for nothing.

I wrapped myself in the blue afghan my mother made me two Christmases ago as I tried to forget the morning that could have ended with my murder. So many questions spun inside my mind, turning and turning like a wheel. After hiding behind the rock the whole time, why did he have to see me after it was over? I thought he was gone. What could she have done to deserve such an awful death? Who were they? Where did they come from? And my fox trap. I squeezed my eyes shut and shook at the thought of him finding me.

But being swathed in the blanket calmed me like a warm hug, and I finally drifted off.

It must have been less than a half hour later when I heard my mother's footsteps and the creak of each stair. Moments later, I felt her standing by my bed. She covered my shoulder with the afghan and left my bedroom. I heard the stir of the water.

"What on God's good earth did you get into?" Her agitated voice carried from the bathroom to my room.

But I had learned that not all that happened on God's earth was good.

Three

It was evening after three nights of hardly any sleep, and my mom was busy preparing dinner. I headed into the parlor and lay down on the floor in front of the warm crackling fire. I reached over and pulled the pillow off the sofa and rested my head on it as I listened to the wind howling. The texture of the floral embroidery against my cheek was cool and a little scratchy. My eyelids felt like tiny iron gates struggling to shut. The heat from the fire guided me to the edge of sleep. When I was wrapped up tight in this warmth, I tried to focus less on the sounds of the wind and more on my knowledge that my mother was in the next room. This helped me to finally shut my eyes. Then I prayed to God and my father that *he* wouldn't come looking for me, the boy he chased through the cornstalks. At the end of my prayer, I drifted off.

"I'm about to dish the stew up," my mother called out from the kitchen.

I jumped and opened my eyes, "What?"

"Supper's ready."

"All right." I rubbed my eyes and pushed myself up off the floor, shuffled into the kitchen, and sat down at the table.

"Here you go, honey." She set the bowl in front of

me and sat down. "Were you asleep in there?"

"Yeah, I think so." I yawned.

"I'm sorry. I would've let you sleep if I had known."

"That's all right, I'm really hungry." The taste of my mother's beef stew had been on my mind all day. I put a heaping spoonful into my mouth. Also, I noticed the aroma of apples and cinnamon; I had forgotten that my mother had made an apple pie that morning. I looked over my shoulder and saw it on top of the stove warming up.

As I stared at the pie, there was a quick, loud knock at the side door. I almost jumped out of my seat. My heart was on the run. Then I realized by the sound of the knock that it was Helen Wilson. She lived in the center of Linden, just a few steps up a hill from Morgan's General Store. As soon as she collected her daily gossip at the store and the post office—which happened to be around the corner from our house— she was off spreading the neighbors' business like milkweeds in the wind.

My mother glanced over at the door and back at me. "It's Helen." She adjusted her dark brown skirt and answered the door. My mother was always nice enough to listen to Helen with an open ear, but she didn't repeat it because she was much too respectful of people's privacy.

My mother opened the door. "Hello, Helen. We just sat down for supper; can you stop back in a little while or so for some tea, and we can talk then?"

Helen didn't seem to have heard her. "Hello, Fritz." She waved to me with mail still in her hand. "Ella, can I see you outside for a minute?" She motioned and pushed a long strand of gray hair back into the pile of her hair, which happened to look like a bird's nest sitting on her head.

"Can't this wait?" my mother asked. "We just sat down to eat."

"No, something awful has happened," Helen replied with urgency and gently grasped my mother by the arm and pulled her out the door onto our small porch.

My mother glanced over at me and pointed to my stew. "All right, what happened?" she asked, and then shut the door behind her.

I anxiously rose up from my chair, sat down on the floor below the door's window and listened. I heard Helen say "Frank Harlow," and then she mentioned his field, which sent a frigid chill over my body. I started to tremble, and my heart began to beat within my chest so hard I could hear it. I couldn't make out all of what they were saying because they were talking quietly. After a few minutes of listening to muffled voices, I felt the door move. Swiftly, I sat back down at the table.

"I'll see you tomorrow. Good night now." My mother pushed the door open; her face had lost its rosy color.

My heart pounded. I felt my face flush.

"What happened?" I asked in an unsteady voice. Bloody images flashed in my head. She didn't even notice that my hand was shaking when I picked up my spoon.

"Helen told me that Frank Harlow was out gathering wood and found a dead body near his field." She shook her head in disbelief. "A woman, I guess, and she was in terrible shape." She sat back down at the table.

"He did?" The words barely came out of my mouth. My throat felt so tight.

She didn't answer me. I could tell her thoughts had escaped with her to another place.

"Mom!" I raised my voice.

"I'm sorry, honey—what did you say?"

"Who was it?" My voice quivered.

"Helen didn't know. I don't think they know yet. Helen said the woman's face was badly beaten. She's going to let me know when she finds out more."

I could feel my face turning white. "I'm scared," I whispered. She nodded as if she understood, but I knew that she just didn't know how scared I really was. Nor did she know who I was so afraid of.

Quickly, my mother knelt down next to me and held me tightly. "Listen honey, Frank's farm is almost two miles from here. And I'm sure whoever killed that poor woman is far, far away from here. He wouldn't stay around here. Someone had to have seen him in that area."

I nodded. *Someone did see him.*

She continued to hold me. "Just to feel safer, we'll keep all the doors and windows locked, all right?" I nodded into her soft shoulder. "I'd never let anything happen to you. You know that, don't you?"

I nodded. "I'd never let anything happen to you either," I whispered.

My mother smiled softly and kissed my forehead. "I know." She hugged me again for a moment and pulled away. "We're safe here and we have a lot of good neighbors nearby. Now let's finish up and we'll have some pie." She pointed to my bowl again and grabbed her own bowl off the table. Her stew was only half-eaten, but she placed it in the sink anyway.

After I finished my stew, she cut the pie and handed me a slice. Pieces of apple were oozing out from each side. She looked closely at my face.

"You look really tired," she said. "I think we'll skip your arithmetic lesson tonight and just read for a little while." Since my mother was a school teacher before she married my father, Miss Murphy gave her permission to teach me my lessons at home so that I had more time to learn how to run the family farm. Even with all my farming responsibilities, Mom cared too much about education to give me the night off. She was right. I was really tired—too tired to think about numbers.

"I want you to go to bed a little earlier tonight, too. You have dark circles under your eyes... probably from being sick. And tomorrow, you're supposed to start working with Uncle John, remember?"

I nodded. "Yeah," I replied.

"But I'm not so sure I want you to start tomorrow; you still look a bit run down," she said. "We'll see how you are in the morning."

After I ate my pie, I helped my mother lock the doors and all the windows. Mom lit the kerosene lamp in the parlor, and then added two more birch logs to the fire. We opened our books and began reading. I glanced up from the pages of *The Scarecrow of Oz* and noticed the book my mother was reading: *A Cry for Justice* by Upton Sinclair, her favorite author.

The bright sun sliced through my drapes, and I heard my Uncle John's voice downstairs. I climbed out of bed feeling rested and ready for my first day on the farm.

"Fritz," my mother called up the stairs.

"I'll be down in a few minutes." The smell of sausage and fresh baked bread made its way to my room.

Quickly, I splashed my face with cold water, changed, and headed downstairs.

"Hey, Fritzy." Uncle John patted my back as I sat

down at the table and drank my milk. He brought fresh milk over every morning.

He always reminded me of a big friendly bear, because of the way his beard covered most of his face. My mother told me that he's a lot like my grandfather, who was also a big, strong man.

"Morning, Uncle John," I said. Then I began cutting into my sausage patty.

"Well, you slept late! It's almost nine," my mother said as she pumped water from the cistern into the sink.

"You should have woken me up earlier."

"No, I let you sleep in a little longer. You needed it."

"Fritz, there's been a change in plans this morning," Uncle John said. "Your mother and I have to go into Batavia for a little while before you and I head back to the farm. I stopped in to see Martha on the way over here, and she told me that the sheriff came by the store last night. He told her that the district attorney is having the woman's body shown at Turner's Funeral Parlor today. They want to see if anyone recognizes the woman they found in Frank Harlow's field, and this morning is the best time for your mother and me to go."

I froze for a moment. "What?" I asked. "They still don't know who she is?"

John shook his head. "No, they don't. She wasn't

carrying any papers with her name." He bit into his sausage. "I guess the district attorney thinks that someone around here may have known her."

I shook my head in disbelief. "But her face," I said under my breath.

"What did you say, honey? Please speak up so I can hear you."

"Didn't Helen tell you that she was in really terrible shape?"

My uncle gave my mother a quick look as he took a sip of his coffee.

"Honey, I'm sure the morticians cleaned her up and made her presentable for the public to view." She pulled the towel off the cupboard handle. "They wouldn't be asking otherwise."

I stared down at my plate, and suddenly I was back in Harlow's woods staring at the lady's bashed-in face. Feeling sick to my stomach, I sat there in silence for a minute.

"Honey, are you all right?"

I turned to her. "Yeah, I'm all right." I nodded my head. "I'm just not awake yet."

"You're starting to worry me. Are you *sure* you're all right? You look a little pale."

I rubbed my face. "Yeah, I'm okay."

"Let me feel your head." She reached her hand over and placed it on my forehead. "Well, you don't feel warm."

"No, really, I'm okay, Mom," I said eagerly.

My mother looked over at Uncle John, and then back at me. "A lot of people get off the train here. And I might have seen her at the store."

"Maybe you did," I said, shrugging my shoulders.

"If it were me lying there, I'd hope that there would be good people who would take their time to help me reach my final resting place and take me back home to my family." She wiped the frying pan with her dish towel and placed the pan in the bottom cupboard.

I turned to her. "But you can't stand to see a dead animal. You wouldn't even go into the barn last year to see the deer Dad killed. So I just thought—"

"Fritzy, your mother will be fine. They'll clean her up, as they do with all bodies." John patted me on the shoulder.

"By the way, I ran into Junior on the way over here this morning." Junior was Senior Kessler's twenty-eight-year-old son from his first marriage. His first wife died. Senior and his second wife, Mertie, lived down the road from us. Senior and Mertie had a daughter, Valerie, who was my age and also happened to be very pretty. "He told me that he is working over at Flo's this week, and he could use your help with the hay this morning. Walter is working another farm and he's a little shorthanded."

"Walter is working another farm during apple

season?" I asked. Walter, Florence's brother, worked a lot of other farms. I never understood why he didn't just stay and help his sister with her farm. She had to hire Junior to do her brother's work, and Junior would come and find me to help.

"I guess so, which leaves Florence shorthanded this week, so I thought of you. I knew you'd be available now that we're heading in for the viewing. So as soon as you're finished with breakfast you can head over there until we're back," Uncle John said.

"Are you feeling well enough to help Florence out for a couple of hours?" my mother asked.

"Yeah, I told you that I feel fine, so please quit asking," I replied in a tightened voice.

My mother shook her head.

Uncle John stood up from the table and set his plate and cup in the sink.

"I'll go," I said, and handed my plate and glass to Mom. With my heart starting to race, I anxiously threw on my muddy boots and yanked my jacket off the hook by the door. My mother leaned in and gave me a kiss on the cheek. Then she handed me the key to the door.

"Fritzy," my mother said in a caring voice.

I turned back and saw concern etched in her face. "What?"

"I'm starting to worry about you. You don't seem like you're back to yourself just yet. Don't overwork yourself this morning." She glanced over at Uncle John. "If you're too tired later, you can rest and start on the farm tomorrow, or next week."

I clutched the doorknob and opened the door. The cool air rushed past me into the kitchen. I looked over at my mother as I grabbed my tweed cap off the hook and placed it on my head. "Mom, quit worrying about me... *please!*"

"That's what mothers do; they worry about their children." She tilted her head slightly to the left. Her gaze filled with question. "Also, I know my son."

Her words cracked the wall I was hiding behind. "Just stop at Flo's on the way back," I said, ignoring her prying words. I walked out the door and ambled down to the end of the driveway.

I knew my mother, too. If I told her that I saw what happened in Harlow's woods, she'd want to do one more right thing and take me to see the sheriff so I could tell him everything. Then everyone would know Fritzelle Reynolds was there in the woods and saw the lady get bumped off. My guess was that the man read the newspaper every day, trying to find out who that boy was—the one who could tell his secret.

The sound of a train whistle startled me. I watched each car pass, counting the cars, waiting for the red caboose.

After a couple of minutes, the train passed, and its rumble disappeared into the distance. Once again, the hamlet returned to its peaceful state. I took a deep breath and grasped my pocket watch that was, as always, in my front pocket. I stared at the bridge and listened to the water flowing beneath it.

Suddenly, I remembered my father carrying me down our driveway and over to the bridge with my mom by our side. He pointed to the sky, telling me with excitement in his voice to look up. We watched brilliant flashes of yellow, red, and green lights shoot to the top of the sky. It looked as if there was a glowing green curtain dancing across the night sky. Mom explained that they were Northern Lights from the sun reflecting off the ice at the North Pole.

I pulled my hand out of my front pocket, still holding my pocket watch. As I headed toward Florence Kingsley's farm, my body tingled with warmth. I stared off into the blue skies, knowing my father was looking back at me.

Four

After talking to Junior about the viewing, I no longer thought locked doors and windows were enough to protect me and my mother. If *he* really wanted to break in, *he* knew how to use a tree branch really well. And there were plenty of them to pick from around our house.

It had been about an hour since they left for Batavia, so I figured I had a little time to find extra protection before they returned home. As I ran home from Flo's, I pulled my key out of my pocket. I looked through the kitchen window and didn't see my mother. Nervously fumbling with the key and almost dropping it, I placed it into the keyhole and opened the door.

"Mom," I hollered into the house as I stepped into the kitchen. There was no answer. *Good!* I locked the door behind me. Then I dropped the key back into my pocket. I grabbed my watch, which read 12:05.

It didn't look like she'd been home yet, so I ran down into the basement and grabbed my father's shotgun off the far wall, loaded it, and ran up to my bedroom. I held the gun for a minute, staring at it.

I never held a loaded gun with the thought that I might have to use it on a person. What if I had to shoot him on the way up to my bedroom? What would my father say? He only used guns for hunting animals. He would never shoot at another man. Killing was a sin, the worst kind of sin. The words "Thou shall not kill" were in the Bible.

But would my father kill to protect us? I heard the answer in my head: *"Of course he would."* I shoved the gun under my bed and opened my bottom drawer, pulled out a dark wool blanket, and draped it over the gun so my mother wouldn't see it if she meddled around in my room to clean. But I still had to watch her closely; she was always cleaning something.

There was a noise downstairs. I heard the door shut in the kitchen.

"Fritzy," my mother called out.

I stood at the top of the stairs and didn't answer. I wanted to hear what they were going to say about the viewing.

"I guess he's not here yet. Maybe he headed over to the store," my mother said.

"Junior said that he had left about fifteen minutes ago. So I'm sure he'll be back shortly," Uncle John said.

"It is dinner time, so he'll be hungry when he finally comes home," my mother said.

I sat down on the top step and listened. Then I crept down three more steps. My eyes rolled over the trail of mud, down the stairs through the parlor, and into the kitchen. The dirt trail meant that a load of trouble and I would be spending some time together this afternoon.

"I'll warm up the stew I made last night. Do you want some coffee?" my mother asked as one of them moved a chair over the wooden floor.

"Yeah, I'll have a cup."

I heard another chair move.

"Ella, you didn't say much on the ride back in. Are you all right?" Uncle John asked.

"I'm just really shaken up, that's all... It was hard being back in a funeral parlor. And I never expected the woman to be in that kind of shape. I mean her face... it was just the most disturbing sight. I'm still shaking," my mother answered in a quiet voice.

"It was an awful sight," Uncle John said, and then he coughed to clear his throat.

"Fritzy was right. He knows I don't like the sight of blood," my mother admitted. "I almost fainted."

I shook my head. *She should have listened to me.*

"How could someone... I can't even imagine the suffering she must have endured." My mother's voice faded.

"She didn't suffer, Ella. By the shape she was in, it was a quick death," Uncle John assured her.

I nodded. *It was a quick death.*

"The funeral director said that she was in her late twenties or early thirties... my age," my mother said in a concerned tone. "It's so upsetting; she may have young children waiting for her to come home."

"She could, but we may never know," Uncle John said.

"I'm not sure showing her is going to help anyone identify her," my mother said. "Her face isn't recognizable."

"Someone might be familiar with her clothing. That's probably why they set her handbag on the back of the casket too. They're showing all that they have to show."

"That has to be it. And there were so many people. The news must have been in all the papers throughout western New York," my mother said.

"I heard a few people say that they traveled over an hour or more," Uncle John said.

"I just feel so awful for her family. It is such a tragedy."

"They have no idea who she is yet?" I whispered to myself as I crept down another step.

"Well, Fritzy should be home in a little while. I wanted him to start today, but he can always start tomorrow."

"I think I'd rather have him start tomorrow. He could use the rest. I'm not sure what it is, but he hasn't been himself the past few days. I know he wasn't feeling well, but it's not like him to be so quiet and distant."

"Maybe something has him rattled."

"You're probably right. He was really scared the night Helen came over and told us about that poor woman."

"That could be it," Uncle John said. "Listen, I really should be heading back to the farm. Are you going to be all right here alone?"

"I'll be fine; I'll lock the door when you leave."

I heard a kitchen chair move again.

"By the mud all over the floor, it looks like Fritzy must have stopped home and traipsed through the house with his muddy boots again. I've told him hundreds of times to take off his boots at the door. He doesn't listen very well. He only takes them off when I am in the kitchen watching him." My mother sounded deflated. "He's just like his father." She began to weep a little.

There was silence.

"Ella," my uncle said in a feathery voice.

"All the mud… it's all through the house," my mother sniveled. "Peter used to do the same thing. He would forget to take his boots off no matter how many times I reminded him," she said. "And I miss his muddy boots."

"I know, we all miss him." My uncle's quiet words held me still. "But it does get easier over time."

"It's hard to believe that it'll already be a year in December that he's been gone," my mother said softly.

"It's already been fourteen years since Ruthy died. You have to believe me; it becomes easier as the years pass."

"I have my moments here and there. But today was the first time I've been in a funeral parlor since last December. Being there brought all those feelings back, as if it was Peter lying there."

"That's understandable," Uncle John said. "It hasn't even been a year yet. It takes time."

I didn't hear them talking. All was quiet.

"I know one thing; Fritz will bring in enough mud for the both of them. You don't have to worry about that at all," he said. Then he chuckled softly.

My mother laughed and cried at the same time, and then blew her nose.

"Are you going to be okay?" Uncle John asked. "I can make a call and stay for a while."

"No, I don't need you to do that. I'll be fine. It is the oddest things, things like mud on the floor—of all things, mud." My mother chuckled. "I should be crying because now I have to clean up all this mess, not because I miss it."

"It hasn't been an easy day," Uncle John said, "for either of us."

"No it hasn't," my mother agreed.

"Okay, I better be on my way... only if you're all right with me leaving, though."

"Yes, yes, now go on. I need to make Fritz his dinner. Don't you want to eat before you go?"

"No, I don't feel much like eating," my uncle replied.

"I know, neither do I. But I'm sure Fritzy will be
hungry when he finally decides to come home."

I heard the door open.

"All right then, ring me if you need to."

"I will," my mother replied in a calmer voice, no
longer weeping.

"I'll see you in the morning. Maybe Fritzy will be
up to helping then. And I'll check with Florence on my
way out to see if she needs him tomorrow morning. I'd
rather he helped her out first."

"All right, I'll see you tomorrow. Bye now."

The door shut.

I didn't want my mother to know I was listening.
She always said that it's not polite to eavesdrop. So I
crept over to my bedroom window, opened it an inch at
a time, and stepped out onto the roof. The only window in my room was perfectly placed for sneaking out.
I crawled across the roof and prayed my mother didn't
hear me as I grabbed the thick tree branch hanging
over our second-floor rooftop. I climbed to the center of
the maple tree.

"Hey, Fritzy!" A voice called out from below. "Why
the hell're you climbing out your window in the middle of the day?"

It was Leon Chapman. "Would you hush?" I gestured with my hand and whispered loud enough for him to hear me. "I don't want my mother to know I'm up here!"

He stood there with his hands in his front pockets, chuckling because he knew I was up to no good.

Leon had just turned sixteen last year, before my father died. It was then that he started to act like a big brother to me. He brought me hunting a few times. He also taught me how to hop a moving train at Belknap Crossings. Helen Wilson found out and rushed right over to my house to report the latest Linden news to my mother; my mother was not pleased. She told me if I ever did it again, I would be punished like I've never been—whatever that meant. But I was in no hurry to find out.

From the treetop, I could scan all of the thirty-five houses in Linden.

"Would you scram before my mother sees you talking to this tree?"

"What's wrong with talking to a tree?" Leon laughed.

"Real funny, Leon. Now scram before my mother looks out the window!" I said as loudly as a whisper could be.

"No, I want to know why you're sneaking out your window."

"Get away from the damn tree before my mother sees you!" I pointed toward the post office as I began to climb down, branch by branch. Small dead sticks broke and fell to the ground.

Then I jumped out of the tree and looked around. No one saw me. I met Leon, who was waiting for me in front of the post office.

"So you're sneaking out of your window in the middle of the day... Why?" Leon asked as he lifted up his cap. Then he itched his reddish-brown, wavy hair.

"I was listening to my mother and Uncle John talk about the viewing of that lady that Frank Harlow found on his farm. The viewing was this morning. And I didn't want them to know I was home."

"Oh yeah, I heard about that. Did they figure out who she was?"

"From what it sounded like, I don't think so."

"What a horrible way to go... I mean, her face." Leon shook his head and looked down at the dirt road.

I glanced over my shoulder at the post office. "So where you headed to?"

"The post office. My father's waiting for a letter from the bank," he replied. "So you been doing any hunting since I saw ya last?"

"Just a little trapping, but ain't got nothing yet."

"I was looking for you the other day to shoot some turkeys. There were about eight turkeys in our back field on Monday." He nodded his head and made a tisk sound out of the side of his mouth. "You missed out."

Maybe I did miss out. But I wasn't going to let

him know that. Leon always enjoyed razzing me whenever he could. "I've been trying to trap some foxes, but I ain't had much luck. I was hoping to have enough pelts to make a coat for my mother for Christmas."

"Do you know how many that would take?" Leon let out a laugh.

I shrugged my shoulder. "Well, no... not really."

"I'd say you'd need at least fifty or more to make a coat, a small coat."

"That many?" My eyes widened. "Well, I guess she won't be getting a fox coat this Christmas," I said, disappointed.

"Looks that way." Leon shrugged his shoulders. "Well, my father's probably wondering where I am." He started to walk toward the post office steps. "I'll come find you when I see the turkeys again. Or a fox... if I can trap a few foxes, I'll give them to you for your mother's coat."

I nodded. Then I flashed him a quick smile. "That would be swell, Leon. Thanks. Come and get me if you see 'em." I turned around, and I headed back toward my house. As I stepped onto our side porch, I grabbed the cold, tarnished door knob, and jiggled it. It was locked. I reached in my pocket to grab my key and saw Mom rushing toward the door with a dirty towel in her hand. I knew a load of trouble was waiting for me in the kitchen.

Five

Three more days had passed, and no one knew any more about the lady who lay dead in the casket at H.E. Turner's Parlor.

"Fritzy," my mother called out.

"I'm in the barn," I yelled back.

Moments later, my mother was standing in the barn doorway, holding her purse and watching me climb up the bales of hay. "I thought I saw you run in here. Did you just get back from Florence's?"

"Yeah," I replied as my eyes swept every nook of the barn.

"What are you doing up there?"

"I saw a tomcat run in here, one that I haven't seen around our yard before. He jumped onto the hay and then disappeared," I replied as I searched between the hay bales.

"I've seen a couple strays running around here too. Leave them alone." She gestured with her hand. "They're good for catching the mice." She stepped inside the barn and looked around.

"We don't need more of them. If they start having kittens we'll have a whole mess of them running around."

"What're you planning to do with it when you

45

finally catch it?" she asked.

"I'll take it over to Chapman's. Heck, they won't even notice," I replied.

"Did Florence say when her brother would be back?"

"No," I replied as I listened for the cat.

"Did you ask?" my mother asked in a slightly lower voice.

"Didn't think of it."

"Well, try and find out tomorrow so I can let Uncle John know, all right?"

"Yeah, I will."

"So, what did you and Junior help Florence with today?"

"We worked in the orchard, cutting dead tree branches," I replied as I climbed onto another bale of hay.

"Frankly, I don't know how Florence runs that farm by herself."

"Well, she *does* have help."

"I know, but she's old enough to be my grand-mother, maybe even my great-grandmother."

"Yeah, I guess." I shrugged my shoulders as I pushed one of the bales over toward the wall so I could see between the two stacks of hay.

My mother casually walked over to the bundles of straw and looked up at me. "All right, since you haven't found the cat, do you want to come with me to

Morgan's?" Mom asked. "I need to pick up my grocery order. Martha said that her coffee order would be in on the noon train and your Uncle John is coming for supper. You know he likes his coffee after a meal."

"I guess I'll go." I began to climb down. "I want some candy," I mumbled. I liked to visit Grandma Harrison. Martha and Gerry Morgan had two sons: Harrison, who was given Martha's maiden name, and Cliff, who seemed to inherit Martha's musical talent. Grandma Harrison told everyone to call her Grandma, so that's what we did.

Since I could remember, Grandma spent her days sitting in her rocking chair by the window with her apron pockets stuffed full of candy that she'd hand out to all the children.

Cliff and Harrison were grown. Harrison was in his twenties. He moved to Buffalo at the end of last summer for work. Cliff was a few years older than me, and he spent most of his time on his studies and piano lessons. Cliff told me that after he graduated, he was going to the Eastman School of Music in Rochester. I told him that he sure had some big plans for himself.

My mother and I left the barn and headed down Linden Road. As we crossed over the railroad tracks, my mother glanced up at the cloudy sky. "It's starting to rain." A cool raindrop hit my bottom lip, and another hit below my eye. "I was hoping the rain would hold off until we made it back home," my mother said quietly.

"I felt a couple drops, too."

"If it rains any harder, maybe Merle can drive us home."

The question waiting to slide through my lips made my heart pound a little harder. "So, did you find out any more about the lady who was found on Harlow's Farm?" I asked as we walked up the steps onto Morgan's long wooden porch.

"No, but Martha or Helen may know something," my mother replied, holding the door open for me.

"Hello, Fritzy," Martha said. Her cheery smile spread across her round face. "How're you today?"

"I'm swell, thanks." I nodded, smiling back at her as I removed my cap. Grandma Harrison wasn't sitting in her rocking chair. "Is Grandma here?"

"She's upstairs lying down. She has a headache," Martha replied as she began to unpack one of the many crates piled next to the counter.

Martha Morgan was plump as warm dough and stood about three fingers taller than me. She also wore dark colored dresses every day. Either that was the only one that she had, or she had a closet full of identical ones. And she always wore her hair short, which was different than most women, who wore their long hair wrapped on top of their heads like a nest.

I reached over, and I set my cap on the side counter that was lined with seven stools. The store was where the neighbors from the area gathered after supper to listen to radio shows. Once in a while, my father would go to the store to listen to the shows too. Then he'd head over to the Mill to play cards and drink cider with Senior and Anton Mitchell. My mother became angry at him if he had too much cider.

I once asked my mother why she never became angry at me for drinking cider. She said that was because the cider I drank was fresh and that the cider my father drank turned men into drunkards.

"Fritzy." Martha pointed to the small glass bowl next to the register. "Grandma left some butterscotch candy: take some," she said before turning to my mother. "Ella, how're you doing today?"

"I'm well, thank you. How're you?"

I grabbed a piece of candy, and I popped it into my mouth. "Thank you," I said as I swirled the hard candy around with my tongue. I sat down on a stool, reached across the counter for my cap, and set it in front of me.

"I'm doing well," Martha replied to my mother with a smile as she pushed the bowl of candy toward me.

"Where's Merle today?" my mother asked, sitting down on the stool next to me.

Merle Smithers was a friend of mine. He started working for Martha over the summer, after he turned fifteen. More than half the men in Linden worked on farms, but Merle never wanted to do that type of work. He hung around the store almost every day last summer. He helped Martha unload the crates as she filled the orders. She finally decided to hire him as a clerk.

"He has the day off today. He left with his parents to visit his cousins."

"Now that you have Merle working almost every day, have you thought of working fewer hours?" my mother asked.

"After the first of the year, I was going to start cutting back an hour or two in the afternoon after the 3:00 train rush," Martha replied. "Merle can handle the store after 4:30."

"What about Gerry? Is he ready to slow down any?" my mother asked.

"Not yet. I don't know what he'd do with himself at home all day," Martha replied.

I heard the back door swing open as I continued to tumble the small piece of creamy, vanilla butterscotch candy around my mouth.

A tall, thin figure leisurely walked toward us from the back of the dark store. "Hello ladies! And Fritzy," Helen smiled as she strolled up to us. She stopped in the counter walkway.

My mother turned her stool toward Helen.

I looked over my shoulder and smiled. "Hallo," I said and waved.

"Hello, Helen, how're you?" my mother asked.

"I'm well, thank you. I just came back from visiting with Gracie Harlow," she said.

I bumped my mother's shoe with my boot and glanced over at her. Her eyes met mine for a moment, and she gave me a slight nod. Just then, the copper kettle whistled on the back stove.

"Would any of you like some tea?" Martha made her way past Helen toward the stove.

"I would," Helen turned and answered as she removed her long gray coat and set it over the counter.

"No thank you, Martha," my mother answered.

Helen grabbed a teacup off the back shelf, the one with fancy flowers painted on it that she always drank out of. I watched her grab the tin can sitting next to the row of tea cups. She popped open the can, pulled out a tea bag, and then set it into the cup.

"I have your coffee right here, Ella." Martha held up the bag. "As soon as I saw you walk in, I knew I forgot to do something. I just need to grind it for you." Martha poured the beans into the coffee grinder on the back counter and turned the crank at the top. The aroma of the coffee beans brushed my nose as she turned the handle.

"Have either of you learned any more about the woman Frank found on his farm?" my mother asked.

"Well, I can tell you *all* that I found out this morning," Helen said. There was a bit of a flicker in her eyes, one that I'd seen before. I was sure that she liked being the flame-keeper, and she took pleasure in spreading the burning news to all the corners of Linden.

I gave my mother a quick glance. Then I turned back to Helen, waiting to hear what she had to say.

"Gracie told me that people have been traipsing through her field since Frank found that poor woman." Helen stepped over to the back counter, pulled out the drawer for a spoon, and then placed it in her teacup and stirred. "Some of the woman's belongings were found not far from where Frank found her body. Gracie told me that a gentleman found a few hairpins, a cameo, and a bloody handkerchief. The gentleman, kindly, turned them in to the sheriff's department." Helen shook her head, and she sipped her tea.

I glanced over at my mother, but she didn't look over at me.

"The sheriff stopped by to see Gracie and Frank, and he told them to keep their eyes open for more of the woman's personal items." Helen set her teacup back on the counter.

"They probably figure the more items that they have, the more likely someone will recognize them," my mother said.

"The sheriff told Gracie someone also found a bloody razor blade in the cornfield and turned it into the department," Helen continued.

My eyes widened as I bit down on the buttery vanilla candy, crushing the small, sugary piece with my back teeth. I wanted to ask Helen if anyone found a fox trap, but that question would surely lead to my name being printed in the *Batavia Daily News*.

"Why would people go traipsing around in their field? A woman was killed there," my mother said in a disturbed tone of voice as she shook her head. "It's a place to set flowers, not a place to dig for treasure." Her voice was filled with disgust. "I understand that people are curious, but they need to have some respect for the deceased."

"Gracie said that there were two sets of footprints in the field leading into the wooded area."

I gasped as a chill ran through my body, and then I looked down at my boots. *Did they find my footprints too?* My mother gave me a quick look, then she turned to Helen.

"Gracie also told me that a woman who lived down the road reported that she saw the couple walk past their house. The man was walking a little ahead of the woman and she heard them shouting at each other."

"Now, what day was it that she saw the couple?" Martha asked as she poured the kettle of hot water over the tea bag sitting in her cup.

"Monday the twelfth," Helen replied. "Gracie said that the district attorney does know that couple was seen at the New York Station around 11:00 that Monday morning. And no one seems to have any idea who they were." Helen shook her head and sipped more of her tea.

"The viewing didn't help much, then?" Martha asked.

"No, the first one didn't. Maybe the next one will," Helen replied as she set her cup down on the counter.

"Next one? Are you telling us that they are going to hold another one?" My mother's eyes widened along with her mouth.

"Yes, and it starts tomorrow. The sheriff told Frank that the district attorney hired an artist to reconstruct the woman's face out of plaster," Helen said.

"Out of plaster?" My mother tilted her head slightly, and she gave Helen a puzzled stare. "You mean the same plaster that walls are made of?"

"That's the only plaster I know of," Martha said as she opened the coffee grinder and began to pour the coffee into the small sack.

Helen shrugged her shoulders slightly. "Me, too."

"It's hard to believe that it'll resemble her face," Martha said as she set the sack of coffee on the counter along with a sack of sugar and a sack of flour. Martha pressed the cash register keys and totaled my mother's order.

"I agree with you, Martha. I think it's going to be difficult, maybe even impossible, to mold plaster into a smooth face," Mom said as she opened her handbag.

"No one can blame the district attorney for trying. If no one recognizes her after this second viewing, I think they'll have to bury her without a stone," Helen said.

I turned to my mother. "Mom, I want to go to the viewing tomorrow." The words slipped out of my mouth before I could catch them.

"You what?" My mother's deep-blue eyes widened. "What for?" She stared at me with her hand on her hip. Her mouth hung slightly open as if she wanted to say more but didn't.

I replied with the same answer she gave me for going to the viewing. "Maybe I saw her at the depot."

Helen gestured with her finger. "He has a point, Ella," Helen nodded her head in agreement with me and finished her tea.

I read the expression on my mother's face like a newspaper headline. She wanted to tell Helen to mind her own concerns, but she was too nice.

"Helen, it's up to Ella," Martha interrupted, breaking the tension that was suddenly pulsing between my mother, myself, and Helen. Martha then placed my mother's money into the cash register drawer and set our grocery items into a basket.

"Ella, really, what's it going to hurt?" Helen glanced at me as I placed another piece of candy into my mouth and began to tumble it around with my tongue. "What's it going to hurt if Fritzy goes to the showing? All the damage that was done to her face will be covered. Maybe Fritzy did see her before. A lot of people exit the train here."

"Helen!" Martha snapped.

"Thank you, Helen. I'll talk it over with my brother tonight and see what he thinks. But I can't see it doing much good." The heat from my mother's eyes flushed my skin. She picked up her basket, moved the stool way from the counter, and tugged my arm to leave.

"Are you all set, Ella?" Martha asked.

"Yes, thank you," my mother replied with a smile that held discomfort. Then she rose from her stool. By the look on her face, I thought I better do the same.

"Are you two leaving already?" Helen asked with a tinge of surprise in her voice.

Mom nodded. "Yes, I have to start supper. John's coming over after he's done working."

Martha looked at my mother and rolled her eyes. "You two have a good night." She smiled.

"Thanks, Martha," my mother said as we headed toward the door.

"I'm sorry that you have to be on your way so soon, Ella," Helen said. "Enjoy the rest of your day."

"Thank you, Helen, you too," my mother said with a half-hearted smile.

My mother held the door for me. I looked up at

her. Her eyes were locked on mine, and she had a scowl on her face. I knew that I had a load of trouble coming my way. I took a deep breath, stared straight ahead, and clenched my teeth as we walked down the porch steps, hoping she'd forget whatever was going on in her head. When we were far enough away from the store and over the railroad tracks, she stopped and turned to me. "Do not put me in a situation like that again!" she scolded.

"What do you mean?" I replied, innocently.

"I don't appreciate you putting me in the position to make a decision like that in front of Martha and Helen."

"I'm sorry, Mom," I said with remorse. "The words just came out of my mouth before I could stop them." I stared at the ground for a moment.

My mother placed her finger below my chin and lifted it until my eyes met hers. "That's all right, honey. I understand. Sometimes our thoughts slip out before we have a chance to think," she said in a soft voice. "And I think it happens to Helen *all* the time," she added.

"That's what happened!" I assured her as we began to walk.

"I'm more upset with Helen. I love her dearly, but sometimes she goes a little too far."

I nodded. "She does that sometimes."

"Your uncle should be here in another hour or

so," my mother said as we headed toward the bridge.
Then she glanced up at the sky. "It looks like the rain
passed us by."

When we reached the bridge I looked over at her.
"I still want to know," I said with trepidation. "Can I
go to the viewing tomorrow?"

"After supper, I'll talk it over with Uncle John.
Honestly, I really don't want to go back to the funeral
parlor. It was a hard day for me. No one should ever
see a face in that type of shape. And just seeing the
casket reminded me of your father lying there. I had
a hard time sleeping. Why are you so interested in
going to the viewing, anyway?" she asked, looking at
me out of the corner of her eye, and her lips pressed
into a lopsided line.

"I told you, maybe I saw her at the depot," I replied, feeling the guilt slither around inside my head.

"Well, there's a chance you did, but I don't think
that's the real reason that you want to go," my mother
said as we stepped onto our porch, and she placed the
key into the lock.

I felt a chill shoot through my body, and it landed
in my stomach. "Why do you think I want to go then?"
I asked in an unsteady voice.

She looked directly into my eyes. "I think you're
curious. Since the woman was found, everyone here
has been talking about it, and most everyone in Linden has traveled into Batavia for the viewing. And I

think you feel left out." She turned, and she pushed the door open.

"Maybe," I shrugged my shoulders, and we stepped into the house. I placed my coat on the hook and shook off my boots.

Left out? If you only knew... If you only knew.

Six

The wax from the burning candles dripped down the tarnished brass sconces. One of the golden-yellow tapers was slightly tilted, dripping spots of wax onto the hardwood floor.

In the dimly lit room, there was a woman standing by a black and white marble-topped table. She was clutching a handkerchief in her hand. Our eyes locked for a moment. Then she dabbed the tear running down her cheek. A tall man with white hair wearing a dark suit was standing in the doorway to another room. He motioned me toward him.

I turned back to find my mother and Uncle John, but I didn't see them. Suddenly, I was standing at the side of the wooden casket. My eyes crept like a spider up the lady's tattered black boots with broken laces, over her dark blue skirt, above her crossed arms, and hands. One hand had a rosary woven through her fingers.

My eyes continued to creep up to her shattered face. Her body began to twitch. I gasped. Slowly, her fingers began to move. The rosary slipped out of her hand. Her arms began to loosen and uncross. Her head turned toward me. Her bottom jaw seemed to unhinge and her mouth fell open. A pool of dark blood filled her mouth. The blood began to trickle out, and it dripped down her neck. Swiftly, I felt a sharp clench-ing pain on my arm. Unable to move my arm, I looked down and saw her bloody nails digging into my skin. I shook loose from her grip. I turned to run out of the room and there *he* was, again.

Gasping for breath, I opened my eyes. I saw my bedroom's dusty blue walls. My bed sheet was wound tightly around my arm where I felt the lady's nails. The gloom of the morning sky leaked through the crack in the drapes, letting me know the day was new again. The sound of rain hitting my window whis-pered relief. I lay there gathering my thoughts as a gust of wind slammed the rain against the window like a bucket of nails.

"It was only a dream," I whispered. I unraveled my sheet and looked closer at my aching arm. There were no nail marks or blood. I reached back under my head and felt my pillow. It was damp, and my fore-head was sweaty. I sat up and rubbed my face. Then I threw my covers to the side.

I ambled over to the window to see if there was any sign in the sky that the rain would stop, but all I saw was gloom. It had to be well past 7:00. I grabbed my pocket watch out of the front pocket of my trou-sers, which were lying on my small deep red velvet chair that once sat in the corner of my grandparents' bedroom. 7:40. Uncle John planned on picking me up early. He was probably waiting for me in the kitchen.

After my dream, I wasn't sure if I should go to the viewing. My own private viewing was probably enough. As much as I didn't want to admit it, my mother was probably right. I just wanted to see what everyone was talking about, especially now that they fixed her face.

And with her face fixed, there was hope that someone might recognize her.

Uncle John, his other farm hands, and I finished the first milking by 11:00, leaving John plenty of time to drive back to my house, pick up my mother, and drive us to the funeral parlor. John made me take off my wet, soiled clothes in the kitchen entryway. I grabbed my clean clothes off the kitchen chair and placed my work clothes in a sack by the door. My hands were a little dirty, so I walked over to the sink, pumped the water, and washed my hands. The house felt cold and damp, so I placed another piece of wood into the fiery ashes and stood close to the woodstove to warm my bones for a couple of minutes and began to dress.

"Fritzy," Uncle John yelled from upstairs.

"What?"

The stairs creaked as John took each step. He entered the kitchen as he adjusted his dark brown suspenders, and then he looked up at me. "I thought you were going to come upstairs and wash up before you changed your clothes."

"Nah, I just washed my hands."

My uncle checked my face and brushed his hand through my hair. "I guess you look presentable."

I nodded as I finished buttoning my shirt and placed my tweed cap on my head.

"Are you sure you want to go to the funeral parlor today?" John rubbed his beard as he looked over at me.

I hesitated for a moment. *I wanted to see her face all fixed.* I thought for a moment, and then nodded. "Yeah, I want to go," I replied as John held the door open. "Maybe I saw her get off the train," I replied with the best excuse I had. "And I want to see what all the fuss is about," I added, even though I was pretty clear on what all the fuss was about.

Through the kitchen door window, I saw my mother sitting at the kitchen table, drinking her tea as she waited for us to arrive back from Uncle John's farm. I swung the door open; a gust of wind snatched the doorknob from my hand, causing it to hit the wall.

"Fritzy, how many times have I told you to hold the door when you open it?" my mother scolded.

"Sorry, Mom, I'll try to remember next time."

"Try to remember next time, please. I don't want the glass to break." She shook her head with displeasure. Then she sipped more of her tea from her favorite cup, the white one with a painted red rose on each side. "You're back sooner than I thought you'd be."

"I know." I looked at my mother, removed my boots outside the door, and left them on the porch.

"Throw the sack downstairs and go wash up good. You smell like a barn," my mother insisted.

"Ugh! I already washed up." I groaned and glanced over at John.

"I thought I looked presentable!"

Uncle John gave me a slight nod. His focused eyes said to do as I was told.

"You may *look* presentable, but you don't *smell* it. Now run up there and go wash up." My mother pointed to the stairs as she stood up. Then she placed her cup into the sink.

I tossed the sack of soiled clothes down the basement stairs, and I watched it tumble to the landing at the bottom. Then I ran upstairs while unbuttoning my shirt. As I finished washing up in the tub, the lady's shattered bloody face flashed in my head over and over again.

My heart began to pound harder.

My chest tightened.

It was hard to take a breath.

Sweat beaded on my forehead and neck.

I splashed myself with water. I could taste the bile that burned my throat. I spit the yellowish wad into the tub and drained the water. Slowly, I stepped out and grabbed my towel off the sink, then made my way to my room and lay down on my bed. I covered up with the towel, but I was still shivering, so I pulled up the blue afghan sitting at the end of my bed and threw it over me for a few minutes until I could breathe again. It was over ten minutes before I felt well enough to dress.

"Let's go," John yelled upstairs as I was pulling up my trousers.

"I'm ready." I ran down the stairs into the kitchen where my mother and uncle were waiting for me by the door. My mother handed me my wool coat and cap. My dress shoes were waiting for me next to the pulled out kitchen chair.

The rain had dwindled to a few sprinkles, but the sky still held the misery of the day within the layers of grayness. John opened the car door for my mother, and I jumped in the seat behind them. We headed out of Linden, past the post office and the schoolhouse I used to attend, and we headed left around the bend across from Florence Kingsley's farm. My mother and I waved to Florence as she stepped into her barn carrying a tin pail in her hand. I turned, and I looked out the back window. Junior was carrying a shovel as he walked toward the apple orchard.

"Florence has always been one to keep to herself. I never see much of her unless I'm driving by and see her outside, working," my mother said casually.

"With neighbors like Helen, it's probably good that she keeps to herself," Uncle John said, and then let out a brief chuckle. "She doesn't give a thought about telling you about someone's business."

"No, she doesn't." My mother nodded in agreement. "But we all know Helen means well. She calls on everyone in need."

"Yes, she does, and after she calls on them, she takes an earful with her!" My Uncle eyed my mother for a moment. Then he looked back at the road as he shook his head.

"I'm not going to disagree with you, John, but after knowing her for so many years, I know she sees everyone in the hamlet as her family. I truly believe that she wouldn't concern herself with anyone's business if she and Travis had children. And if she did have children, she'd be a busy grandmother by now. She wouldn't have time to concern herself with everyone else."

"She doesn't call on the Chapmans," I said. "I don't think Leon's family likes her too much."

"I know that Helen can go a little too far at times. So I am careful what I tell her. I'm sure it was something like that with the Chapmans. I'm sure that over time it will all be forgotten."

I stared off in the distance at patches of woods and the open fields until the cold, brown earth met the dreary sky.

"That reminds me: Mertie stopped by for tea this morning. And she was telling me that Junior received a letter from the bank yesterday. He brought it over to her last night so she could read it to him. I told him a number of times that if he would just come over two or three nights a week after dinner, I would teach him to read." My mother looked back at me. "Would you please remind him of my offer?"

"I don't think it's going to do much good. I've told him that before. He always says that he ain't got any use for reading."

"Well, if he's having Mertie read his mail to him, then apparently he *does* have a use for it." My mother glanced back at me again. I nodded, agreeing with her. "He might end up in a situation with someone who should not be trusted. If you can't read, then you don't know what you are signing."

"Junior has always been a hard one to figure out," Uncle John said in a puzzled tone. "He's a nice fella, but he's an odd one."

"The Kessler boys were young when they lost their mother, and with Junior being the youngest, life was probably the hardest for him," my mother said. "I'm sure that's why he left school at such a young age too. I recall Mertie saying that Junior has been working on farms since he was six or seven years old. She assured me that Valerie—"

"He's been working on farms for twenty years?" I asked in a slightly high pitched voice.

"That sounds right. He's almost thirty, so yes, about twenty years," my mother replied.

"That's a long time," I said. "I don't know if I want to do farm work for the next twenty years."

Uncle John let out a laugh. "You're only eleven, so everything is a long time to you. And if you decide that running the farm isn't what you want to do down the road when I retire, we can sell it. Farming is hard work and long hours."

My mother nodded. "It *is* hard work. And no one said that you have to work on the farm all of your life. That's why I insist that you get a high school diploma. There are other ways to earn a living."

"Yeah, I know. But for now, working on the farm is all right."

John glanced over at my mother. "Weren't you going to say something about Valerie?"

"Yes, I was about to, but somehow we started talking about the farm. What I was going to say is that when Mertie and Senior were married, the boys were all grown and had just started living on their own. She did tell me that Valerie *is* going to finish high school. Of course, they could use the extra money if she was hired as a house girl when she turns thirteen or fourteen. But they would rather see her graduate and work as a secretary." My mother glanced over her shoulder at me. "By the way, have you seen Valerie lately?"

"No, not lately," I replied casually, hoping that my tone conveyed a lack of interest to hide how lovely I thought she was. She looked so beautiful when she wore her long blonde hair back in a blue bow that matched her eyes. Every time I would look over at her sitting at her desk at school and she'd smile at me, my heart would beat a little harder.

"Since you don't see her at school anymore, you should visit her sometime. I'm sure she'd like to see you."

I nodded and then turned to look out the side window at the buildings that lined the city of Bata-via. "Yeah, maybe I'll stop and see her sometime," I mumbled.

Talking about Valerie almost made me forget where we were going. Uncle John pulled up in front of what looked like a huge white house with a large porch. My palms and forehead moistened, and I could hear my heart pounding against my ribcage. I began to sweat as I stepped out of the car. I walked ahead of my mother and John. When I reached the top of the steps, I wiped my hands on my trousers, removed my cap, and then entered through the parlor door. The parlor was quiet and bright. There were no candles on the walls dripping wax onto the floor. And there was no woman crying.

A tall man with reddish-blond hair and a mustache, wearing a black three-piece suit, stood guard in front of the double glass-paned doors. "Is that your mother and father, young man?" he asked, gesturing behind me as my mother and Uncle John entered the foyer.

"It's my m-m-mother and, and my Uncle John." I stuttered my words.

"Please wait for them; we don't allow children in without a parent," he said in a soft, smooth voice.

I glanced over my shoulder, and I stood still, waiting for them to catch up to me. My mother came over to me and grabbed my hand like I was five years old. "Are you sure you want to go in there?"

I hesitated for a moment, took a deep breath, and nodded, hoping she wouldn't feel my hand shaking. "I may have seen her get off the train," I said quietly, and then used the back of my other hand to wipe my forehead.

My mother turned, and she nodded at the man. He pushed the door open.

There was an old woman in a dark green dress wearing a matching hat with a black feather sticking up and two men in dark suits, all of whom were standing near the open casket. The old woman turned around and looked at us. The two men stepped aside as the woman shook her head. Her eyes narrowed. My mother gave her a brief smile appropriate for a room with a dead body lying in a casket.

I heard my Uncle John's voice behind me talking to the man guarding the door. My mother and I slowly stepped toward the casket. I could feel the walls of my stomach clench and twist. I could feel the wetness in the palm of my hand. My mother's grip was firm. I let go of her hand so I could wipe my sweaty palm on my trousers again. Then she reached for my hand again. I began to think that *she* was the one who needed to hold *my* hand.

As we approached the casket, I looked directly at the lady's new face. I stared at the molded plaster, which looked like bread dough with too much water. The eyes were painted on its milky white surface. They were out of place.

My eyes moved over the body of the lady. I remembered her dark blue skirt, her purple velvet hat that was tilted to the side as she walked through the trees on that sunny day. However, I didn't remember her small leather handbag that rested on the back of the casket, or the small cameo, or the hair pins sitting next to it, all lined up for someone to recognize.

My mother shook her head. "There isn't any way that anyone could know who she was from this face." My mother let go of my hand and placed her arm around my shoulder. "I could be staring at my own mother and not know it," she whispered.

I shook my head. "It doesn't look like her," I said

under my breath.

My mother turned, and she stared down into my eyes. "What do you mean, it doesn't look like her?" she asked in a deep whisper that demanded an answer. "It doesn't look like *who*?"

I could feel the heat rush over my face as coldness clutched my stomach. "A lady that I saw at the train depot," I replied in a shaky tone. "I saw her a couple of times when I was going to the store."

"Saw who, what lady?" My mother's eyes held on for a confession.

"A lady... But she was taller, much taller."

"Someone you know?"

I shook my head no as guilt crawled all over me. But the lie needed to be told.

"Why didn't you tell me what you were thinking, and that it might have been someone that you *specifically* remember seeing in the hamlet?"

I shrugged my shoulders with my mother's eyes fixed on me. "I did say that. I told you that I might have seen her get off the train. Then I kept seeing this lady in my head. So I kept thinking it might be her." My guilt had slid down my throat and wrapped itself around each word that fell out of my mouth.

My mother's face softened, and her eyes dropped to the floor for a moment before resting back on mine. "All right, I understand what you are trying to tell me." My mother gently grasped my hand again, and we turned to leave. "At least you can put your thoughts to rest." My mother gave me a solemn grin. "And now, I know I finally understand why you insist-ed on coming here."

I nodded before we walked through the foyer and left the funeral parlor. My guilt began to feel like a disease, sickening my every thought. All of a sudden, the man in the road staring back at me flashed in my head. He was reading my face like the front page headline.

Seven

1922

Iopened my eyes and saw that the bright sunshine had filled my room. I lay there, tired and
worn out from the six-day work week at the farm. I
was too tired to do anything. I thought back to the
days when I'd wake up at the first peek of the sun,
excited to go hunting and trapping. But after that day
in Harlow's woods, something changed. Killing an
animal—even though it was for a good reason—over
time, lost its appeal. Leon would always ask me, but
I'd make up an excuse that I was too busy working.
He understood because he was busy working on his
family farm too. Maybe it was the blood and guts that
reminded me of the lady who died in Harlow's woods.
Or maybe it was because I felt like the animal being
hunted that day I witnessed the lady's murder. The
thought reminded me: I still needed to go back and
find my trap. But every time I thought about going
back there to look for it, I couldn't bring myself to go
back into those woods and have to remember.

That day in Harlow's woods—already five years in
the past—found a place in an old trunk in the attic of
my mind. The trunk's latch was broken, allowing the
memory of that day when I hid behind the large rock

to crawl out and disturb me from time to time.

As for the lady with the plaster face, she was buried in the Batavia Cemetery with the word Unknown on her headstone. The Presbyterian Church donated the money for her burial. Sadly, her family never learned of her life's tragic end, and probably never would.

Around Linden, the unknown lady's murder also found its place in the past. And the fear that kept everyone's doors locked had turned to dust, and the murder settled on the shelves in their minds alongside the rest of their faded memories.

Everyone moved on, including my mother. Last year, my mom brought Uncle John to see his doctor, Dr. O' Hara. She ended up meeting his son, Joseph O'Hara, who happened to be in his father's office that day. He had recently graduated from the University at Buffalo's Law School and had just been hired by the Genesee County District Attorney's office.

At first, it was difficult for me when Joseph started calling on my mom. Even though Joseph seemed like a good man, it was uncomfortable to see my mother spending time with a man other than my father. But it was clear how content she was with him. Not only was she *content*, she was *really smitten* with Joseph. He would always take her to the finest places including the fancy Richmond Hotel in Batavia for dining and dancing. As the months passed, and mom's joy continued, I realized that I had to set my feelings aside because it wasn't fair to her. She was a widow. My dad was gone. And my mother deserved to be happy again.

One night after supper, my mother and Joseph were talking about the unknown lady. He was telling us that he wrote about the unsolved case in college, and how he had spent a lot of time reading all of the news articles that were stored at the Richmond Library.

I realized that, although I knew more than anyone else about what actually happened that day in Harlow's woods, I didn't know anything about the investigation. So that next day, I drove to the library, and I read all about it, hoping that maybe I could finally close that trunk that sat in the back of my mind and lock it for good.

I learned that the investigators knew that the couple exited the train at the Lehigh-Valley Railroad Station on Ellicott Street at approximately 11:00 that morning. The man was seen again entering New York's Central Station forty-five minutes later. The investigators believed that the man had enough time to commit the murder. I could, of course, verify that he had. I also read that they believed that he must have visited Harlow's woods at least one other time before the murder in order to dig the shallow grave. No one claimed to know who they were or recognized them

in a town where everyone seems to know each other.
I thought that explained the lingering belief that the
man and the woman were not from the area.

After reading through the articles, I gathered
that even if I met with the sheriff and investigators
and told them that I was there in the woods that day,
I could not have described his face. I don't remember
looking back at him as he chased me. But I assumed
he had seen my face well enough. At least it was a
lot safer to assume he did, which had left me with
no choice but to spew out lies to protect myself from
the man who would see my name in bold print on the
front page of the *Batavia Daily News*.

I lay there staring at the ceiling for a while, trying
to fall back asleep. *So much had changed over the past five
years.*

"Fritz, are you awake?" mom called up the stairs.

"Yeah, why?" I replied in a voice that was barely
intelligible.

"Valerie's here: she wants to know if you would
like to go to church with us. Martha is singing today."

Since Valerie Kessler and I graduated high school
at the end of May, I'd called on her a couple of times
because she was the prettiest girl I knew, but there
was more. We were good friends, and I enjoyed spending time with her. But we never admitted that we *liked*
each other, even though I think we both did.

Church? I put the pillow over my head for a moment and then turned my head toward my bedroom door. "Yeah, I guess. Give me about fifteen minutes." *Who came up with this idea?* Martha sang at church every Sunday! So Valerie just happened to come over without her parents to ask me and my mother to go to church with her? *Leave it to two women, to come up with a plan.*

After I washed up, I found my dark brown trousers and cream-colored shirt and threw them on. I poured a little Brilliantine hair oil into my hand, rubbed my palms together, and smoothed the oil into my hair. I parted it to the side, and I slicked it back with my comb, then headed down stairs. Valerie and my mother were sitting at the kitchen table, sipping tea.

"Hallo." I smiled as I walked into the kitchen, catching a whiff of cinnamon and apples.

"Good morning, honey. Did you sleep well?" my mother asked. She seemed to have an extra cheery smile spread across her face.

"Yeah, but my plan was to sleep another two or three more hours," I said and let out a chuckle. "But a couple of scheming ladies had other ideas." I set my tired eyes on Valerie's lovely face.

Valerie smiled at me. "I'm so glad you're coming with us," Valerie said with sparkling blue, delighted eyes. Strands of her golden blonde hair had fallen out of the loose pile on her head. *What a doll! I guess she is worth losing a couple hours of sleep.* She looked prettier than ever.

"Well, I didn't have much to do this morning other than sleep, so why not take a lovely lady to church." I rested my eyes on Valerie.

My mother placed her hand on her chest. "Am I suddenly being excluded?"

"Oh, you too, Mom. I meant to say ladies!" I leaned over and gave my mother an apologetic kiss on the cheek. "Mmmm, Ma: you made apple pie this morning?" I asked, noticing the two pies sitting on top of the woodstove.

"No, I brought them over. Last night, I helped Helen bake pies for the church bake sale today," Valerie said. "So I brought a couple over for you and your mom."

"Well, thank you for thinking of us." I strolled over to the stove, broke off a piece of glazed crust, and bit into the cinnamon-flavored pie shell. "So where're your mom and dad? Did they already leave for church?"

"My dad isn't feeling too well this morning, so my mother decided to stay home with him," Valerie replied, a touch of aggravation rattling through her voice.

"What, too much cider last night?" I asked and chuckled.

She nodded. "Well, yeah." Valerie's reply held a

trace of embarrassment. "They've been arguing all morning, and my mom is just too angry at him to worship. Even though I told her she needs to go pray for him today."

"Peter liked the cider too, just like all the men around here do." My mother gestured with her hand. "Ever since prohibition started, they seem to drink each glass of cider as if it were the last drop on earth. If they'd take a look around, they'd see the apples haven't stopped growing around here," my mother said, shaking her head as her expression turned solemn, and she became quiet.

"My father can be a lot to handle sometimes."

"Your brothers can be a lot to handle too," I said. "Speaking of, I haven't seen Junior in a couple of weeks. Where's he been working?"

"He's been working in Alexander. He was over for supper last night, but I didn't see him because I was over at Helen's," Valerie explained.

"Well, I'm glad you're coming with us." My mother glanced over at me. "Maybe you can start going with us every Sunday."

"I'd have to be persuaded." I gave Valerie an inviting grin as I bit into another piece of crust and leaned against the counter.

My mother looked over at Valerie. "Your hair looks nice like that. With your hair twisted up, I think you look a lot like the Gibson Girl."

"I do?" Valerie smiled.

My mother nodded. "Don't you think so, honey?" and then turned to me as I bit into another piece of pie crust.

I nodded as I savored the sweet, cinnamon flavored crust inside my mouth. "Yeah." I nodded. "Who's the Gibson Girl, anyway?"

"Never-mind." My mother slightly pressed her lips together and shook her head. "You look very fashionable, Valerie." My mother stood up, grabbed both teacups, and placed them in the sink.

"Are we ready?"

"Yeah," I replied as I grabbed my jacket and cap and slipped on my shoes. Then I helped Valerie on with her coat, and we left for church.

We drove a couple miles down Middlebury Road to the Middlebury Baptist Church, which was located across the road from the cemetery where my father was buried. We strolled in the door of the church just as the elderly Pastor Clive McVay began the service. I smiled at Helen Wilson. She smiled and waved back at me, and then she turned and whispered something to her husband, Travis. I saw Leon sitting next to his father, Everett, and his mother, Clara. Felix and his wife Millie were sitting in the row ahead of them. The pastor finished his reading, and Martha gave me a quick grin and began to sing the hymn as Cliff played the piano. He played beautifully.

After the service, my mother and Valerie stopped to talk with Martha as we stood outside in the fall sunshine. I spotted Leon standing with his parents next to their brand new Model T Coupe.

"I'll be right back," I said to Valerie, my mother, and Martha before ambling over to Leon as he lit up a cigarette and began walking towards me.

"I didn't expect to see you here!" Leon shook my hand and took a drag off the cigarette. The smoke curled around his head and then disappeared.

"Valerie asked me and my mother to go to church with her this morning. She said Senior got bent last night, so Mertie didn't feel like coming."

"Merle told me they'd be over at the Mill last night, but after I got home from Felix's I dozed off early, so I didn't end up going."

"So how've you been?" I asked.

"Swell," he replied as he removed his bow tie and shoved it into his jacket pocket. "I've been busy help‑ing Felix with the new barn that he's building."

"I'm not home much either. I've taken over most of my uncle's chores at the farm since he broke his leg a month ago."

"Well, it's going to be your farm in a few years, so you need to know how to run it."

"Yeah, maybe. Sometimes, though, I'm not sure that I want to take over the family farm." I turned and looked back at my mother. "It's a lot of long hours."

Leon dragged off of his cigarette. "So Valerie came to your house to ask you to go to church, huh?" His lips moved to the side as smoke leaked out of his mouth.

I nodded. "Yeah, she did. Or I'd still be in bed right now."

Leon glanced over at my mother and Valerie talking to Martha, Helen, and Travis on the church sidewalk. "She sure is the cat's meow!"

"You ain't telling me anything I don't know." I glanced over at Valerie for a moment.

Leon's slicked-back, reddish-brown hair caught the sun as he adjusted his cap, scratched his head, and tossed his cigarette on the ground. "Ain't it about time you made her your squeeze?" He looked over at Valerie, smiled and waved. She smiled and waved back. "If you don't—"

"Don't you even *think* about it." I shook my head and pointed at his chest as I started to laugh at his idea.

"Fritzy, I'm just razzing you. But you better make a move or someone else will."

"Well, you're not funny." I set my eyes on him. "And I'm working on it," I said. "Well, I better head back over there."

Leon glanced over toward the sidewalk. "It looks like the old hen is talking about you. Helen just pointed over here." Leon shook his head, annoyed.

"Yeah. She doesn't know when to quit, does she?"

"She needs to stop squawking," Leon said. "I'll be over at the store tonight until about 7:00. Then I was going to head over to the Mill if I'm not too tired. Stop by if you want to tip a few. And keep it hush because ol' lady Kingsley told the dry agents that Anton's been selling his cider."

"She told them?" I asked, my eyes wide as quarters. I knew that her brothers, Walter and Willard, always bought cider from him.

"Yeah, she did. Last week the dry agents came in and asked ol' lady Kingsley if she knew who was making the giggle juice around here. She gave them Anton's name, so they questioned him." Leon shook his head. "He's lucky they didn't throw him in the can."

"I guess he is lucky. I'm just surprised that she gave them Anton's name."

"Well, she did. And Anton was blazing mad," Leon said. "So keep hushed about it."

"I'm not going to say anything," I assured him. "I'm not sure if I'll be there tonight. It depends on how I feel. "

"All right. We'll probably be there till at least 10:00 if you decide to show."

"I wouldn't count on Senior being there tonight," I scoffed.

"We'll see. He might want to cut the ball off the

chain by 7:00 or 8:00."

"Yeah, but then he won't have a place to sleep tonight."

"Don't let your mother's attorney friend know what we're doing either. We don't need those agents sniffing around here again," Leon said and turned. Then he looked back at me to make sure I understood.

"Don't worry," I said, and he walked away.

I heard footsteps behind me and turned around. It was my mother and Valerie walking toward me.

"What're you two talking about?" Valerie asked. "I heard you laughing."

I shook my head. "Nothing, really. Leon just being Leon."

"Well, Helen and Martha were shocked to see you in church today," my mom said. "I told them that they might start seeing you here more often."

"Come on, let's go. I'm hungry and that apple pie is awaiting," Valerie said, grabbing my arm.

"I was thinking about that apple pie, too."

. . .

After we arrived back home, my mother served us shavings of roast beef and gravy piled high on toast. Then Valerie and I each ate warm, oozing slices of apple pie.

"Do you two have any plans for this afternoon?" my mother asked as she leaned against the sink, drying a plate.

"Do we?" I glanced over at Valerie.

"Not that I know of," she replied casually.

"Do you have to go home soon, Valerie?" my mother asked.

"I should, but I can just tell my parents that I stayed for dinner and visited for a little while. I really don't feel like going home to listen to them arguing," Valerie replied.

"You want to go for a walk, then?" I asked.

"That would be nice." She grinned, stood up from the table, and set her yellow embroidered napkin next to her plate. My mother grabbed our plates, set them on the sink, and began to pump the water.

Valerie and I walked out the door and down the hill until we reached the bridge. We leaned against the railing and watched the waterfall.

I glanced over at Valerie as a strand of her blonde hair caught the breeze and rested on her soft pink lips. "How long before you have to be home?" I asked.

"Well, I shouldn't be away for too long. My mom will want help with the wash and supper. And she likes me around when my father does this so she has someone to complain to."

"How long does it take for your dad to move back into your mom's good graces again?"

"Maybe a day or two."

We both folded our arms on the railing of the bridge, and we stared off at the waterfall for a moment. I reached over and placed my hand on top of hers. She smiled at me. My heart began to hit my chest a little harder.

"Come on." I grabbed her hand, and we continued our walk. We wandered through the trees and made our way onto the rocks next to the tall, thin waterfall. The sound of the water hitting the rocks below echoed off the hill. The cool breeze swept faded orange and yellow leaves across the water.

I looked down into her eyes and leaned in to kiss her. My heart pounded against my chest, either from excitement or nervousness... probably a little of both. I opened my mouth slightly, and our tongues touched. I let go of her hand and reached over to the back of her neck. Softly, I placed my fingers in her hair. Then our lips drifted.

"I've been waiting so long to do that," I whispered.

"Me too," Valerie blushed.

I leaned in and kissed her again. Our mouths opened, and our tongues crossed, and they swirled together. I felt her touch my back, and then she moved her hand down to my waist. My spine tingled with excitement. Her gentle touch sent my blood rushing through my body.

The longer I kissed her, the more my body felt like it was on fire. I moved my fingers through her hair, pulled out the hairpin that held her hair up, and placed it in her hand as I kept kissing her. Valerie's long, wavy tresses fell onto her shoulders. She pulled away as she moved a few strands of hair away from her wet lips.

"I like when you wear your hair down."

"My mother said at my age, it's more proper to wear my hair up as ladies do."

"It's too pretty to hide all wrapped up."

"You mean like the Gibson Girl?"

"Yeah, just like her," I replied and kissed her supple lips again.

Valerie pulled away, stared into my eyes for a moment, and smiled. Then she glanced over her shoulder and looked toward her house. "Well, as much as I don't want to go, I should head home. I'm sure my mother called your house already, wondering where I am."

"Probably," I whispered and pulled her closer. I kissed her again and kept kissing her. Our breathing became heavier. I didn't want to stop.

Valerie pulled away. "Come on, or we'll be here until the stars come out." She smiled, pulled at my hand, and turned toward the bridge. "Wait!" Valerie whispered, pulling me behind a group of piney bushes.

"What?"

"It's Helen!"

We watched Helen dash over the bridge.

"Is she going to my house?"

"No, I think she's going over to Springer's to help

Doty this afternoon. Victoria is coming in on the train today. Charlie has to go into Batavia to pick her up this afternoon."

We watched Helen walk past my house and the post office and down the road toward Springer's house on the left side of the bend, diagonally across from Florence's house.

"Okay." I grabbed her hand. We climbed up the slight hill and strolled past my house before finally stopping behind the row of pine trees next to her house.

"Well, I better head inside." Valerie leaned over and gave me a long goodbye kiss. "Come over after you're done with work tomorrow?"

"I won't be home tomorrow night. I told John that I'd take turns with him staying overnight in the barn. One of his cows is calving."

"I should be home after 6:00 on Tuesday." I leaned over and kissed her one last time.

"I've wanted to ask you for a while... would you be my girl?" I whispered.

She stared into my eyes, smiling, and kissed me again. "Does that answer your question?"

I nodded and kissed her.

Valerie broke our embrace and then turned and walked toward her house.

As I headed home, I could feel the joy radiating from the grin on my face. The day was so perfect; I almost expected to see a few beautiful white horses galloping down the road. Then, as I stepped into my house, I heard, "Hwhoooo hooooo." I looked over my shoulder: there, sitting in the dark hole of our old maple tree, was a white owl.

Eight

After dozing off for a couple of hours after supper, I decided to go meet Leon and the others at the Mill. Seeing that white owl in the tree stuck in my mind, and the cool air sent a chill through my bones as I buttoned my coat. I remembered my dad saying something about seeing an owl during the day. He said it was an omen, but I couldn't remember what he told me, and my mother didn't remember either. I'd like to think it was a message from my dad giving me his approval on Valerie. Maybe he couldn't find any white horses, so he sent the white owl.

The fall moon hanging in the night's deep blue sky dusted the hamlet with a haze of light. It was well past 7:00, so I knew Leon had to be at the Mill already. I ascended the hill, and I stepped over the tracks, the flicker of fire from a kerosene lamp on the porch of the Morgans' store caught my attention. I saw the shadowy figures of Martha and Helen sitting on the rocking chairs. I ambled over to the steps.

"Hello, Fritzy," Martha said as she sipped from a steaming mug.

"Hallo," I said with a nod and a smile. "Leon's not still here, is he?" I asked.

"No, honey. He left with Cliff and Matt about a

half-hour ago," Martha replied.

"I'm sure they're over at the Mill." Helen pointed across the road. "I know you boys are up to no good, again."

"Oh, Helen, leave the boy alone," Martha said to Helen before looking back at me. "Cliff told me they were going to play cards tonight, so I'm sure they're across the road."

"Okay; I'll head over there, then," I said and rested my eyes on Helen as I adjusted my cap. "Helen, you know me, I don't participate in any nonsense."

"Telling lies like that ain't good for the soul, Fritzy," Helen said frankly, then she sipped from her mug.

"Don't listen to her," Martha said with a smile.

Helen rolled her eyes, and she slightly shook her head. "It looks like you found yourself a pretty young lady. I couldn't help but notice you two at church this morning."

I nodded with a grin.

"Valerie is a wonderful girl, Fritzy," Martha said in agreement.

"Yes, she is, and we approve," Helen added, and then she set her mug next to the lamp.

"That's swell."

"Can we expect to see you and Valerie every Sunday?" Helen asked.

"We'll see. Uncle John has me putting in a lot of

hours on the farm. Sunday is the only day I have to sleep in. I'm sure God will understand if I can't make it *every* Sunday. Sunday was his day of rest, too," I reminded her.

Martha laughed, and she turned to Helen. "Helen, he has a good point." Martha looked back over at me. "You're as witty as your father was."

"Thank you, Martha. I'll take that as a compliment." I nodded. "Well, I better go find the guys."

"Have a good time, Fritzy, and tell Cliff I don't want him coming home too late. And tell him to be quiet when he comes in. I don't think he knows what quietly means."

"Have a good night, Fritzy," Helen said.

"Will do, and I'll be sure to tell Cliff what you said." I waved and headed across the road.

I swung the Mill's wooden door open and ran up the stairs. When I reached the top of the loft, the scent of aged apples swept past my nose and a haze of smoke surrounded me. Large barrels of cider were lined against the back wall next to an old rickety table and chairs where the guys were all seated.

"Hey, how's it going?" I asked the guys. Anton, Leon, Cliff, Matt, and Senior were all there. I was surprised to see Senior, and I'm sure it showed on my face.

"How did you get out of your house tonight? From what Valerie told me, I thought for sure Mertie put the old ball and chain on you last night," I mocked as I unbuttoned my coat, shook it off, and hung it on the back of the only empty seat at the table.

"Now, how was I supposed to get rid of the aching headache? I've had it all day, so I came for my medicine." Senior lifted his glass and swigged down all of his cider.

"Mertie must have some big angel wings to put up with your hooey," I said as I sat down and poured a glass of cider from the jug that sat in the middle of the table.

"Yes, she does. I'd have to agree with ya there, Fritzy, boy," Senior nodded while dragging from his cigar.

Leon looked over at me with a glass of cider in his hand and a cigarette hanging from his lips. "Hey, I waited for you at the store. What kept you?"

"I dozed off for a while."

"I thought maybe you went over to Senior's to see Valerie," Leon said.

"I thought maybe you did too. My daughter is sweet on you. She came home after church giddy as could be," Senior said.

I grinned, and then sipped from my glass. The sharp apple taste sent a burn down my throat. The first couple of sips were always the hardest. "Hey, Cliff, I just saw your mom; she told me to tell you not to come home stumbling in the door like a drunkard,"

I said.

His eyes widened. "She said that?"

"Well, she didn't say stumbling or drunkard. I added that because that's what you are every time you leave here," I said and laughed.

"You're a real jokester, Fritzy," Cliff said as he shook his head. "Last time you were here, you almost fell down the stairs. You're lucky Leon was in front of you."

"I don't remember." I glanced over at Leon. "But, I remember you telling me about it, Leon."

"Hey, Fritzy." Anton dragged off his cigar and let the smoke seep out of his mouth before he continued. It curled above his head and melted into the haze above the table. "Does that lawyer who calls on your mother know that I sell the juice?"

"No, I never told him about it," I replied and looked over at Leon, again. "But from what Leon told me earlier, you'd better watch it. Those agents will throw you in the cooler!"

"Everyone knows that you sell the juice, but they keep it hushed," Cliff added as he shuffled the cards, hit the deck on the table, and began dealing. "They all drink it."

"Yeah, well, I ain't so sure 'bout that." Anton's eyes fixed on each of us one for a second. "Those sniffers came to my house last week poking around. I was glad the wife and the kids were over at my mother's when

they showed up. Ol' lady Kingsley squealed on me."
Anton's face was sour, and it wasn't from the taste of
the cider.

"The word is that she don't want her brothers
drinking it. Springer told me that she was blazing
mad when Willard came home and fell up the porch
steps," Senior said as he picked up his hand of cards.

"Ain't nothing worse than someone getting in your
business," Leon said. "Christ, her brothers are in their
sixties! And Willard doesn't even live there. The only
hen that should be squawking is his wife." He shook
his head in disgust, picking up his hand.

"Ya know, someone ought to kill ol' lady Kingsely,"
Anton said. He had a serious glare in his bloodshot
eyes.

Leon shot a look at me. "Maybe you ought to stop
by and tell her to stay out of Anton's business," Leon
suggested.

"Yeah, like she's going to listen to a sixteen year
old." I flashed him an irritated look as I shook my
head and stared at my hand of cards. I glanced over at
Anton. "Just keep quiet. It'll all go away."

A couple of hours passed, and I pulled out my
pocket watch. I had a hard time focusing on the
numbers because they kept moving, but the one hand
looked like it was on the ten. After I got them to stay
still, I saw that it was 10:20.

"I better be heading home." I set my hands on the

table's edge and stood up. The room seemed to move as I clumsily shoved my arms into the dark hollows of my coat. I stared down at the buttons. I didn't see how I was going to slip the buttons through the small holes, so I gave up the whole idea. I staggered a little as I shuffled toward the stairs.

"See ya, Fritzy," Senior yelled.

"Yeah," I said.

I slowly made it down each step without falling, and then I pushed the door open. The cold air hit my face like a slap, which I needed. The road and the train tracks seemed to be moving the way the room had been, so I leaned against the outside wall of the Mill and let the cold air sober me up.

My mouth began to water. I began to feel a hot rush over my body. I leaned over and vomited.

"Shit," I mumbled, and then wiped my mouth with the back of my sleeve. My throat burned. It didn't taste good the first time, and it tasted even worse the second time around. I kept spitting the bitterness out of my mouth.

I waited a few more minutes, and then I finally began to head home. I tripped over the train tracks but managed not to fall. I took small, steady steps down the hill and wished that one of those white horses that I had imagined earlier would show up and take me home.

Nine

I stared off into the western sky as I drove around the bend. The burning sun's rays left behind melted hues of lavender, pink, and orange mixed in the gentle clouds.

I turned right onto Linden Road and noticed a cluster of cars parked in front of Florence Kingsley's farm. As I drew closer, I saw two New York State Troopers' sedans and two other touring cars, along with a hearse parked behind Martin Nelson's car, who was our Justice of the Peace.

"What the hell?" I said under my breath. The sight formed a tight knot in my stomach. *Did someone die?*

Slowly, I pulled my car over to the side of the road and stopped in front of Springer's house, across the road from Flo's farm. A sheriff was talking to Martin Nelson on the porch. Willard and Walter, Flo's twin brothers, were standing on the lawn not far from the steps that led down to the fruit cellar. The door was open.

A man in a suit marched up the cellar steps with a state trooper following behind him. They both had notepads in their hands. I kept watching, trying to figure out what was happening. Then I saw someone coming up the stairs carefully, but backwards.

My eyes followed his arms down to the stretcher they were holding. Trembling, I opened my car door, stepped out, and ran across the road.

I stood by the tall pine trees and watched the two men who were holding the stretcher. It was Florence Kingsley. Her long beige skirt was hanging off the stretcher, almost touching the ground. I gasped and moved a little closer. All was quiet. My eyes locked onto Florence's body.

The right side of Florence's head above her ear was crushed. Her nose, eye, and cheek were buried into her face. Dried blood coated her face, neck, and wiry gray hair. A large piece of her skull was gone. Part of her brain was torn away. Her bottom jaw was hanging as if it was a broken door that was dangling from its hinges.

Suddenly, in my mind, I was eleven years old again, staring at a shattered skull. I began to feel hot. Blackness fell over my eyes. My knees began to weaken. Abruptly, I felt a soft grip on my arm. Feeling dazed, I was being gently guided toward the house.

"Son, have a seat." A man gestured to the front steps. "Keep your head down. I'll be back shortly."

I nodded and hung my head between my legs. After a few minutes, my feverish skin turned to a cold sweat, leaving my neck and back damp. A little while later, the man came back.

"Are you all right, son?"

I looked up and saw that the man was in uniform, a Genesee County Sheriff. "Yeah, I'm starting to feel a little better." I rubbed my face.

"I saw that you were turning white, so I brought you over here as quick as I could," the sheriff said with concern. He reached out his hand. "I'm Deputy Ornsby."

"Thank you," I said and extended my hand and shook his. "My name is Fritz Reynolds. I live down the road." I pointed, trying to hold back the tears. "I live just around the corner. What happened to Florence?"

"That's what we're trying to figure out," Ornsby replied. Someone in the house turned the porch light on. "So, I gather you knew Miss Kingsley?"

"Yeah, I used to work for her," I replied in a shaky voice. "Can you tell me what happened to her?" I pleaded.

He glanced down at his notepad and hesitated for a moment. "Well, we know that Miss Kingsley was last seen outside last night around supper time. Her neighbor, Mr. Springer, became concerned when she didn't answer her door this morning, and all of her doors were locked. So he called one of the neighbors down the road who had a key. They let themselves in and found the house undisturbed, but there was no sign of Miss Kingsley. They attempted to call her brothers, but realized that her telephone wires had been cut. It was then that Mr. Springer called us.

After searching a good part of the day, Miss Kingsley's body was finally found close to 6:30."

'Someone ought to kill ol' lady Kingsley.' I could hear Anton's voice as if he was sitting right beside me.

"Listen, son, I need to head back to the station," Ornsby said as the hearse drove away. "I noted that you once worked for Miss Kingsley, so I am sure that you'll be hearing from District Attorney Keller in the next day or two. You may have information that will help this investigation."

I nodded. "Okay," I whispered with tear-filled eyes.

"I'm sorry, son." He patted my shoulder, headed over to his car, and then drove away.

I looked over my shoulder and saw that the front door was open. The cool air carried the voices and cries coming from the house as the sky hung on the edge of night.

Shocked, I ambled over to my car feeling like someone was going to shake me at any second and wake me up. Or that I must have taken the wrong road, taken the wrong turn, and ended up in the wrong place, because this couldn't be happening, not again.

When I opened the door, I exchanged looks with my mother and Valerie, who were sitting at the kitchen table. Their eager expressions read like a list of questions. A smile and the word hallo didn't even come to mind because I was in a nightmarish daze.

"Were there still cars over at Florence's?" my
mother asked.

I nodded. "Yeah," I replied quietly.

"Did you stop?" Valerie asked.

I nodded. "Yeah, I did."

"Did they finally find out where Florence was
today?" Valerie asked.

"Gloria came by around noon and asked if we had
seen Flo, and then she came back again around 3:00
and asked again, and we hadn't seen her," my mother
said.

They didn't know. I looked over at my mother, hoping she would read it on my face.

"Fritz, what's wrong?" my mother asked quietly.

"They found her," I said under my breath as I
shrugged off my coat and untied my boots.

"That's good! They found her. We were so worried
about her," Valerie said in a higher cheery tone.

"No, Valerie! Stop! It's not good." I raised my voice
and watched the smile slide off her face.

My mother stood up nervously and pulled out
a seat for me. "Honey, sit down. I'll dish up supper,
and you can tell us what happened." She stacked the
bowls and placed them on the counter. She opened the
lid of the pot, filling the entire kitchen with the aroma
of beef stew. Then she cut slices of bread from the
freshly baked loaf sitting on the cutting board.

I waited for my mother to finish and looked over

at her. "Can you sit down?" My chin quivered as I battled with the image of Florence lying dead on the stretcher.

"Sure, honey." My mother nodded, set the knife down next to the bread, placed the cover back on the pot, and sat across from me. Her eyes were filled with anxious anticipation.

"Yes, they found her. She's dead." My voice began to break as my eyes blurred with tears. But I held my composure. "They found her in the fruit cellar, beneath the house. She was beaten to death," I whispered.

Valerie gasped. "What?" Pools of tears overflowed from her eyes and began to stream down her flushed face. "You mean someone killed her?" Red, blotchy patches started to appear on her neck and cheeks, which always happened when she became nervous or cried.

I nodded. "Yeah," I replied nervously.

My mother's eyes were wide as she held her hand over her mouth. "I don't understand. Who would want to hurt Florence?" she asked, trying to stay calm.

I reached over and grasped Valerie's hand. I could see the fear in her eyes.

My mother took a deep breath, shaking her head in disbelief. There was a loud silence in the kitchen. Valerie began to sob.

A minute or two later, my mother stood up, opened

the top kitchen drawer, and pulled out three handker-chiefs. She handed one to me and Valerie, and then sat back down.

"Did you see her?" Valerie asked as she wiped the tears that were running down her face.

"Yeah. I was driving by when they were bringing her body up from the cellar."

"Was someone trying to rob her?" my mother asked.

"I don't know. The deputy told me that the house was locked."

"I feel so awful for Florence's brothers. Were they there?" my mother asked.

"Yeah, they were there. But I didn't talk to them. I only talked with the deputy."

We sat there in silence. I could hear the sound of the ice box humming. Anton's words repeated in my head. I envisioned him pulling Flo down her cellar stairs and yelling at her, accusing her of telling the dry agents about his cider. I could see her with her finger in his face, telling him how ashamed he should be for breaking the law. Neither one was going to back down. Then in a fit of rage he struck her and she fell to the ground. He found a board or stick to hit her with and began beating her to death—eerily echoing what I witnessed in Harlow's woods.

"Wasn't it about four or five years ago, around this time of year, when that woman was murdered on Frank Harlow's farm? Remember? You had Uncle John and I take you to the funeral parlor." My mother glanced at Valerie, and then back at me.

"Yeah, I remember." My voice faded.

"Do you think it could have been the same person?" my mother asked.

"I don't know, but I don't think so. Weren't they from Buffalo or something?"

"They could have been," my mother said. "But to think two people, beaten to death..."

"I'm really scared!" Valerie cried out.

"I know. I am, too," I said, stroking her hand. "We'll have to keep all the doors and windows locked. And I'm going to grab a couple of guns from downstairs. You should take one home, too, Valerie."

"I've used a shotgun before. Junior taught me how to load and shoot. A few months ago, we shot at glass bottles stacked on hay bales out in the field," Valerie said.

"It has been a long time since I used a shotgun, but I think I remember," my mother said as she rose up from the table and began to dish up the stew. "Your father showed me."

"I'll show you again, just to make sure you remember," I said.

Even though I was sick to my stomach, I managed to eat some of my mother's beef stew. I ate some quick mouthfuls, and then dipped my bread in the beef broth and bit into the soggy crust. My stomach ached as the food hit the bottom, and soon I couldn't eat any more.

Neither Valerie nor my mother finished their stew, either. Valerie set our bowls in the sink as my mother began to pump the water. As soon as we sat back down at the table, there was a knock at the door. I jumped out of my seat and saw that it was Valerie's mother, Mertie.

"Mom!" Valerie's eyes widened. "Did you hear?"

"Yes." Mertie gave Valerie a long hug. "Yes, Junior was over for supper. He was really shaken by the news. He told us that he ran into Charlie Springer on his way home. I didn't know if you had heard, so I came right over."

"I'm scared, Mom," Valerie said.

"I think we all are," Mertie said.

"Who could do this to her?" Valerie cried.

Anton's words still rang in my ears. *But was he fiend enough to kill her? Anton was a lot of things… but a murderer?* Questions swirled inside my head as I stood there, watching Valerie wipe her tears.

Valerie dabbed her eyes with the napkin and turned to her mother. "Fritz said that we need to keep our guns close. Do you know how to use a shotgun?"

"It has been years, but, yeah, I do know how to fire a gun," Mertie answered. "My father did a lot of hunting and he taught me and my brother when we were young."

"That's right, I remember you telling me about it," Valerie said with relief.

"As soon as Junior left, your father loaded all three of his shotguns. He has one in the parlor, one in the kitchen, and he put one by our bed."

I turned to Valerie. "I was going to give you one, but I guess you don't need it after all. I'm going to go grab ours real quick." I ran down the basement steps. The four shotguns were sitting on the gun rack. I pulled two off the rack and set them on my father's work table. Then I opened the workbench drawer, grabbed a box of bullets, and loaded them both. I carefully held them against my shoulder and ran back up the stairs with the box of bullets in my other hand.

By the time I stepped back into the kitchen, Mertie was holding the door open. "Are you ready?" she asked Valerie.

Valerie nodded and ran over to me. "I'm going back with my mom."

"All right," I said, and then leaned in and kissed her on the cheek. Suddenly, she threw her arms around my neck and gave me a long hug. "Everything's going to be okay," I assured her.

Valerie nodded and pulled away. She then left with her mother. Gazing out the door, I watched them walk up the road and around the pine trees. It pained me to see her leave my house. I wanted her by my side where I could keep her and my mother safe. As the man of the house, it was what I needed to do. I wasn't going to let anything happen to the people I loved. *Loved?* Did I just—I thought for a moment. I *did* love her. I loved Valerie. And I'd never let anything happen to her. I shut the door, locked it, and set the key on the counter. Then I handed one of the shotguns to my mother and threw another log on the fire in the parlor.

I set one of the guns down against the sofa and sat down. I took a deep breath. Flashes of Florence's face overwhelmed my mind. *Why? Why?* I sat there staring at the fire, but all that I could see was Florence's body on the stretcher—and her partially crushed skull. I began to shake. Tears began to fall down my cheeks. I tried hard to hold them back, but they wouldn't stop. I sobbed into my hands so that my mother wouldn't hear me.

"Fritzy," my mother said gently from the kitchen doorway.

I looked up at her and wiped my tears.

"Oh, honey." My mother came over to me and sat down. "I know, I know," she said and reached over and hugged me. "She didn't deserve this."

"How could someone do this? I don't understand," I cried on her shoulder, comforted by her presence as the grief overcame me.

"I don't know. As I've grown older, I've learned that sometimes terrible things happen to good people,

people who don't deserve it."

I nodded, pulled away, and wiped my eyes again. The tears had stopped. The trunk that I had tucked away in the back of my mind slid forward. It began to shake. The lid began to lift.

The dark memory of that day in Harlow's woods slithered out and coiled itself inside my head. It began to unravel itself as if I was back there again: the sound of the horse, the cold rock, the scent of the dried leaves, the voices of the man and the woman, the bloody tree branch, her shattered face, and the man staring back at me as I stood frozen in the sea of dead cornstalks, then him chasing his next kill—me.

I stared painfully into my mother's eyes. "Mom, I lied to you," I said softly as I began to tremble.

My mother stared at me, puzzled. "Honey, what are you talking about? You lied to me about what?"

"You know the lady that was found on Harlow's farm a few years ago?" I could feel the sweat on my neck and back as my bones shook.

"Yes, of course I remember." My mother tilted her head slightly as her eyebrows twisted.

"I've been keeping this a secret for so long. I never told anybody."

"What secret? I don't understand." My mother's hand was shaking as she reached over and grabbed my hand. "Honey, please tell me what this is all about?" she asked.

"I'm trying to tell you, I was there," I sobbed. "I was there that day. I was in the woods on Harlow's farm when he killed her!"

My mother's face drained of color. Her face was white and filled with horror, a look that I'd never seen before. She placed her hand over her mouth. "You were there?" she cried out.

I nodded as I trembled. "I was there setting my trap. I saw the couple coming so I hid. There was a huge rock there so I hid behind it. I didn't know what they were going to do. So I just stayed there."

"Did they see you?" she asked with tears running down her cheeks.

"No, but when it was all over, she was lying there dead. I waited until he was gone, and when I ran out of there... the man was standing by the road. He saw me! So I ran away as fast as I could."

Relief ran through my body. My entire soul seemed to lighten. The weight of the dark secret was no longer with me. I felt better. But I realized that wasn't all that mattered. Tears were streaming down my mom's face. It pained me to see her cry. It was then that I realized that the only thing I did by telling her was pass the burden of that day on to her. I regretted telling her. She'd had enough pain to carry over the years.

"Did he chase you?"

I nodded. "Yeah, I ran through the field toward the

next farm house and hid in the woods behind a barn. Luckily, there were two dogs outside barking, and then the owner came out of the house. I watched the man walk to the edge of the field looking for me, but I don't think he saw me. With all of the barking and the owner outside, he gave up. I watched him run down the road toward Batavia. I thought that if I told anyone he would find out who I was and come after me."

My mother threw her arms around me and just held me. "Oh honey, I am so sorry that you had to go through that. This breaks my heart that you had to witness such an evil act. All I ever wanted to do was to protect you—protect you from anything that would cause you harm or suffering. I'm sorry. I'm so sorry." She continued to weep.

"It's okay," I said as I tried to console her and regain my emotions. "I tried to forget about it. And then today, I just couldn't hold it in any longer. I had to tell you. But I don't want you to be upset. I'm okay."

"And I thank God for that..." My mother looked me in the eye for a moment as she began to gain her composure. Then she reached over and gently brushed my hair away from my eyes. Her mind seemed to be on recall. "This is all becoming clear to me. That was the real reason you wanted to go to the viewing, right?"

"Yeah, I wanted to see if they fixed her face." I nodded. "And today, after seeing Florence's face...

the whole side of it was crushed like the lady in the woods." I brushed my hand over the side of my face as I looked over at her. "Do you forgive me?"

"Forgive you? Sweetheart, you don't need to ask for forgiveness! Of course, I forgive you!" My mother began to sob again and threw her arms around me "My baby! You must have been so scared."

"I really thought if word got out, my name would have been in the newspaper and then he'd find out where I lived and then—"

"No, no. I wouldn't have let that happen," she assured me as she wiped her tears away. "Did you see his face?"

I shook my head. "No, I really didn't. I was behind the rock and he had his back toward me, so I really never got a good look at him. And when he was chas‑ ing me, I didn't look back at him. I just kept running."

"But you saw him standing at the edge of the road... How close was he to you?"

I thought for a moment. "He was maybe a baseball field away, or maybe a little less."

"Being that far away, I guess neither of you really saw each other's faces that well."

"Back then, I never thought about how far away he was from me. I just knew that he saw me. And I was scared!"

"Of course you were. Anyone would have been. I'm just so glad he never saw you hiding in those woods behind that barn."

"I know, those dogs saved me," I said softly. "Do you think I should tell the sheriff?"

"Now, let's think about this for a minute. Do you have anything to tell them that will help catch him? Did they use any names?"

"Well, no. I don't remember hearing any names."

My mother sat quietly for a moment, shaking her head. "I remember hearing about people who reported that they saw the couple. Those reports didn't help the authorities find the man that was responsible. So you weren't the only one who saw them, honey." She reached over and grasped my hand.

"So you're saying it's probably not going to help at all?"

"I really don't think so. Joseph told me that they came in on a train from Buffalo, but that doesn't mean that they were from Buffalo. They could have ridden in from another city and switched trains in Buffalo. No one knows. It is still a mystery."

I nodded.

"Even with all the news that covered all of western New York, and even beyond, no one came forward to identify her. There were people who drove for more than an hour or two to attend the viewing, and still no one identified her. And now with what happened to Florence, be careful who you tell. Helen is one of my closest friends, but you know how she is with news."

I nodded and sat silent for a minute as I imagined Helen knocking on every door in Linden spreading the news. "I wasn't planning on telling anyone else. But I'm sure I'll eventually tell Valerie. Right now, I think it would upset her even more... Are you going to tell Joseph?"

"I'm sure I'll end up telling him at some point. If you told me something that would help the investigation, such as a name, I would have you talk to him tonight. But since you do not have any information that would help, there isn't any reason to connect your name with a news story that happened over five years ago."

I looked over at my mother. "I have to tell you something else," I said quietly.

Her eyes revealed her concern. She took a deep breath. "Yes, what is it?"

"The other night at the Mill, Anton told us that he was angry about Florence reporting him to the dry agents."

"Martha told me about that. Florence blamed Anton for her brother's consumption."

"Yeah, but it's what he said to us," I said as my pulse began to speed up.

"What did he say?"

"He said, 'Someone ought to kill her.' And now, someone *did* kill her."

Her eyes widened. "What? He said that?"

"He sure did."

"I know that he's been in trouble with the law before, but do you think he would actually *murder* someone?"

I shrugged my shoulders. "I don't know. I would hope not, but I really don't know."

My mother eyes turned serious. "Listen to me honey; people say things out of anger all the time. And then again, you never know what someone is really capable of. Knowing what Anton said, you need to give the authorities this information, okay? You can't keep this one a secret."

I nodded. "Yeah," I replied softly, feeling a little afraid of Anton finding out I told the authorities about what he said. What if he *did* do it?

"Who else was there that heard him say it?"

"Senior, Cliff, and Leon all heard him."

"If they all heard it, there is no doubt in my mind that everyone in Linden already knows what he said." She grabbed my hand and gave it a squeeze. "I'm sure by the time you talk to the authorities, they will have already heard it a number of times."

"Yeah, you're probably right. I just didn't want to be the only one telling them because maybe… I don't know what Anton is capable of." *Was he fiend enough?* There were only two people who knew that answer, and one of them wasn't breathing.

"All right." My mother rose up from the sofa,

kissed me on the forehead, and then headed back into the kitchen.

It was then that I heard a quick knock at the door.

"I'll answer it." I grabbed the gun and swift-ly walked into the kitchen, unlocked the door, and opened it.

"Martin, come in," my mother said from behind me as she tried to find an appropriate expression for his call. Justice of the Peace Martin Nelson lived two doors down from the post office and not far from Flor-ence's house.

"No thank you, Ella, I just stopped by for a min-ute," he said as he glanced over at me and the shotgun in my hand. "I know that everyone is really shaken up and scared, and they've been dusting off their guns like you all did. I can't say I blame you or anyone else. My reason for calling is to let the neighbors know what happened, if they don't already know, and also that there's been an arrest."

My eyes widened. I slowly looked back at my mother standing by the sink. Our eyes met. *Anton.*

Ten

"They made an arrest?" The words darted out of my mouth.

"Martin, please come in and sit down." My mother gestured toward the seat.

"Just for a minute or two," Martin said as he stepped inside and sat down at the table. My mother sat down across from him. Her eyes sharpened as she sat forward. "I don't know many of the details, but this is what I can tell you: shortly after they removed Florence's body, a couple of the neighbors reported to one of the troopers that they saw three Negroes walking past Florence's house late yesterday after-noon. Using their description, the troopers found one of them in the area, not far from the county home, and brought him in."

"Do they think that they were the ones who killed Florence?" I asked as I sat down next to him at the table.

"Well, I don't know. The Negro man was taken to jail, and they're looking for the other two, so I assume they're suspects," Martin replied. "Like I said, I don't have all the details."

"Well, we really appreciate you stopping by to give us the news," my mother said.

"We all have the right to protect ourselves," Martin nodded in agreement. "Especially with the county home just down the road. We don't know what kind of trouble one of the residents could bring us." Martin rose from his seat. "Well, I better be on my way."

"Thank you again, for stopping over," my mother said.

"Yeah. Thank you for letting us know about the arrest," I added.

Martin opened up the door. "I'll give you a call if I hear any more news. And say your prayers for Florence and her brothers."

"We will," my mother replied.

Martin shut the door behind him.

"Three Negroes?" My mother shook her head in disbelief. "I wasn't expecting him to say that."

"Neither was I." I turned around and left the kitchen, lay down on the sofa, and shut my eyes.

□　□　□

"Ella!" I heard Helen's voice over the knocking on the door.

I rushed into the kitchen and opened the door. Helen and Travis were standing on the porch.

"Hi, there, Fritzy," Helen said. She held her knitted, gray shawl together at her chest.

"Honey, who is it?" my mother yelled down the stairs.

"Helen and Travis," I replied, gestured for them to

come in, and shut the door.

"I'll be right down," my mother said.

"Hey, there, young man." Travis removed his hat, exposing the white halo of hair that matched his long white mustache that curled up on both ends. He set his hat on the hook by the door before shaking my hand. He helped Helen remove her shawl and placed it on the back of the chair. He then pulled the seat out for Helen, and she sat down.

Helen turned to me. "Did you hear about Florence?" she asked. "They found her in her cellar, beaten!"

"Yeah, we know. It's really awful and scary. I mean, just down the road from us."

"Normally, I would have come over for tea by myself, but after Doty called me with the dreadful news about Florence, I was too afraid to walk alone. So I asked Martha if she wanted to come with me when she stopped over to get her milk, but she said that she was tired and wasn't feeling up to it."

I heard my mother coming down the stairs. She entered the kitchen and glanced over at Helen. "Hi, Helen."

"Hi, Ella," Helen replied.

She walked over to Travis sitting at the table. "Hi, Travis. It's good to see you," my mother said and gave him a kiss on the cheek. Mom placed the tea kettle onto the stove and sat down across from him.

"It's good to see you, too," Travis said. "Had to escort my wife. It ain't safe out there."

"No, it's not... No, it's not safe at all." My mother agreed. Sadness was woven through her faded words.

The table felt a little crowded, so I hopped up on the kitchen counter.

"Ella, I'll get the cups for you," Helen said and rose from the table. She turned to me. "Would you like some tea, Fritzy?"

"No, thank you. I don't drink tea," I replied as the kettle began to whistle.

Helen poured the hot water into the three cups as Travis pulled out his pipe. They were all so quiet—too quiet for a visit, especially from Helen who never ran out of people to talk about.

"I am still shaking," Helen blurted out. "Just down the road." Helen gestured eastward. "Florence Kings-ley, murdered in her own cellar."

"On Fritzy's way home, he saw all the cars at Florence's, and that's when he found out what had happened. He came home and told me and Valerie," my mother said.

"Helen was waiting for me at the door, holding her iron skillet," Travis said as he puffed his pipe. His smoke curled above them, filling the kitchen with a pleasing smoky cherry aroma.

"Can you blame her?" my mother asked, taking a sip of tea.

"No," Travis replied, puffing away on his pipe. "Just never expected such a thing, that's all."

"Gloria called Martha at the store around dinner time, and then later stopped over to our house, asking if we had any idea where Florence was. And never once did I think that... that... they'd find her dead. Let alone beaten to death," Helen said in a shaky voice and watery eyes.

"Did Martin stop by to tell you that they made an arrest?" my mother asked.

"No, he didn't. They made an arrest?" Helen's eyes widened as she held her cup near her lips.

My mother nodded. "I guess a couple neighbors reported seeing three Negro men walking past Florence's house yesterday afternoon. They found one of the men right away and arrested him. They're still looking for the other two."

"It's those vagrants that get off the train here." Travis dragged from his pipe and shook his head. "They're no good!"

"Travis, do you have a gun at home to keep close by?" I asked.

"Naw, I ain't never been a good shot. I must have something in the barn... Something better than an iron skillet." Travis glanced over at Helen, who looked as if she had sipped vinegar. Sweet smoke swirled around the light and melted into the haze that filled the kitchen. "I think I have an old adz handle in the barn somewhere. I'll keep it close, case one of those vagrants shows up at our door," Travis said. "That'll hurt 'em good."

"Well, that's something at least," I said.

"Yeah, you ain't never know. One might try to rob you. They ain't got nothing but the rags hanging off 'em," Travis said.

"Well, being up on the hill, we have a good view of everyone walking this way. I'm going to keep a closer eye on who doesn't belong here. I never paid much attention to the vagrants before," my mother said. "They never seemed to bother anyone."

I pulled out my pocket watch. 8:20. I hopped off the counter and opened the icebox. I pulled out the jug of milk, poured myself a glass, and walked into the parlor. All that was left in the fireplace was burning coals, so I added two more birch logs, lay on the sofa, and shut my eyes while my mother visited with Helen and Travis.

I was awakened by the ring of the phone, and then I heard my mother talking in the kitchen. I knew it was Joseph by the tone of her voice. I shut my eyes again and drifted off.

"Honey," my mother said, shaking my shoulder. "Why don't you go upstairs and go to bed?"

I opened my eyes and looked up at her. "What time is it?" I asked with a yawn.

"It's a little after nine. Why don't you go upstairs and go to bed. You'll be more comfortable."

I sat up. "Where's the gun?"

"Right here." She handed it to me. "I'll keep one down here with me."

I looked over and saw the other gun leaning against the wall. "Aren't you going to go to bed too?"

"In a little while. Joseph is just leaving the office and driving out here."

"This late?"

My mother nodded. "Yes. He should be here in about twenty minutes."

"All right, I'll go to bed." I rolled off the sofa. "Are the doors locked?"

"Yes, we're all locked up."

I headed upstairs with my gun in hand. I set my gun on the floor and climbed into bed. A little while later, I woke up and heard Joseph and my mother talking. They were keeping their voices down so I couldn't really hear what they were talking about. I was too tired to leave my bed, so I turned over and closed my eyes, trying not to think about Florence.

I woke up suddenly. My heart was thrashing. I knew I was dreaming, but I couldn't remember about what, which was probably for the best. The morning light began to wipe away the darkness. I grabbed my pocket watch off my night stand. 5:20. Quickly, I washed up and dressed.

Before going downstairs, I opened my mother's bedroom door. "Mom," I whispered. "I'm leaving."

She turned her head toward me, yawned, and stretched. Then she threw her covers off. "Okay, let me make you breakfast."

"I'll eat with John," I said as we headed downstairs. "What time did Joseph leave?"

"It must have been close to eleven," she replied as we entered the kitchen.

I saw the shotgun leaning against the wall under the window. Then I noticed a glass on the counter with a flask-shaped bottle half full of an amber colored liquid.

I strolled over to the counter. Then I opened the bottle, held it under my nose, and whiffed. The scent burned my nostrils. I set it down and glanced over at my mother with question.

"It's bourbon whisky," she said. "He brought it with him." She swiftly placed the glass in the sink and the bottle in the cupboard, making it disappear.

My mother followed me to the door. I slipped my boots on, and she handed me my jacket. I grabbed the gun and handed it to her. "Keep this by you all day and lock the door behind me."

"I will," she said and gave me a kiss on the cheek, and I stepped out the door.

The sky had fully ripened into morning. But the news of Florence's death had turned Linden into a darker place: terror, an unwelcome guest, had moved into our lives, holding everyone's minds hostage.

Eleven

After work, I pulled into the driveway next to Joseph's car. As I entered the house, the aroma of beef gravy greeted me at the door. Joseph was sitting at the kitchen table with the same man who I had spotted walking up Florence's cellar stairs.

"Hello, Joseph," I said. My heart sped up a bit as I looked around for my mother.

"Fritz, this is District Attorney Ronald Keller." Joseph and Keller rose from their chairs. Keller extended his hand to shake mine.

I turned to Joseph. "Where's my mom?"

"She's upstairs changing," Joseph replied.

"Fritz, I just have a few questions for you regarding Florence Kingsley," Keller said and sat back down. He had a pad of paper in front of him and a pencil in his hand.

"Wasn't someone just arrested?" I asked with confusion. "Martin Nelson stopped by last night and told us there had been an arrest made."

"A man was picked up on vagrancy, and they are holding him. We're still looking for two more men that exited the train here. I'm not convinced that he or they had anything to do with the murder of Miss Kingsley. Right now, we have a lot of questions to ask the residents of Linden," Keller said in a slightly deeper authoritative voice.

"Okay, but I don't know if I have anything to say that's going to help," I replied, breaking into a sweat.

"We've been interviewing everyone," Keller said.

"I haven't had any contact with Florence in the past few weeks, other than seeing her outside working the farm. I haven't talked to her lately," I replied as I shook off my boots and coat, then sat down.

"You and Mr. Gordon Kessler Junior worked for Miss Kingsley as farmhands, correct?" Keller asked.

"Yes, that is correct, sir, we did, but only when she needed some extra help," I replied.

"I spoke to Junior about an hour ago," Keller said.

I looked over at Joseph. "Are you working on Florence's case, too?" I asked before thinking whether I should or should not have asked.

Joseph glanced over at District Attorney Keller and then focused his eyes on me. "Well, no. I finished at the office and was on my way to your house. Mr. Keller told me that you and your mother were going to be questioned, so I came along. Mr. Keller just finished interviewing your mother before you walked in the door," Joseph explained.

"I read Corporal Whitehaven's report. How long has it been since you worked for Miss Kingsley?" Keller asked.

"It's probably been two years, maybe more," I said,

with no idea who Corporal Whitehaven was.

"Do you know if Junior would have reason to hurt Miss Kingsley?" Keller asked.

My blood turned to ice from the shock of the question. "Junior? Hurt Florence? No! No, he would never—"

"Do you know if Junior had any arguments or any frustrations with Miss Kingsley or any of her brothers?" Keller asked.

"No, of course not. Junior has always been kind to Florence and was always neighborly with her brothers. She always paid us for our work. There were never any problems. So no, he never had a reason to have any bad feelings toward Florence or her brothers," I replied adamantly.

"Can you think of any reason, any reason at all, that Junior could have been at odds with Miss Kingsley in the past month or two?" Keller asked.

"No, not at all," I replied. I tried to stay composed about his line of questioning. "Why are you asking so many questions about Junior?" My voice overflowed with aggravation. "He would never hurt or kill anyone," I insisted as Joseph gave a hint of a glare and slowly shook his head. I knew by his eyes that I'd better hold in my anger. Even though Junior was older than me, I always felt sort of protective of him because he was different from everyone. It always took longer for him to understand things. He never had any friends, and not many people liked him. He was never the friendly type, but I always got along with him.

"We have to do a thorough investigation," Keller replied with a lack of emotion, still writing. "Okay, do you know of anyone who had a reason to murder Miss Florence Kingsley?"

I could feel the sweat beading on my forehead and on my back. I did have an answer for that particular question. I nodded my head. "Yes," I replied softly. The answer seemed to tighten my vocal cords.

Keller looked up from his notepad and leaned back in his seat for a moment. His eyes shifted over to Joseph for a second and then rested back on mine.

"Anton Mitchell." The words fell cautiously from my lips.

Keller nodded as if he seemed to already know Anton had a reason. "Why Anton?"

"Flo told the dry agents that he's been selling his cider. He was blazing mad about it."

Keller glanced over at Joseph and nodded, then set his eyes back on me. I couldn't help but wonder what they were both thinking.

"What can you tell me about Anton Mitchell?"

By their behavior, looking at each other and nodding after almost every answer I gave, I was sure Keller and Joseph could tell me more about Anton than I could tell them.

"He's been in trouble with the law before."

Keller kept writing, and then looked up at me. He gestured to me with his pencil in hand. "That's an accurate statement."

I nodded my head. "Yeah, I know he's been in trouble... for stealing, I think."

"By the way, Anton's name has come up today." Keller continued to write. "More than once."

"I'm not surprised," I said. "Some people around here don't care for him much. They think he can't be trusted. And I can't blame them."

"What do you think?" Keller asked.

"I don't really trust him either," I replied. "But even though he was angry with Flo, I don't think he'd go so far as to *kill* her over it."

"Fritz, is that you?" my mother called from upstairs.

"Yeah, it's me," I called out.

"Well, I think I have enough for now. I'm going to be on my way," Keller rose from the seat, and Joseph followed his lead.

My mother entered the kitchen wearing a long black skirt and white blouse. She looked pretty.

"Thank you for waiting," my mother said to Joseph. "I had to change into something much more presentable."

"I'm all through here," Keller said as he tucked his notepad under his arm and placed his pencil in his inside shirt pocket.

Keller opened the door and turned to me. "Fritz, we will talk again."

"All right," I said.

Keller stepped out the door and closed it behind him.

"Joseph, please sit down. I'll dish up your supper."

I watched Joseph as he sat back down with his eyes resting on me. I assumed he was trying to figure out what I knew that he didn't.

Joseph looked directly at me. "Keller was watch-ing your every move," he said with an unsettlingly calm voice.

"Why? I ain't got anything to hide!" I struck back like a cornered snake.

"He can read more about your behavior than what you're saying to him. So be careful. It's his job to figure out who's telling him the truth and who is being deceitful." Joseph stared intently into my eyes. "And I'm starting to become good at it, too."

Silence filled the room. All that I could hear was the sound of the spoon hitting the side of the pot as I thought about what I said to Keller.

"Well, he can keep reading, because I ain't got nothing to hide." My eyes shifted to my mother as she dished up the gravy. I thought she might come to my rescue, but apparently she was staying out of it. I turned back to Joseph. "I thought that an arrest was made and that was going to be the end of it."

"Vagrancy charges are not murder charges. The deputies and the troopers were ordered to pick up every vagrant they find within a ten mile radius of the Kingsley Farm," Joseph said.

"Why so many questions about Junior?" I asked.

"Ron thought he was acting rather odd when he questioned him," Joseph replied.

My mother set two plates piled with shredded beef and biscuits, smothered with gravy, in front of me and Joseph. My mouth began to water from the aroma of the gravy.

"Thank you, Ella." Joseph smiled at my mother and turned back to me.

"Thanks, Mom." I picked up my fork. "Junior was always different. That's the way he is," I replied. "I'm sure he wasn't *acting* at all!" I said adamantly.

My mother turned to Joseph. "Junior has always been more of a loner. So Fritzy is probably right. He was acting odd because that's the way he is."

"So they don't think it was a vagrant who killed Florence?" I asked Joseph as my mother set her plate on the table and sat down.

"Right now, it's not looking that way due to the nature of the crime, and nothing seemed to be stolen. There doesn't seem to be a motive. And as for Anton Mitchell, we know that he's no stranger to the law. Mostly petty crimes though, just a nuisance to the sheriff's department from what Ron said earlier,"

Joseph said.

I glanced over at my mother.

"He's been in trouble off and on since I can remember," she added. "A lot of people around here don't like him. He's gruff and has been known to curse at people. I just avoid him when I see him."

"I don't think he knows how to stay out of trouble," I said.

"Oh, Gloria called earlier," my mother said. "The service for Florence is going to be in her home on Thursday. Let's just hope they make an arrest soon."

There was a knock at the door. I stood up from the table and opened the door. Valerie was standing with a shotgun over her shoulder with an anxious look on her face.

"Valerie! Is everything all right?" I asked, staring at the barrel of the gun.

"I'm sorry, I didn't mean to interrupt your supper," Valerie said to my mother and Joseph and then turned to me. "Can I talk to you for a minute?"

I looked back at my mother and Joseph. My mother nodded. "That's fine, Valerie. Honey, shut the door. I don't want the cold air in here."

"Okay, I'll be back in a couple of minutes." I slipped on my boots, stepped out onto the porch, and looked at Valerie. "Is everything okay?"

"Yes, everything is fine. I just stopped to tell you that Mrs. Adleman called my mother. She's scared to be alone, so she asked my mother if I could stay with her. That's why I'm bringing the shotgun," Valerie replied.

"She did? Well, I guess I can't blame her."

"My father showed me how to use the gun again before I left."

"Well, keep it with you, and make sure all the windows and doors are locked."

"I will. She sleeps in the downstairs bedroom. So I'll just sleep on her sofa with the gun next to me," Valerie replied.

"I know how scared you were. Are you sure you are going to be all right over there?"

"I feel better now that my father showed me how to use this." She raised the gun off the ground. "I remembered everything Junior taught me."

"Speaking of your brother: I was just questioned by the District Attorney, and he asked me a few questions about Junior."

"He did? Why would he ask about him? He would never hurt Florence," Valerie said with a huff.

"I think it was because Junior used to work for her. Anton's name came up, too."

"I'm not surprised about that. My father said that he probably did it."

"I don't know. I'd hate to think... I'd hate to think that anyone I knew could kill someone." I shook my head. "Come on, I'll walk you over." I reached for Valerie's hand, and we walked down my driveway and across the road. We stopped on the small sidewalk that led to the porch. I leaned in and kissed her. Then I wrapped my arms around her and held her for a minute. Her warmth felt good against my cold body. "I'm just across the road if you need me."

She nodded and glanced over at my house.

"Well, you better head inside. She's probably wondering why we're standing out here—and me without a coat." Shivering, I leaned over and gave her another kiss. "Call me if you need me. Or yell out the front door. I'll hear you."

"I will," Valerie said, and then she turned and headed towards the door. Then she opened the screen door and knocked. When the door opened, she looked back, waved to me, and then shut the door behind her.

I put my hands in my front pocket as I ambled back to the house. I was about to place my foot on the first step of the porch when I heard a stick crack. Out of the corner of my eye, I saw a shadow.

I froze.

I couldn't be sure, but it looked like a silhouette of a man standing near the grove of trees at the end of our property. I ran up the steps, flung the door open, and quickly closed it behind me. I was out of breath.

Mom and Joseph stared at me, puzzled. Without saying a word, I turned off the kitchen light and looked out the window above the sink. There was no one there.

Twelve

Merle's eyes fixed on mine. He nodded as he leaned against Florence's porch railing. His parents and sister were already in the line for Flo's memorial service.

"Hey, Merle," I said as I walked up the porch steps with one hand in my pocket and the other holding Valerie's hand. I let go of her hand for a moment, reached out, and shook Merle's hand.

"Hello, Mrs. Reynolds. Valerie," Merle nodded.

"Hello, Merle," my mother said quietly before strolling over to his mother and father.

Valerie briefly smiled at Merle. "Hi, Merle."

Mertie came around behind us, reached her hand out, and warmly patted Merle's shoulder as she passed by him, clutching Senior's arm.

Valerie and I stood with Merle on the porch. There was a lack of words to say. I took a deep breath and nervously pulled out my pocket watch. 9:22. The service was to start at 9:30.

"We planned on being here earlier to make sure we found a place to sit," Merle blurted out. "But I told Martha I'd wait for a delivery she had coming in on the nine o'clock train. So I locked up for her after it came in. We just got here about ten minutes ago."

"I'm sure she appreciated that," I nodded. "Did Grandma Harrison come with them?"

"No, Martha thought it would be too much for her."

After waiting a couple of minutes, Valerie, my mother, Mertie, Senior and I entered Florence's house. All of the folding wooden chairs were almost filled in both of Florence's front rooms.

Colton Daly, the new pastor of Middlebury Baptist Church, was standing near the casket directing people to the few remaining seats in the room across from the parlor.

Valerie gasped and buried her face into my shoulder. She began to cry. "Her face, her face, it's—"

"Shhh, I know." I placed my hand on her soft golden hair and tried to comfort her. I flashed a look at my mother and felt heat come over my face. "They didn't close it?" I whispered.

My mother stared at the casket. I could see the disbelief on her face. She turned to me, noticeably shaken and pale. "I never expected—" Tears filled her eyes. She glanced over at Florence's family with sadness as we made our way to the last few empty seats and sat down.

"Why didn't they close the casket? This isn't the way we should all have to remember her!" I whispered to my mother.

My mother placed her finger near her lips. "Shhh.

It must be what the family wanted," she replied quietly, and then pulled her handkerchief out of her sleeve
to dab her eyes.

"I don't know what they were thinking," I whispered in Valerie's ear.

"I had no idea her face..." Valerie wiped her eyes.
"What kind of person..."

"I know," I whispered.

"The whole side her face—" Valerie cried.

"Just try not to look."

I looked into the parlor across from us and saw
Gerry and Martha. Helen and Travis were sitting
behind them. Then I saw Helen tap Martha on the
shoulder and point toward us. They sort of smiled at
us. My mother gave them a slight wave.

With a keen eye, I scanned both rooms, hoping to
find Junior. I didn't see him in either room. I didn't
see Anton either, but I didn't really expect him to
show up.

"Do you see Junior?" I whispered to Valerie.

"He's not here?" Valerie asked and looked around,
avoiding the casket.

I leaned over to make sure I saw everyone seated
and noticed a couple of men who were unfamiliar to
me standing against the back wall. "No, he's not here."

"He stopped over for supper last night. We talked
about Flo's service, and he acted like he was coming,"
Valerie replied.

"Your mother told us that he was really shaken by what happened," I said. "Maybe it's too much for him."

"I know, but that's not a good excuse. He should be here," Valerie said with anger.

"It doesn't look good for him, not being here and all," I said, shaking my head.

"Why? What do you mean?" Valerie asked.

"I told you that Keller was asking questions about him." I glanced over my shoulder to look at the two men who were still standing against the wall closest to the door. One was a sheriff and the other was in a suit. I could tell that they were there on business. "I'm sure the authorities are taking notes."

Valerie stood up, looked over at the two men, and scanned the two rooms again. She leaned over to her mother.

"Mom, where's Junior?" she whispered. "I thought he said he was coming."

Mertie gave a quick scan of both rooms. "I don't see him."

Valerie leaned over her mother's lap. "Dad, Junior's not here. Don't you think it looks bad that he's not here? He worked for Florence for years, and he's not attending her funeral?"

"Well, yeah, I suppose so," Senior replied, lifting his head and briefly glanced around. Senior's eyes were fixed on mine. "I don't see Anton either." His eyes told me all that he couldn't say out loud. There were two people's absence that would not go unnoticed. I was sure of it.

I nodded. "Yeah," I whispered before looking back at the sheriff and the other gentleman again. I leaned toward Senior. He leaned toward me.

"Do you know who the other gentleman is standing next the sheriff?" I asked.

Senior coughed and turned around to see who I was talking about. "I think it's the detective Keller hired. I ran into Charlie at the store yesterday and he said that Keller hired a detective out of Rochester. I think his name is Dawson, Detective Thomas Dawson. They needed someone with more experience in an investigation of this type."

The house had become uncomfortably warm by the time Pastor Daly began to address the people. He was standing just a few feet from the casket. During the readings, I watched the people occasionally turn their heads to look at Florence's face and quickly turn away. Probably wondering, like me, why the casket was opened. I listened, waited, and wondered if he was going to talk about her gruesome death.

"...as we allow Florence to leave us to be with God who has welcomed her with open arms into his kingdom of angels, let us pray," Pastor Colton said, and he closed his eyes.

I closed my eyes; the cries of the men and the women could be heard from both rooms.

"Psalm 23, The Lord Is My Shepherd," Pastor Colton Daly said, holding his Bible.

The words of the psalm were slowly drowned out by the images in my head of Florence lying on the stretcher. "The Lord Is My Shepherd" didn't give me any comfort. Daly's words faded in and out. Then I heard him say: "though I walk through the valley of the shadow of death, I will fear no evil." *Ain't that something? 'I will fear no evil.' We're all shaking with guns by our beds.*

As we stood up to leave, the parlor slowly emptied, Willard closed the pocket doors to give the family time to say their private goodbyes to their beloved sister and aunt. Oddly, not a word was mentioned about the way Florence died. But by the condition of Flo's face, did Pastor Daly really need to say anything? We were all left to sort through the tragic end of her life, and Daly's unsuccessful attempt to soften the true horror of it all.

I would have ended the service by saying, "Keep your doors locked and a weapon close by, because the evil that ripped away this life before you may be your very own neighbor who greets you every day with a smile and a friendly hello."

Thirteen

After Florence's burial, and after I arrived home from the farm that night, the late afternoon was on the edge of darkness. I parked my car in our driveway and headed over to Junior's house.

"Junior," I called out as I knocked on the front door of his meager, one-bedroom house.

The door swung open. "Hey, Fritzy, I'm on my way over to my parents'. What can I do for ya?" he asked as he placed his cap over his slicked-back brown hair and walked out the door.

"Why didn't you go to Florence's service today?" I asked as I stepped off his porch and walked with him. "You told Valerie you were going."

"No, I never said I was going. And I don't like funerals," he replied casually.

"Does anyone like funerals?" I asked, annoyed by his foolish answer.

He shrugged his shoulders as we headed toward the bridge.

"After working for her all those years, you couldn't show up to pay your respects to her?"

Junior shook his head and gazed at me, puzzled, and we continued on over the bridge. "Why're you here asking me 'bout Flo's funeral?" Junior stopped and stared me in the eye. "I went to the cemetery after supper last night to pay my respects." His voice faded with undeniable sadness.

I took a deep breath. "I'm glad to hear that you *at least* went to her grave site." We stood there in silence for a moment while Junior gathered his composure. "I don't know if your sister told you, but the District Attorney was over at my house the other night, asking me questions about who might have killed Florence. And you know who he was asking me about?" My eyes were locked on his.

Junior stared at me, waiting for my answer.

I pointed at his chest. "You! That's who he was asking questions about."

"Yeah, I talked to him, too." Junior casually turned and continued walking. "I ain't concerned 'bout it. I ain't the one who killed her."

"Well, I know you didn't. But you not showing up today makes people think you're guilty."

"I just told you; I ain't concerned 'bout it."

"Well, I think you should've been there today, that's all."

"The only funeral I ever went to was my mother's. And that's because I was seven and my father made me go."

"I don't get you!" I said heatedly. "And I don't know how I'm supposed to defend you to Keller. By not going, you made your situation worse! They will throw you in the can if they think you *might* be guilty!"

We walked past my house and the line of pine trees. I stopped at the edge of the road as Junior kept walking, apparently without any interest or concern in what I was telling him. At that moment, I clearly understood why people had a hard time liking him.

Junior narrowed his eyes. "You ain't got to defend me, Fritzy!" he said with irritation in his voice. "The word is that Anton is the one who's goin' to need defendin'!"

Our eyes met with agreement, and then I nodded. "Yeah, you might be right, but still: justice isn't always just. And it could turn on you. Guilty people *do* get away with murder."

"Like I said, I ain't concerned about it." Junior walked up the steps to Mertie and Senior's front porch. "See you, Fritzy. And thanks," he added.

I nodded. The front door opened, and Mertie stepped out and waved. "Valerie is over at Mrs. Adleman's for the night."

"Okay, I'll stop over and see her." I turned and headed back down the road.

"Fritz!" Valerie called out as I approached Mrs. Adleman's.

The porch light was on, and Valerie was standing at the front door waving me over. I smiled, waved and swiftly headed over to her.

I stepped onto the porch and kissed her.

"I saw you walking with Junior over to my house. I thought you were looking for me."

"After I got home, I headed right over to see him. It bothered me that he wasn't at Florence's funeral. I told him how bad it looked that he wasn't there." I shrugged my shoulders. "But he didn't care much."

Valerie crossed her arms. "So, why—why didn't he go?"

"He doesn't like to go to funerals."

Valerie rolled her eyes. "That was his reason!" She placed her hands on her hips. "Well, I didn't want to go either! I even told my mother that at breakfast. She told me there'll be a lot of things in life that we don't want to do, but we have to do anyway." Valerie scoffed. "Then, after seeing her face, I've been sick to my stomach since. After seeing her lying there, well, it was the last place I wanted to be."

"You know, some people around here already don't like your brother. So by him not being there, it just gives people someone to point their finger at."

"I know. But you know Junior, he doesn't pay attention to what anyone thinks, and I don't see him changing any."

"I don't either." I took a step closer to Valerie. "I should be heading home. My mother is probably wondering why the car is in the driveway, but I'm not there."

"Yeah, I better head back inside. I have to clean

up the kitchen. We just finished supper."

"Where's your gun?" I asked.

"It's by the door." Valerie pointed behind her. "Don't worry: I keep it with me all night."

I turned and looked around to make sure no one was walking by. "Just make sure you do! You don't know who might be walking around here." I looked over my shoulder again. The idea of someone walking past me or through my yard—especially if I couldn't see them—made me anxious, even though I knew everyone in Linden. My gut told me that maybe I didn't know everyone as well as I thought. "The other night, after I left you, I thought I saw someone standing in my backyard by the tree. But after I ran inside and looked out the window, I didn't see anyone."

"Do you really think someone was in your yard?" Valerie asked. Her eyes were wide as quarters.

"I don't know. It only took me a second or two to get to the window, and I think I would have seen someone behind the post office or walking through the field, but I didn't see anyone at all. It was probably just the shadows from the tree branches. Or my mind playing tricks on me."

"We're all so afraid. *Everything* scares us now."

"I think you're right." I reached over and grabbed Valerie's hand and leaned in to give her a soft kiss. "I better go."

"All right. I'm sure Mrs. Adleman is wondering

where I am, too."

"Call me if you need me." I stepped off the porch and headed toward my house. At the edge of Mrs. Adleman's sidewalk, I stopped for a moment and turned back as Valerie waved and closed the door.

As I stood in the middle of the road, just a little ways away from the bridge, I could hear the waterfall off in the distance. The hum of the water soothed my thoughts as I reached inside my pocket and grasped my watch. *Dad, I sure hope you're with me right now.*

I glanced up at the deepening blue sky as the day slowly slipped into a memory. Above the trees, smoke from the chimneys melted into the dusk. The aroma of burning birch swept past my nose. I took a deep breath. A feeling of warmth seemed to hold me for a moment. *Dad.* Then it was gone.

As I walked up the road toward my house, scattered leaves carried by the wind skidded past my feet. Suddenly, from behind, I heard rustling leaves and snapping twigs. I gasped, looked over my shoulder, and stopped. There was a large doe standing completely still at the edge of the embankment. I stood motionless, captivated by her power and grace.

Fourteen

*The People of
the State of New York*   *Plaintiff*
-against-
John Doe   *Defendant*

As I walked up the steps to the Genesee County Court House, I felt sick to my stomach. *What more could I tell them?* When the phone rang shortly after last night's supper, I had a strange feeling it was about the John Doe Proceeding that Joseph was telling us about, and sure enough it was the call. Keller's secretary just told me when and where I needed to be. It was not an invitation that I could decline. I kept waking up every couple of hours thinking about the proceeding. What I said at the proceeding could help Anton be arrested. I only knew what he said, but that didn't mean he killed her. Also, Joseph had made me paranoid about reading my behavior. Keller knew when he was being lied to. Being so nervous, I was scared that I was going to look like I was lying even when I was telling the truth.

I reached into my pocket and grasped my pocket watch as I stepped into the court house. "I need you with me, Dad," I whispered as I felt the sweat begin to bead on my forehead.

The copper nameplate outside the door read "District Attorney Ronald Keller." As I pushed the wooden door open with my sweaty hand, a young secretary with deep crimson hair and black, round-framed glasses glanced up from her typewriter. With a pencil grasped between her fingers, she looked down at a paper on her desk, and then over at the grandfather clock against the far right wall. 3:40.

"Are you Fritzelle Reynolds?"

I nodded nervously, recognizing her voice from talking to her on the phone. "Yes, I am." My bones were trembling. I took a deep breath, trying to stay calm.

She wrote something on the paper and set the pencil down. "Let me see if they're ready for you." She rose from her chair, knocked on the wooden door, and then gently clutched the tarnished gold doorknob, and opened it.

"All right," she said in a quiet voice while nodding her head. She then turned toward me and stepped away from the door. "You may go in." She smiled pleasantly.

I entered District Attorney Keller's office and was greeted by a faint haze of smoke that filled the large office. My heart sounded like a galloping horse that was trying to get away. Thoughts of jumping on its back and riding away crossed my mind. I did not want to be there.

Keller and the detective that Senior had told me about both stood up from the rectangular table. There were two tin ashtrays that were already filled to the brim with ashes and finished cigarettes. Keller stepped toward me and extended his hand. I shook it firmly.

"This is Detective Thomas Dawson," Keller said, gesturing to the man sitting next to him.

Dawson extended his hand, and I shook it. "I saw you at the service the other day." The words tumbled out of my mouth.

Dawson nodded and stared at me for a few seconds. He scrutinized me. "I think I remember seeing you there."

"This is Justice of the Peace William Taton, and this is Francine Whittle, our court stenographer."

The gray-haired woman glanced up from her small recording machine, smiled, and nodded.

Keller looked over at Justice of the Peace Taton, who was standing in front of the bookshelf that covered the wall, and waved him over.

"Fritz, would you please place your hand on top of the Bible?"

I walked over to the Justice of the Peace and set my shaky, sweaty palm on top of the tattered black leather book. I noticed that the pages were trimmed in gold.

"Repeat after me," Taton said. "I, Fritzelle Reynolds, being duly sworn under oath, avow under penalty of perjury and pursuant to the laws of New York State that the following statements are true and accurate to the best of my knowledge."

I nodded, and repeated the oath.

"Fritz, please have a seat." Keller pointed to the black leather chair at the end of the table.

I sat down, as did Keller and Dawson. Taton sat down in the chair across from Keller's large desk. It was a good thing they asked me to sit down, because I was starting to feel light headed.

"There's been a lot written in the *Daily News* about people of interest, and there's been a lot of talk. I want you to understand whatever you say here is confidential. We will not tell anyone about it," Keller said.

After Keller told me that all I had to say would be just between the people in the room, I felt my bones relax a little. "As you probably recall, last week, I met with you and a number of residents of Linden regarding the murder of Miss Florence Kingsley. The information that Detective Dawson and members of law enforcement collected has led us to this John Doe Proceeding so we can determine who committed this murder."

I nodded.

"Detective Dawson and I will be asking you a number of questions. If you could just answer each question to the best of your ability, we will move on to the next question."

"I-I will do my best to answer your questions, Mr. Keller."

"Any questions?" Dawson asked.

"No, I'm ready," I said as I wiped my palms on my trousers.

"How old are you?"

"Sixteen."

"Where do live?"

"4820 Linden Road, Linden, NY."

"Are you a farmer?"

"I guess you could call me a farmer. I work on our family farm with my Uncle John." I could hear Francine Whittle tick, tick, ticking, typing every word I said.

"How far from the Kingsley farm do you live?"

"I'd say about a half a mile. Maybe a little more, but not much."

"What direction?"

"West. Well, more northwest."

"Do you live near the railroad tracks?"

"Heading in that direction. Our house faces the bridge, and the tracks are up the hill."

"How long have you lived on Linden Road?"

"All my life. Sixteen years."

"How many are in your family?"

"It's just my mom and me living there. My father

died about six years ago."

I didn't know what Keller was trying to discover with all these simple questions. They didn't have anything to do with who committed Flo's murder. Keller knew where I lived, and I was sure he knew it was just me and my mother living there.

I wiped my sweaty hands on my trousers again and placed them back on the table, folded in front of me. As I sat there listening to the questions, the smoke curled above Dawson and Keller's heads from Dawson's cigarette. Then the swinging pendulum caught my attention inside the large grandfather clock on the wall behind Keller and Dawson.

"Do you work on the Kingsley farm?" Dawson asked.

"I haven't in a while. I only worked there because Junior asked me to when Flo needed extra help during apple season."

"Did you work on shares?" Keller asked.

"No, but Junior did. Florence just paid me for a day's work."

"How much did she pay you?"

"Fifty-five cents a day."

"Did she pay you at the end of the day?"

"Yes; she wanted to settle at the end of each day."

I didn't understand why Keller was asking all these questions that didn't have to do with the murder. *This could go on for hours.*

"How often did you see Miss Kingsley at her home?"

"When I worked for her and when I had the time, I'd stop by to see if she needed any help."

"When was the last time you saw Miss Kingsley alive?" Dawson asked and set his cigarette on the edge of the ashtray, sending a wavy stream of smoke into the haze.

My mouth was starting to feel dry, and the smoke began to sting my eyes. I started to cough a little.

Dawson glanced over his shoulder at Taton. "Can you get him some water?"

Taton nodded, stepped out the door, and returned a minute later with a glass of water and set it down in front of me.

"Thank you," I said and took a needed sip. The cold water soothed my scratchy throat.

"I think it was the Saturday before she died, on my way home from the farm. I saw her outside working, as she always did." My voice faded as I began to remember all the times I would drive by Flo's farm and see her working. I'd wave, and she'd wave back at me. I took a deep breath and tried to keep my wits about me.

"Did you ever have any words with Miss Kingsley?" Keller asked.

"No, she was a good woman. I never had any reason to have words with her."

Keller nodded, then he placed his eyes intently on mine. "On Monday, the sixteenth of October, the day on which we think Miss Kingsley was murdered: you didn't see her that day?"

Finally, I realized the reason for his line of questioning. Joseph's words started to make sense. Keller was reading my behavior, and I was sure that Dawson was too. Keller was asking me a lot of questions that I would have no reason to lie about. Then he could watch my reaction to the ones that mattered.

"I wasn't home on Monday; I left for the farm early that morning and stayed the night."

"Do you normally stay at your Uncle's during the week?" Dawson asked.

"No, I don't like to leave my mother home alone. But my uncle had a couple of cows that were calving, so he asked me to stay."

"Do you know of anyone who has had trouble with Miss Kingsley's farm dealings?" Keller asked.

"No, not that I know of or heard about."

Keller wrote on his notepad and flipped the page. He seemed to be reading and then flipped the page again. He looked up at me.

"Was Miss Kingsley a hot-tempered person?"

"I'd say she was quick to tell you what was on her mind."

"Quick tempered?" Dawson asked as he squished his cigarette into the ashtray, leaving the tips of his fingers covered in ashes.

I nodded. "Yes, sir, quick, but it wouldn't amount to anything. She would laugh about it a few minutes later."

"Do you think she was a person who, if some stranger came in, would flare up and try to push them off the premises?" Keller asked as he held the end of his pencil near his bottom lip.

"I think so."

"She wouldn't be afraid?"

"No, I don't think so."

"There has been some talk about a man seen around there that day. It was reported that he was carrying a trunk and was trying to sell some items. He wore a long black overcoat and had shaggy hair and whiskers."

"I didn't hear anything about that."

"Do you know of anyone who answers to that description?"

"No, I don't."

This was all news to me.

"In recent days, have you noticed any strange tramps going down the road?"

"Once in a while, I see a tramp, or a Negro, or a foreigner."

"Did you ever see a stranger on the Kingsley farm?"

"No, sir."

Keller looked down at his notepad and started writing. The ticking of the stenographer's keys had stopped as Keller continued to write. I glanced over at Dawson. His eyes were on me, and I wondered what he was thinking. I took a deep breath and swallowed.

"Did you know Elvin Kingsley, Florence Kingsley's older brother?" Keller asked.

"No, I never heard her mention him."

"During your acquaintance with Miss Kingsley, did you ever hear her say anything in regards to her brother Willard, who lived with her?"

"Everything was Willard with her, she'd say."

"By that, they got along well together?" Dawson asked.

I nodded. "Yes, she was always talking about how Willard said so and so, and whatever Willard said was good with her."

"Did you and Willard ever have any words?" Keller asked.

"No, never."

"Did you ever hear Walter or Willard speak about ownership of the property?"

"No, sir."

"From your relationship with Walter and Willard, and Miss Florence Kingsley, did you ever see or hear of any trouble between them?"

"The times when they drank—she didn't like that at all."

"Have you known of any occasion, recently, that Walter or Willard had been drinking?"

"No, I haven't. I guess if one of them got bent everybody would know it. They always show up at the store or someone's house. But I haven't seen either of them do that in a while."

"Do you know Anton Mitchell?" Keller asked.

Keller's question sent a flash of heat over my skin. "Yes, sir."

"How long have you known him?"

"All my life."

"Do you think he had anything to do with this crime?"

"I don't think so…" I sat there quietly for a minute. "Honestly, I can't see him committing murder."

Keller looked up from his notepad. His inquisitive eyes rested on my face, which began to flush. "Do you know if he had any words with her?"

"No, I'm not sure. But I *know* he was angry at her for squealing on him about his cider making."

"There has been a great many people that have mentioned him in connection with this crime, for various reasons. What's his reputation in the neighborhood there?"

"It ain't good, not a very good reputation at all. I don't know him to have many friends."

"Did you ever have any words or trouble with him?

"No."

"Why doesn't he have a good reputation?"

"He has a foul mouth."

"You mean profanity, or talking about people?"

"Yes, both. Always talking about his neighbors, and he doesn't use good language—quick to start an argument with people."

"Do you think there is a kind of general feeling among the residents of Linden about Mitchell?"

"Yes."

"Are they afraid of him?"

"I don't think they are *afraid* of him. I don't know why they would be. No, I never heard anyone say they were afraid of him."

"Do you think Walter or Willard had anything to do with this crime?"

"Florence's twin brothers?"

"Yes: do you think they were involved?"

"No, they thought too much of their sister."

"The general opinion of the neighbors seems to be rather mixed. Some think Willard did it, and some think Mitchell did it. Is it your opinion that a stranger did it?"

"I don't know. I have a hard time believing any-one in Linden would commit such a crime. But at the same time, I don't know what any stranger would gain from killing her. The word is, nothing was stolen from her house—so that's my answer, I just don't know."

"When did you first hear of Miss Kingsley's death?"

"Tuesday evening, on my way home from the farm. When I saw all the cars and police cars, I stopped to see what happened."

"What was Junior's relationship with Miss Kingsley?"

"He worked for her for years, picking apples and threshing hay."

"Did he ever have words with Miss Kingsley?"

"None that I know of. He thought a lot of her."

"If he thought so much of her, why wasn't he at the service?" Detective Dawson asked with intensity in his light aqua eyes.

"I was surprised that he didn't go, and I was a little angry about it. So after I got home from work I went over to see him to find out why he wasn't there. He told me that he doesn't like funerals and so he just doesn't go to them. My thought was, no one likes funerals, and it was a poor excuse for not going. But that's just how he is."

"So by him not attending, do you think he was involved with this crime?" Dawson's eyes were directly on me.

"No, not at all, because I know Junior. He didn't do it."

"It is the general opinion among the neighbors that Gordon Kessler, Junior, was not involved with this crime," Keller said.

"I know he wasn't." *So why did you ask?* I held my tongue.

Dawson turned to Keller. "Do you have any more questions?"

"No," Keller replied.

"Mr. Reynolds, that will be all. Thank you," Dawson said.

I walked out of the office. A car horn sounded off as I exited out the set of double wooden doors. The light gray limestone courthouse was surrounded by Main Street, Ellicott Street, and Court Street that made a triangle. I stood at the edge of the steps and took a deep breath, enjoying the cool air on my sweaty skin. I watched the automobiles traveling east and west down Main Street and appreciated my relief of finally being out of Keller's office. It was then that I noticed Joseph walking up the Main Street sidewalk, carrying his briefcase.

Joseph saw me standing at the top of steps. He waved as he ascended up the steps. "Fritz, I'm glad I ran into you."

"I'm glad that I ran into you, too." I gestured to the large wooden doors behind me. "I was just interviewed by Keller and Dawson. They know Junior wasn't involved."

"Yeah, it took some time to rule him out, but they seem confident that he was not involved in the murder."

"I've been telling you that all along. But you seemed to think that I was lying to you," I said, with a touch of resentment in my voice.

"No, I just think you know more than you're telling us," he said casually.

I stared into his dark brown eyes. "I don't... I don't know any more than I'm telling you or Keller. But I do know squealing can get you killed in Linden," I said in a steady voice. I wasn't sure if he realized it, but the world was a very dangerous place.

Joseph tightened his lips and gave me a slight nod. "I know," he said quietly.

"I'm just glad that Junior's been cleared."

"I understand. He's Valerie's brother." He paused for a moment before continuing. "I've been thinking... this murder has not been solved yet, and I worry about both of you living out there."

"Didn't my mother tell you? My father had shotguns."

"Yes, she told me, but that doesn't make me feel any better."

"Why?"

"Let me ask you this: do you think it would be hard to grab a gun out of your mother's hand if someone was attacking her?"

"Well, now that you say it like that... I don't know."

"Fear can paralyze you. Just because you know how to use a gun doesn't mean that in any given situation you'll be able to fight back or pull the trigger. I'm not confident that your mother could shoot anyone."

"I'm so used to shooting a gun, I never thought about her not shooting if she—"

"I think you're smart to have the guns nearby, but I can't see your mother using a gun, at least not with any confidence."

"You're probably right; she'd be too nervous. Gosh, Florence was murdered the night I stayed at my uncle's house." I shook my head with a somber gratefulness.

"I know, I thought about that too."

An uncomfortable silence held its place between us as I imagined my mother standing at the top of our stairs, holding a gun at someone. The trigger sticking and—I wouldn't allow my mind to complete the scene. "Well, I better head back to the farm. Uncle John is probably wondering where I am."

"Your mother called earlier and asked me over for supper. I'll probably be there around five-thirty or six."

"All right, I'll see you tonight. I probably won't be there until closer to seven."

Joseph stepped toward the wooden doors.

"Do you think there will be an arrest soon?" I asked apprehensively.

"I can't say. That's the reason for the John Doe proceeding."

"What about the three Negroes?"

"They were arrested on vagrancy charges and let out last Friday. They didn't have anything to do with Miss Kingsley's murder. They only picked them up because they didn't belong in the area."

"I was just wondering because Dawson probably has more experience with these types of cases."

"Just understand that Keller isn't questioning strangers in this proceeding; he is questioning your neighbors about your neighbors." Joseph's eyes held mine for a moment. I understood what his eyes were saying: it wasn't a vagrant who stepped off the train—it was someone I knew. Then he pulled out his pocket watch, looked at it briefly, and shoved it back into his front pocket. "I better head inside. I have a meeting in ten minutes."

"All right, I'll see you tonight." I waved and ran down the steps. It was then that I noticed a shorter, burly man, probably in his forties, wearing a black fedora hat and a long dark grey coat, heading toward me.

"Hello," I nodded.

"Hello." The man stopped. "Young man, can I ask you a question?"

He was jittery and fast speaking, but I shrugged my shoulders. "I guess."

"My name is Frank Henderson." He extended his hand and I shook it briskly. "I am a reporter for the *Batavia Daily News*."

"I'm Fritz, Fritz Reynolds. It's nice—"

"Would you happen to be here for the John Doe Proceedings?"

"Yes," I replied nervously. "I just met with District Attorney Keller about ten minutes ago."

"If you don't mind me asking, why were you questioned?"

"I used to work for Florence Kingsley."

"I see... So who do you think murdered her?" He asked as he swiftly pulled out a notepad and pencil from his coat pocket and waited for my answer.

"I don't know."

"I always ask... I have to ask. If you want answers, you have to ask."

"Well, I don't have anything to tell. I just told Keller and Dawson what I knew, which ain't much."

"You must've been one of the last witnesses to be questioned, because I called District Attorney Keller five minutes ago to ask him if he was going to be giving a formal statement to the press regarding the John Doe Proceedings, and he told me to be at his office at five o'clock."

I pulled out my pocket watch: 4:35. "It looks like you're early."

"I'm always early. You'll want to buy a copy of the

four o'clock *Daily* tomorrow. Keller's statement will be in there."

"I'll be sure to pick it up," I said hesitantly. I turned and headed toward my car.

"So far, it's been a fearful mystery; maybe tomorrow we'll know a lot more." Frank lit his cigar and ran up the courthouse steps.

As I approached my car, I looked back at the courthouse doors as they closed behind Frank Henderson.

Shaking my head unconvinced, I grasped my pocket watch. *Twenty-three hours from now ought to be interesting.*

Fifteen

The next evening after work, I drove around the bend and past Florence's empty farm. My mind drifted back to the last time Flo waved to me. It was the last time I saw her alive. For a moment it was as if nothing had really changed: the juicy apples hanging in the orchard, the threshing of hay out in the field, and the ripened pumpkins waiting to be pies lying across the field. There was a stillness to the time I spent there, like a painting with brush strokes of laughter, hard work, and red apples floating among the dark green, rustling leaves. As I glanced back at the farm, it was gray. So I tucked the painting away on a shelf inside my mind.

I pulled my pocket watch out of my trousers. 6:12. I needed to read the four o'clock paper to see what Frank Henderson had to report. *I hope Martha has one left.* I pulled my car into our driveway, ran to the door, and turned the door handle. *Locked!* "Mom? Mom!" I called out as I knocked on the glass. "The door!"

"I'm coming!" She rushed into the kitchen and placed the skeleton key into the keyhole, jiggled it, and then opened the door. "Did you forget your key?"

"Yeah, I guess I did." I stepped through the door and could smell the turkey soup, then noticed three apple pies sitting on the counter. "Do you have the newspaper?"

"No, I never made it to the store today. I've been busy cooking all day. I made soup for supper and baked three apple pies—one for us and the other two for Martha and Helen."

"All right, I'm going to head down to the store, maybe there's one left. Keller's statement is supposed to be in there today."

"That's right: I remember Joseph saying that. Well, if you're going to run down there, take the two pies with you." She walked over to the kitchen counter and handed them to me. "Just put them on the seat next to you and don't drive too fast."

"Okay. Do you need anything else while I'm there?"

"No, I don't think so."

I set the pies on the seat next to me. The smell of apples and cinnamon filled the car. As I drove off, my mouth began to salivate just from the aroma. I pulled up to the front of the store and saw Merle standing at the door.

"Hey, Merle, do you have any copies of the *Daily* left, the four o'clock?"

"Yeah, why?"

"The John Doe proceeding… Keller's statement is supposed to be in there." I grabbed the two pies from the car and ascended up the four steps. Merle held the door for me. I set the pies on the counter. "These are from my mother: one's for Martha and Gerry, and the other is for Helen and Travis."

"When Helen was here earlier she was talking about the proceeding. Keller interviewed her too; you knew that, didn't you?"

"Yeah, I'm sure he interviewed just about everyone around here except my mother. Keller didn't bother with her."

"Well, I'm sure that having an assistant district attorney as her caller probably had something to do with it."

"Yeah, I'm sure you're right. But just the same, she didn't have anything to say. She only knows what people tell her."

Merle glanced over at the newspaper sitting on the back counter. "I already read the article. Keller stated that... wait; I have the paper right here." Merle walked around the front counter and picked up the folded newspaper. "Here it is! Let me find the paragraph... right here! I'll read it:

District Attorney Keller said that the John Doe Hearing failed to bring out anything of importance in the search for the murderer, but that it served to completely clear the persons whose names are mentioned in the statement. He said that each one of those persons had a perfect alibi and they were able to establish that they were in other places than the vicinity of the Kingsley home from the time that Miss Kingsley was last seen alive until her body was found."

"Let me see that paper!" I grabbed it out of Merle's hands and read it for myself, then tossed it on the counter next to the pies. I sat there for a moment, just shaking my head. "I can't believe it," I said under my breath.

"I don't like it either, Fritz." Merle shook his head.

"So does this mean they don't have any suspects, at all?" I asked. "We both heard what came out of Anton's mouth that night—even though I have a hard time believing he was evil enough to commit murder, he still said it."

"I know. And I told Keller what he said, and I wasn't the only one. So, I have no idea if they have any other suspects. Maybe you should ask Joseph that question. He would know."

"Yeah, he would," I said as my words faded.

I heard the back door open. I looked toward the back of the store.

"Why hello, Fritzy," Martha said with a smile as she carried a tin pail of sloshing milk. "Helen and I were just talking about you."

"You were?"

"Yes, we were talking about the interviews with the district attorney. Your mother told us that you were over at the courthouse yesterday."

"Yeah, I was there."

"How'd it go?" Martha set the pail of milk by the stairs that led to their living quarters.

"According to the paper, it was a waste of everyone's time. Did you read Keller's statement?"

"No, I haven't had a chance. I've been upstairs with my mother most of the day. What did it say?"

"The John Doe Proceeding that was supposed to *help* figure out who killed Florence actually cleared everyone of interest." I pointed to the article. "Everyone has an alibi."

"And all that talk about Junior and that other one down the road." Martha waved her finger toward the door.

"Anton?"

"Yes. It's hard to say a kind word about him after the way he spoke to Gerry the other day, so I won't say any."

"What did he say?" I asked.

"Nothing out of the ordinary… he was cursing about his order not coming in when I told him it would. It's just who he is," Martha said while shaking her head. "He wouldn't be so popular with you boys if it wasn't for the cider, and I'm talking about my own son, too," she added with aggravation.

Merle and I nodded with agreement, and a feeling of guilt came over me. Martha was right: we liked to drink his cider.

"He's not that bad of a fellow, Martha," Merle said

in Anton's defense.

Martha glanced over at Merle with disagreement in her brown eyes. "Ask me in a month or two, and maybe I'll agree with you," Martha said as the squeak of the back door opening broke the tension. We all turned to see who it was.

"Martha, I forgot to buy coffee earlier," Helen said as she approached us.

Martha stepped behind the counter and began rummaging through the shelves that were filled with spices, flour, and kitchen items. "I thought I had a couple of pounds out here. Did you sell it today?" she asked, looking at Merle.

"Yeah, I did. I meant to restock it, but I must have forgotten."

"That's all right, honey: let me go grab it. I'll be right back," Martha said and headed to the storage room in the back of the store.

"Hello, Helen," I said. "I have an apple pie for you. My mother made one for you and one for Martha."

"Thank you. Travis loves your mother's apple pies. I'll call her after supper to thank her."

"Is there anything else that you need, Helen?" Merle asked.

"No, just the coffee. Travis can't go to work without having his coffee," Helen said.

"It'll be forty-seven cents," Merle said and hit the cash register keys.

Helen placed the money in his hand, and Merle placed it into the cash register.

"Did you read the news today?" I asked Helen.

"No, Travis was reading the paper when I left. Why do you ask?"

"You'll want to read it. There's an article about yesterday's proceedings."

Helen nodded. "I'll read it when I get home then. Most of my conversation with District Attorney Keller was about Anton, which was not a surprise to me. We all know that he's up to no good most of the time. Did he ask you about Anton too?"

"Yeah, just a few questions. I figured that he had a good reason for asking about him," I replied as I pulled the stool away from the counter and sat down, eager to hear what Helen had to say.

"Well, I saw him the night of Florence's murder." Helen gave a slow nod that seemed to assure me that she did, in fact, see him. "I met up with Jill as she and the kids were leaving Anton's mother's house. She told me that they'd just finished supper over there. I was on my way to the post office, and I walked down the road with them. I was curious why she was walking alone, just coming from her mother-in-law's, so I asked her where Anton was. Jill told me that he had left a few minutes before they did to go finish the chores and do the milking. Then, as we came down the hill, we saw Anton standing by the bridge waiting for them."

"Then that explains his alibi," I said quietly.

"I told them that I saw Anton standing by the bridge. It was starting to turn dark, but it wasn't that dark. It was him. I even spoke to him," Helen said with assurance.

"Did Keller ask you if you thought Anton murdered Florence? Because he asked me."

"Yes, he asked me. And I told him that I don't believe things until I know it is so. And it is so that he was standing by the bridge waiting for Jill and the kids." She glanced over at Merle and then back over at me. "I also told them that I don't *meddle* because I want to keep myself out of trouble."

My eyes were on Merle, who was standing behind Helen. He rolled his eyes and kept shaking his head in disbelief.

"No, I never knew you to *meddle,* Helen," I said with a straight face.

"There's no point in it. Meddling just leads to trouble," Helen said.

Merle covered his mouth. I watched his shoulders bob up and down as he held in his chuckling. He turned and walked toward the back of the store, passing Martha along the way while trying to contain his fit of laughter.

"Helen, here you go," Martha said.

"All right, I'll grab my pie and be on my way. Travis is probably wondering where I am."

"Pie?" Martha asked.

"Ella made them for us," Helen said.

"I thought I smelled apple pie," Martha said and then glanced at the counter as Helen strolled over to where the pies were sitting. "They smell delicious. Would you please thank her for us, honey? I'll call her later, too."

I nodded. "I'll tell her."

"Well, I'll see you all tomorrow." Helen held the pie in one hand and the tin of coffee in the other. She left out the back door as the loud whistle of the 6:50 train passed through Linden, rattling the glasses on the back shelf.

"I'd better be going. My mother has supper waiting for me."

"Don't forget to thank your mother for us." Martha smiled.

"I'll tell her," I said as I rose from the stool and pushed it back toward the counter.

"Fritz, I'll follow you out," Merle said.

"Merle, can you lock up on your way out?" Martha asked. "Gerry should be home any time, and I need to set the table."

"Yeah. I'll see you in the morning."

Merle opened the door, and we stepped out onto the porch. The half-moon hung in the deep blue sky. The scent of burning birch filled the brisk evening air.

"I didn't want to ask in front of those two, but Anton stopped in earlier and asked if a few of us wanted to play some cards tonight. Ya want to go?"

I turned and looked through the store window. I didn't see Martha. "I don't know," I said with hesitation.

"What's the problem? He didn't do it, Fritz! You heard what Helen said."

"I know... I heard her. But I don't know... I mean, I don't *think* he did it either. I even told Keller that. But I don't know... I'm not so sure—"

"Helen just told you, she saw him that night. Anton was with his family."

"It just makes me wonder... I don't know what to think anymore," I said with frustration. "If he was having supper at his mother's and wasn't by Flo's farm, then—"

"Have you taken a gander at the vagrants that get off the train here? Maybe it was a robbery gone sour."

I shrugged my shoulders. "It could have been." I placed my hands in my front pockets.

"So are you coming to the Mill tonight?"

"Yeah, I'll probably head over there after I see Valerie."

"Is she still staying over at old lady Adleman's?"

"Yeah, she's there every night. Valerie has been doing all the chores and cooking all of her meals. Mrs. Adleman's son pays her weekly for staying there."

"That's good. Valerie has a job and it also helps Mrs. Adleman out. All right, I'm going to lock up. I'll see ya in a little while," Merle said as he opened the wooden screen door.

I left the porch, headed toward my car, and opened the car door. "Yeah, 'bout 7:30 or so," I said, and shut the door. I pulled away from the store and headed home.

I drove into our driveway and turned off the car. Out the car window, I could see two deer grazing just beyond the trees in our backyard. There was a time when I'd want to run inside and grab my shotgun. I just didn't feel the same way about hunting anymore. My desire was gone. I stepped out of the car and ambled toward the steps.

"Mom!" I knocked on the door and saw my bowl sitting on the table waiting for me.

"Just a second," my mother yelled from the parlor.

She placed the key in the keyhole and let me in. "What kept you so long?"

"I was talking to Helen and Martha. They said thank you for the pies," I replied as I set my hand on the wall and shook my boots off. "Smells good! I'm starving."

My mother picked up my bowl from the table, filled it, and set it back down. "I already ate. I wasn't sure when you would be home." She sat down.

I sat down across from her. "Did Valerie call?"

"No, but she did stop by on her way to Mrs. Adleman's. She wants you to call her."

"I'll stop over there when I'm done."

"So, what did the paper say?"

"Nothing other than that everyone that Keller talked to who might have been a suspect had an alibi."

"So what does that mean? Do they have any other suspects?"

"The paper didn't say. But honestly, I don't think they have any idea who did it." I placed a big spoonful of soup into my mouth. "Even though I don't think Anton could ever kill someone, I still question it. But he wasn't anywhere near Florence's house that night; he was with Jill and the kids at his mother's house. Then, I guess, he left his mother's house a little bit before Jill and the kids did to go finish the chores, and waited for them by the bridge. Helen saw him herself, standing by the bridge waiting. She was walking with them." I placed another spoonful of soup into my mouth.

"It wouldn't surprise me if it was someone that got off the train passing through. I've seen some of them, and they don't look too trustworthy," my mother said.

"That's what Merle said, a vagrant. If Keller and Dawson can't figure out who did it after talking to everyone, then maybe you're right." I slurped some turkey broth.

"I'm still keeping your father's shotgun close by."

"I'm not so sure I trust you using dad's gun."

My mother's eyes widened. "Honey, I can assure you I know how to use it."

"I was talking to Joseph about that. Knowing you, you'd be too nervous and not be able to find the trigger or something, or even drop it."

"I think just having it pointed at someone would scare them. And then I'd hit him with it."

"Hopefully, none of that would ever happen." As I thought about those words, the idea of my mother having to point a gun at someone to save her life made me sick to my stomach. I imagined the whole scene in my head so that I could see his face. But all that I could see was the back of him walking up our stairs. I nodded my head and sipped the last spoonful of my soup, then tipped the bowl up to drink the rest of the broth.

"Would you like another bowl?"

"Nah, I'm full. That was good."

"Do you want any pie?"

"I do, but I'll have some later, after I get back."

"So you're just going over to see Valerie?"

"Well, after that, I'm going to go play some cards with Merle."

"At the Mill?" she asked in an irritated tone. "And with Anton?"

"That's where we play." I avoided looking at her and did not respond to the second part of her question.

I felt the heat of her eyes on my face.

"You're becoming more like your father every day, and right now, I don't mean that in a pleasant way."

"I'm my father's son." I flashed her a grin.

"With all that's happened, and after all this talk about Anton's remark last week, you're going over to the Mill to drink with him?"

I stood there trying to come up with an answer. "It's been a long week, and I want life to go back to the way it was."

"I understand, but it's going to take some time."

"Besides, I want to hear what Anton has to say about the John Doe Proceeding. I know he was interviewed." I grabbed my bowl and spoon off the table and placed them into the sink. "I'm going to go change."

"Remember to take your key tonight. I don't want you banging on the door at eleven o'clock for me to let you in."

"All right, I won't forget. Is Joseph coming over?"

"No, he has a hearing to prepare for. He'll be here tomorrow night."

After I washed up and changed, I headed back downstairs. I could hear my mother washing the dishes in the kitchen.

"Where's the key?" I asked as I grabbed my shoes by the back door and slipped them on.

My mother pulled the key out of her apron pocket

and set it on the table.

"I won't be too late." I gave my mother a kiss on the cheek.

"Okay, honey, love you. Are you taking the car?"

"Love ya too. And no… I'm gonna walk." I grabbed my coat off the hook and stepped out the door. The cool air felt good after being in the warm kitchen. I saw that the light was on at Mrs. Adleman's house, so I ambled down my driveway and knocked on the door. It took a minute, but then the porch light flicked on; Valerie peeked through the front window and smiled, then opened the door.

"I stopped by earlier and your mother said that you were over at Morgan's."

"Yeah, sorry I missed you," I said and leaned in and gave her a quick kiss. "Can you come out here for a few minutes? And could you turn off the light?"

"Okay, let me check on Mrs. Adleman first. I'll be right back."

The light turned off and Valerie stepped out the door with her coat on. "She's fine. She's listening to the radio show."

"Good. I've wanted to do this all day." I threw my arms around her, kissed her soft lips, and slowly walked her to the side of the porch wall, away from the window. Slowly, I opened my mouth a little and gently slipped my tongue inside her mouth. Our tongues swirled together as one. As I kept kissing her, my body heated up. I felt my heart speeding up, sending blood pulsing though my veins. I pressed my hardness against her.

Valerie pulled away, giggling. "Oh my! I wasn't expecting that!"

"I missed you," I whispered and kissed her again.

"I missed you, too."

I kissed her again.

Valerie slowly closed her lips and pulled away. Strands of her hair were blowing across her face from the cool breeze. A strand was stuck to her moist lips. I reached my hand up and pulled it off of her lip. Her eyes were on mine and read of seriousness. "Okay... okay. I've been waiting to talk to you. What did the paper say about the proceedings?"

"Yeah, not much came of it except that it cleared everyone."

"What about Anton? A lot of people think he did it."

"Yeah, there was a small part of me that thought maybe, but he's not *that* bad of a guy. And besides, he was over at his mother's the night Florence was killed. Helen even saw him by the bridge after supper, waiting for Jill and the kids. Florence was last seen before five-thirty, and they figured that she was murdered around five-thirty, six o'clock, so he had an alibi."

"Well, I hope they find the person. I lie awake at

night, worried that someone is going to break in here."

"That's why you're here; you're not helpless like Mrs. Adleman is. Do you have the shotgun with you?"

"Yes, I keep it next to me all night."

"Are you comfortable using it?"

"If I have to use it, I can. Junior brought me out into the field to practice shooting again today."

"That's good. I want you to be comfortable using it."

"I am. If anyone tries to break in here, he will be a dead man!"

"Looks like I have a dangerous lady in my arms. I better behave myself," I said and laughed. "Hopefully, you won't even have to point it at anyone. But if you ever did, make sure it's not your father or Junior coming to check on you."

Valerie gasped, and covered her mouth. "That would be horrible. I never thought of that. I'll make sure it's not someone I know. But... what if it *is* someone we know?"

"The only people who should be coming here are my family, you and your mom, and Mrs. Adleman's son. Other than them, I'm not letting anyone else in."

"Valerie!" Mrs. Adleman's faint voice could be heard through the door.

Valerie pushed the door open. "I'm out here, still talking to Fritz."

"Can you make me some tea?" Mrs. Adleman

asked.

"I'll be right there," Valerie replied and shut the door. "I have to go in a minute." Valerie gazed into my eyes, threw her arms around my neck, and kissed me.

"All right, I won't keep you."

"Are you going back home?"

I hesitated for a moment. "No, I'm going to meet Merle at the Mill to play some cards."

"Cards? Ha!" She pressed her lips together and shook her head. "Is my father going to be there? My mother will hang him like a goose if he goes!"

"I don't know. Merle just asked me a little while ago."

I leaned over and kissed her again.

"I better go or I'll be out here all night." She smiled.

"All right," I glanced down at the wooden planks on the porch floor for a moment and then into her sparkling eyes. "Hey... I just want you to know... I love you," I said softly, gazing at her pretty doll face.

She smiled. "I love you too," she said tenderly, and then kissed me once more.

I pulled away for a moment. "I know you have to go."

Valerie nodded. "Yeah, I better, but I really don't want to."

"I know." I leaned in and kissed her again, then left. I turned, watched the door close, and listened for it to lock. With my hands in my pockets, I walked down the road toward the bridge, listening to the sound of the waterfall echo off the rocks. As I stepped away from the bridge and onto the road, I saw a figure, outlined by the moonlit sky, standing at the top of the hill in front of the train tracks.

Sixteen

"Hey, Fritzy!"

Leon. I ambled up the hill toward his dark silhouette. "Hey, Leon," I replied. I could see the orange tip of his cigarette clutched in his fingers as the smoke leaked from the side of his lips, curling above him then fading into the cold air.

"Where you headed?" he asked, then placed his cigarette between his lips and adjusted his cap.

"My guess is the same place you're headed," I replied as I stepped over the railroad tracks.

"It's been a long day. I just got done milkin' 'bout an hour ago. And I helped deliver a calf well before sunup, so yeah: I'm ready for a few."

"Yeah, I could use a couple too." I glanced over at Leon as he dragged off of his ciggy. "Anyone else supposed to show tonight?"

"I don't know. Merle told me to stop by," Leon said. "And Anton probably wants to celebrate that his ass ain't in the can right now."

"Or celebrating that he got away with it," I said with sarcasm.

"That's what I meant. I can't help but think that the son of a bitch bumped her off and got away with it." Leon shook his head.

"Yeah, I know. But people *do* say things they don't mean. And Keller knows exactly where Anton was that night, so they couldn't pinch him for it. He had an alibi. You can't be having dinner at your mother's, finishing up chores, and waiting at the bridge, and still have time to walk over to Flo's to hide out in her fruit cellar."

"Is that where he said he was?"

"Yeah, Helen saw him."

Leon opened the door to the Mill. "Hey, I'm smellin' some ripe giggle juice!"

I began to feel uneasy as I stepped through the door as I was hit by a strong scent of apples. I hadn't seen Anton in a couple of weeks, not since before the murder.

"It's the bee's knees!" Anton yelled down. I could tell he was feeling good.

"Is Merle up there with you?" I asked up as our boots hit the wood-planked stairs. The sound of Anton's cheery voice seemed to ease my nerves. Not much had changed from the last time: Anton had the cider and was happy to share it. As gruff as he was, the hard cider had softened him.

"Yeah, I just got here," Merle replied.

When I reached the top of the stairs, I entered a haze of smoke.

"Hey, Anton," I said. I noticed a few gray whiskers in his beard among the darker, scruffy ones. He sat at the table, dragging off of his cigar with a tall glass of cider in front of him. He was still the same Anton. I looked at his bloodshot eyes and tried to see a killer in them. But I just couldn't see it. He was a lot of things: no one could deny that, but a brutal murderer? It was hard to imagine.

"Good to see ya, Fritz... Leon." He pointed over to the chairs against the wall. "Pull up a couple of chairs."

We each grabbed a seat and pulled them up to the cracked wooden table that was spotted with burns. I shucked my coat off, threw it over the back of my chair, and sat down. Leon wandered over to the shelf that held a big jug of cider and poured us each a glass.

"Where's Senior?" I asked.

"I saw him earlier, and he didn't think he would make it tonight. Didn't say why," Merle replied as he sipped his cider.

I nodded.

"Here ya go, Fritzy." Leon set the two glasses down on the table and sat down. He turned to Anton. "I wasn't sure we'd be comin' here this soon," he said with a big grin above the glass that he was about to take a drink from. "I thought there would be some bars between us the next time I saw you."

I flashed Leon a tilted grin and shook my head slightly. *Here we go... Can you ever keep your trap closed?*

Anton's smile fell, leaving his face carved with irritation. "I ain't the one who killed Florence Kingsley! Don't start with me, Leon," he said in a raspy voice, then hit the deck of cards on the table as if he had said all that needed to be said. Without another word, Anton began to deal the cards.

I gulped down the rest of my cider, picked up my hand, and stared at it. After a few minutes, a warm feeling traveled through my bones. I glanced over at Anton. "A lot of people been talking," I said, wondering how the words slipped from the inside of my head and off my tongue. Anton's eyes narrowed as he shook his head. *Shit! I shouldn't have said a word.*

"Yeah, ain't it strange she was bumped off right after you tellin' us someone ought to kill that woman?" Leon said with a load of bravery and stupidity. "And fancy that, someone did!" he added with a hard, ironic tone that asked for a sock in the face.

Anton slammed his fist on the table, stood up, and pointed his finger inches from Leon's nose. "You better watch it, kid! I just told y'all I ain't the one who did it!" His eyes swept past each of us. Leon's words seemed to have grabbed ahold of a wild nerve inside Anton. I wasn't surprised. That's what Leon liked to do: he found your sore spot and amused himself with it.

"Anton, sit down. He didn't mean much by it!" Merle stood up, placed his hand on Anton's shoulder, and guided him back down to his seat. "You know he was just razzing you." Merle flashed a look of warning at Leon.

Anton guzzled down his glass as he eyed Leon as if he were prey. "Ready for another one?" He scanned all our glasses.

"Yeah, I'm ready," I said.

Anton stood up and grabbed my empty glass, and filled it and his own.

I knocked Leon's arm with the back of my fist. "Keep your *damn* mouth shut!" I whispered.

Anton had always gone about his business, which sometimes landed him on the other side of the law, without harming anyone. Leon intended to piss you off, and enjoyed it. I wasn't sure who was more criminal.

Leon grinned and sipped from his glass, ignoring me.

Anton set the glasses down on the table and sat back down. "You guys ain't hiding nothing from me. You all think I'm lying. There ain't nothing to lie about," he said, starting to slur his words.

"It's no secret around here," Merle said. "You do sell a lot of cider and Flo didn't like it."

"Yeah, well, she couldn't stand to see her brothers all bent, so she squealed on me." Anton drank from his glass, and then dragged off of his cigar. "Willard told me how angry she was, and that was the reason she squealed like a pig."

"Well, I never heard her say anything about it. Why did she care if her brothers drank?" I asked.

"Yeah, they're grown men: if they want to have a few drinks, they don't need their meddling old sister getting in their beeswax," Leon said, shaking his head. "But, you know how some hens like to squawk," he added under his breath.

"I've seen them bent a couple of times, and I remember Flo was mad about it. But it didn't last long," Merle said. "Maybe she got sick of it."

"You know how some people 'round here make everything their concerns," Leon said, then swigged from his glass. "Especially that squwakin' hen across the way." He gestured with his finger.

"Well, I told Keller that you came into the store around suppertime that night," Merle said, glancing over at Anton. "You bought a loaf of bread. And that was between four-thirty and five o'clock."

"Yeah, had to get the bread, so I went and got bread," Anton said and took a sip of his cider. "...Mom needed the bread." His voice trailed off as he slowly nodded.

"Yeah, Helen told us she was walking with Jill and the kids from your mom's house, and you were waiting for them over by the bridge." I added.

Anton nodded. "That's where I was, and was as close as I got to the squealer's how... house."

"So what did Keller ask you?" I asked and poured

myself yet another glass of cider.

"He... he asked me a lot of shit," Anton replied gruffly as he fumbled his words and gulped his cider.

"Like what?" Leon asked and shot a quick look over to me as I sat back down with my full glass.

"First of all, he asked... he asked me if old lady Kingsley ever had a difference in opinion, and... and the last time I was at her place. I told him that we ain't had no difference. And I ain't been at her place, no time soon." Anton raised two fingers and stared at them and seemed to count them. "Two years."

It was clear to me that the juice was starting to hit Anton.

"Two years, ya sure about that?" Leon asked in a provoking tone.

I kicked Leon under the table and narrowed my eyes at him. "Do you want your nose broken?"

Anton flashed him a vicious look with heavy, bloodshot eyes. He pointed his finger while he held his cigar. "Ain't I told you to watch it, boy?" Wavering, he then slowly found his mouth and dragged on his cigar. "Whatever the hell you and the rest of Linden think... you're all damn wrong... all you all." Anton swigged his cider, burped, and pointed his unsteady finger at Leon. "And I don't need your shit, Leon. I'm coming close to throwing your ass to the road," he said, his cigar hanging from his mouth.

Lucky for Leon, if Anton tried to throw a punch

he'd probably miss and fall to the floor.

"I was just razzing ya, Ant," Leon said, taking the last sip of his cider. He poured himself another glass.

Anton seemed to ignore him and finished his glass of cider. He placed his hands on the table to steady himself as he stood up. He grabbed his glass and staggered over to the jug of cider.

"Shhhh... did all of you just hear a knock?" Leon set his glass on the table and walked over to the stairs to listen.

"Yeah, I think I did," Merle said.

"I'll go see." Leon ran down the stairs.

I heard the squeak of the wooden door opening.

"Is Fritzy here?" My mother's faint voice carried up the stairs.

"Hello, Mrs. Reynolds. Yeah, he's—"

"Mom!" I quickly stood up. My heart started pounding, and I ran down the stairs to the door.

"Is everything all right?" I asked nervously.

"I'm sorry to bother you boys, but Uncle John called and he's not feeling well, so I'm going to take a drive over there."

Her tone of voice told me there was more to what she was saying. "What's wrong with him?"

"He said that he wasn't feeling well after supper. He had the chills and was going to go to bed. It sounds like he has the flu, so I packed a bag. I'm on my way over there now."

I glanced over her shoulder, and I saw the car running.

"Do you want me to pick you up in the morning, or do you want to come with me now?" she asked in a way that unsettled me.

I looked back up the stairs and thought for a moment. "I'll go with you now. Let me go get my coat."

I ran back up the stairs. "Hey, I'm goin' to head over to my Uncle John's with my mom. He's not feeling well." I picked up my glass and drank what was left. "Thanks for the juice, Anton." I nodded before grabbing my coat off the back of my chair and throwing it on.

"Any—anytime!" Anton replied.

"See ya later, Fritzy," Leon said.

"See ya," Merle nodded.

My mother was already waiting in the car. I opened the door, glanced over the seat, and saw the shotgun lying on the back seat next to her bag. I shut the car door. We drove over the train tracks, down the hill, and over the bridge toward our house.

"Do you need anything at the house?" my mother asked.

"No. I have clothes and a pair of old boots at the farm."

"I can smell your breath from here." My mother side-eyed me. By the expression on her face, she wasn't pleased with the odor. "How much did you drink?"

"Just a couple," I replied slowly, trying not to slur my words. "A couple... few," I said under my breath, so I wasn't lying to her.

"So, what did you find out from Anton about his interview with Mr. Keller?"

"Nothing new."

"So who was over there tonight?"

"Just Merle and Leon, and Leon will be lucky if he walks out of there tonight without his nose broke. He doesn't know when to keep his mouth shut."

"Why, what was he saying?"

"He was trying to get Anton to admit that he is the one who killed Florence."

"Well, if he did do it, he wouldn't be here running free right now. Joseph said that they were confident about who *didn't* do it. But what worries me is who *did* do it." My mother flashed me a quick look.

"I know," I said quietly.

"Leon likes to stir the pot and watch it bubble," Mom stated, matter-of-factly.

"Yeah, he sure does. And I don't know how many times you need to get socked before you learn to keep your mouth shut," I said as we approached the bend near Florence's lifeless house.

My mother glanced over at Florence's farm. "Every time I look at that house, it's just so tragic and sad. It overwhelms me at times."

"I know."

"What happened changed everything around here. It's given me a lot to think about," she said softly.

"What do you mean?"

"I was home alone that night... It could have been me." Her voice faded away but left the lingering fear in the air.

"I know. I've thought about that, too."

My mother stopped at the Route 63 crossroad, near Harlow's farm. I could see the small patch of bare trees where the lady had been murdered. I didn't want to mention it; my mother seemed to have enough on her mind.

"I'm scared. I'm just really scared." Her voice cracked. She lifted her hand off the steering wheel and wiped a tear that was running down her cheek.

"Mom, I know," I said gently. "We're all scared. But nothing is going to happen." I tried to assure her.

"I'm sorry... but tonight, it all just hit me. I was sitting at the kitchen table after you left, and I kept thinking about someone trying to break in. Then I tried to keep my mind off of it, so I started to read. I jumped at every crack the house made. Then Uncle John called and told me that he wasn't feeling that well, so I told him that I'd be right over. He assured me that I didn't need to come over, but I told him I would anyway. I just didn't want to stay in the house alone, waiting for you to come home."

"Why didn't you tell me before I left? I would have stayed home. I'm sorry; I wasn't thinking," I said softly, filled with guilt.

"Don't be sorry. You know Joseph is over almost every night. After you left, the house just felt so cold. It's really the first night I've been home alone since—" Her voice faded.

"Why don't you stay at Uncle John's for a few days? I'm sure he'd like having you around to cook and do his washing."

"I thought about that, but I don't want to intrude on him. And you've been home every night. It was just the couple of hours before Uncle John called, that's all."

"I'm sorry," I said, still feeling as though I'd been selfish.

"No, it's all right. I had the doors locked, but I kept thinking about Florence being so helpless. Suddenly, I felt helpless, too. I kept picturing someone breaking into the house. Over and over again, I kept visualizing a dark figure breaking the glass window on our side door."

"I won't leave after I come home from the farm. I'll come home, go visit Valerie for a few minutes, and come right back."

"Thank you, but I don't mean that you have to stay home with me every night that Joseph isn't going to be there."

I looked at my mother and saw the fear in her eyes.

As I sat there, I closed my eyes for a moment. I imagined nests built of rattled bones, broken skulls, dripping in cold blood inside the minds of everyone in Linden—holding everyone's thoughts captive.

Seventeen

1923

The warm afternoon sun fell on our faces as Valerie and I stepped out of the large wooden doors of the Middlebury Baptist Church. My eyes wandered across the road, over to the cemetery headstones, over the tumbling hills, and up to the clear, crisp blue sky.

"What a gorgeous day!" Valerie said cheerfully.

"Yeah, it sure is." I smiled, noticing how the sun made her blue eyes sparkle like deep blue crystals. We continued walking hand in hand toward the parking lot.

I glanced back at the church doors. "Where are they?"

"Oh, your mom is probably introducing Joseph to everyone."

"Yeah, you're probably right."

"Fritz!" my mother called.

I turned, and she waved as she and Joseph strolled toward us, arm in arm.

"So, was everyone interrogating you in there?" I asked, jokingly.

"It sort of felt a little like that," Joseph replied, and laughed about it as he adjusted his fedora.

"I guess it's to be expected, you're a new face around here," Valerie said.

"Oh, you're exaggerating." My mother flashed a smile at Joseph. "There were only a few people asking questions about who you were."

"I'm sure I've put witnesses on the stand through much worse." Joseph nodded and cleared his throat. "I've new empathy for the folks sitting in the witness stand."

I gave a lighthearted laugh.

My mother turned to me. "Now, you remember that we're going to the Richmond Hotel for dinner with Joseph's parents this afternoon?"

"You and Valerie are welcome to come with us. Today would be the perfect day for you two to meet my parents. I know they would love to finally meet both of you," Joseph said.

"Valerie and I have plans this afternoon, but thank you for the invitation," I said. "I'm sure we'll meet them soon."

Valerie turned to me, her head slightly tilted. "We do?"

"Yes," I nodded with a grin. "We do."

"All right!" Valerie gave me a sly look and turned to my mother and Joseph. "I guess we have plans, which is a surprise to me."

"Do you have any idea what time you'll be back from Batavia?" I asked as I pulled my pocket watch out of my front pocket. "It's quarter to twelve now."

"Before supper," Joseph replied. "I have to prepare for trial tonight."

"I'd really like to meet your parents, Joseph; maybe another time," Valerie said.

He nodded. "Yes, of course. Another time," he said and turned to my mother. "Are you ready?"

"Yes, I am." She stepped toward me, kissed me on the cheek, and then kissed Valerie on the cheek. "See you in a few hours. Enjoy your day."

"Okay, let's go!" I pulled Valerie's hand, and we headed toward the car. I looked over my shoulder; I saw my mother and Joseph exit the parking lot and drive down the road.

"Where're we going?" Valerie asked and started to giggle.

We stopped at the passenger side of the car. I placed my hands on her hips and I stared into her eyes. "You're such a doll, you know that?" I whispered and leaned in and kissed her soft pink lips. "I almost leaned over and kissed you in church. But I thought I'd better wait."

"You did?" Valerie smiled. "That certainly would have turned some heads."

I leaned in and kissed her again. Our mouths opened; our tongues twirled and ignited the desire inside my veins.

The sounds of voices were coming toward us. I

pulled away. We both turned to see who it was.

An old lady and her husband were walking arm in arm. The grey haired lady was shaking her head with disgust on her face. Then she shook her finger at us. "You two ought to be ashamed of yourselves," she said in a creaky, offended voice. Her tall, white-haired husband opened the car door for her; she sat down, and he shut the door.

"Don't mind her," he said quietly. "She must have forgotten what it was like to be young... But I remember." He smiled and then winked. "You two enjoy your day."

Valerie blushed, and then we broke out in laughter when the couple drove away.

"Do you know them?" I asked.

Valerie shook her head. "No, I don't think so."

"Aren't you ashamed of yourself?" I asked.

"Yes, very ashamed."

"Me too! Now kiss me!" We kissed and tried not to laugh.

Valerie pulled away. "We should stop. Now, where're we going?" she asked with earnestness.

"It's such a nice day; I thought we'd take a Sunday drive." I opened the car door for her, and she stepped inside. We drove out of the parking lot, down the road, and into the rolling hills.

"What about dinner? I'm a little hungry."

"I packed it for us. It's in the basket behind the

seat."

"That's so sweet! But we have to stop and tell my parents that I won't be home for dinner."

"No you don't. It's all taken care of. I ran into your mom last night on her way to the post office and asked her if it would be all right for us to do something this afternoon. I also told her that it was a surprise." I flashed a quick grin, and set my hand on her knee.

"You're sneaky. But I like it." She flashed a sly smile. "So where're we going?"

"Well, I thought all last night about where to go today. Then my mother reminded me of the place we used to go to when I was young: have you ever been to Silver Lake?"

"No, I don't think so. Is it far?"

"Not too far. It's in Perry."

As I drove through the back roads of Wyoming County, we passed big farm houses with cows and horses grazing off the land, two small pioneer ceme-teries hidden among the sparse trees, lots of woods, and fields of corn and cabbage coming to the end of their growing season.

"I don't think I've ever been out this way," Valerie said as she gazed at the countryside.

"That's good! I was hoping to take you somewhere you've never been to."

We entered the village of Perry and saw the paint-ed wooden signs for the Silver Lake Marina. A couple of miles down the road, I turned into the marina and parked the car.

"What a beautiful lake!" Valerie said as I opened the door for her and focused for a moment on the soothing sound of the water gently hitting the shore. "I didn't realize that it would be this big."

"Well, it's really a small lake compared to the other lakes around us, like Lake Ontario. You can't even see the other side of that lake."

"This is perfect!" Valerie smiled and gave me a quick kiss as I opened the back door and grabbed the basket off the floor. I also grabbed my dad's old wool blanket, which smelled of cedar and reminded me of him.

A few blankets were already spread out across the grass. There were mothers and fathers with their children. There was a father throwing a baseball to his young son. There was a mother holding her baby as she gazed out at the water. Children were running around, chasing each other and laughing, all under the warm sunshine.

"Where do you want to go?" Valerie asked. "Here, let me carry the blanket." She pulled it out from under my arm and held it up to her nose. "Cedar—I love the smell of cedar."

I scanned the area and saw an opening, not far from a tall maple tree shading the grass beside the water and not far from an older man who was fishing on the shore. "What about over there?" I pointed.

"That's a good spot, right by the water!"

We strolled past the families who were enjoying the day. Valerie shook out the blanket and spread it out a few steps from the layer of pebbles lining the shore. The fisherman nodded and waved as he threw his fishing line into the water.

We sat down, and I opened the basket. "My mother baked fresh rolls this morning, and I made turkey sandwiches." I handed Valerie her sandwich, which was wrapped in a gold linen napkin.

"This was such a great idea," she said and bit into the soft roll.

"I also brought a couple apples." I handed one to Valerie.

"Thank you." She smiled. "Did you bring anything to drink?"

"Yes, of course, cider. The sweet cider." I flashed a grin and grabbed the small jug out of the basket. I found two level spots, set the two glasses down, and then poured the cider.

"I saw a sign saying that you can rent boats here. We should come back sometime and rent one," Valerie said as she watched the boats out on the lake.

"There won't be much time this year with me working almost every day, but maybe next summer."

"That's what I meant, next summer. I've never been on a boat before. It must be nice out there on the water."

"It is," I said as I stared at the lake and bit into my roll. Watching the boats on the water, I remembered all the times out on the lake with my mom and dad. I could almost see my father rowing the boat as I sat next to my mother, her arms wrapped tightly around me. She was so scared that I'd fall in the water. She had held me close as she pointed to the sunfish that swam next to the boat.

"I love the sound of the waves hitting the shore." Valerie gazed at the lake as she sipped on her cider. She seemed mesmerized by the sight and sound of the water.

"So, have you seen much of Junior lately?"

"No, not much, but my mother said he stopped for supper last night. He's been working in Attica all week." She glanced over at me. "Have you seen him?"

"No, that's why I was asking: it's been a while. And I can't look at an apple without thinking of your brother. We must have picked a million of them."

"Your mom bringing Joseph to church today, that was a big step for her."

"Yeah, I guess. She's been talking about bringing him for a couple of weeks. I think she was finally ready to make that move. Joseph is good for her."

I watched a mother, father, and young boy rowing across the lake; memories of my parents taking me out on a boat as a child flooded my head once again. I recalled a pile of flat rocks, a fishing pole, and a blue heron. My father had shown me how to skip a rock across the water. He helped me reel in my first sun-fish. And I remembered him pointing to the blue heron that was standing on the shore by a decaying tree that had fallen in the water.

"What're you thinking about?" Valerie asked in a soft voice. "You're smiling."

I nodded. "Yeah, I guess I am," I replied quietly, still staring at the lake, reminiscing. "All these memo-ries of being here when I was young just came flooding back to me."

Valerie leaned over, placed her finger below my chin, and turned my head toward her. "Tell me about them." A slight grin spread across her face. She placed her hand gently on mine and grasped it.

I leaned over and kissed her. I could smell her perfume: a mix of jasmine and rose. "I have so many. We used to come here a lot during the summers."

"Pick the first one that comes to mind," Valerie said eagerly.

"Well, I remember one time we were out on the boat. My dad had showed me how to row... I must have been five or six then. I tried so hard to move the oars, but I couldn't do it; I wasn't strong enough, and the boat hardly moved. Then my father told me that his arm was hurting from rowing out to the middle of the lake and he wouldn't be able to row us back in. My mother assured me that she wasn't strong enough to row. I remember being so scared, I think I even began to cry. My parents had me going for a couple of minutes!" I started laughing. "So after they realized how scared I was, my dad placed his hands over mine and we rowed the boat back to the dock together. He assured me that we wouldn't have made it back to shore if it wasn't for my help."

"That's sweet and funny. It's a little mean, too, but funny."

"I know, but I felt really strong when we made it back to the shore." I pressed my lips together and couldn't help but smile about that memory.

"I wish I could have seen your face when you thought you had to row the boat all the way back to shore. I will have to ask your mom about that."

"I forgot all about it until a few minutes ago. The day was just like today."

"Those are the memories that you have to hold on to." Valerie kissed me on the cheek.

"Beautiful day, ain't it?" a man's voice asked.

I turned and saw the fisherman walking toward us.

"Yes, it is," Valerie replied.

"Having any luck?" I asked.

"I caught a few earlier. Just came over to say hello and introduce myself. Henry Benson." He reached down and shook my hand. "You can call me Hank."

"I'm Fritz, and this is Valerie."

"It's nice to meet you both. Is this your first time here? Most faces I know."

"I used to come here with my parents when I was younger." I gestured over to Valerie. "This is her first time here."

"I was just asking because I fish a lot here. My wife and I live down the road." Hank pointed. "So, where're you folks from?"

"Linden. It's about twenty miles from here."

"Linden?" He asked with interest. "Ain't that where that woman was found murdered?"

I glanced over at Valerie, then back at Hank. "Yeah, we knew her. I used to pick apples on her farm. She was a good woman," I replied.

"That's a damn shame for something like that to have happened." He shook his head. "So they ain't never found out who did it, did they?"

"No, not yet. No one has been arrested for it."

"Well, I know there've been murder cases open for years, and somehow they catch 'em."

"And sometimes they don't," I said in a fading voice.

Hank nodded and scanned the lake for a moment as he wiped his forehead, maybe at an unexpected loss for words. "I'm gonna let you two get back to enjoying your meal. It was nice meeting you, Fritz, and you too, Valerie." Hank looked at me and pointed to Valerie.

"You have a lovely lady there."

Valerie smiled at me, and then looked up at Hank. "Thank you."

"Thank you," I replied. "Are you done fishing for the day?"

"Yeah, I'm sure my wife is wondering where I am. Dinner's waiting for me."

"Maybe we'll see you around again," I said as I sipped my glass of cider.

"Yeah, we are going to come back and rent a boat sometime," Valerie said.

"Why don't you take a walk down to the rental shop and see if you can rent one today?" He pointed over to the small gray shed to the left of the dock. "You'll want to talk to Charlie. He's a good friend of mine. He'll take good care of ya."

Valerie nodded and smiled.

"Maybe we will." I reached in and pulled out my pocket watch. 2:15. "We have some time."

"Enjoy the rest of your day," Hank wandered away, picked up his fishing pole and tin bucket, and then headed toward the road.

"Would you want to rent one today?" Valerie asked.

"Sure, if he has one available."

"Did you bring any money?"

"Yeah, I have a few dollars with me. Let's pack this up and go see about the boat," I said with enthusiasm and jumped to my feet.

Valerie finished her cider and placed the jug and the glasses into the basket. I grabbed the two apple cores and threw them into the trees while Valerie grabbed the napkins and placed them into the basket. She stood up, shook out the blanket, and folded it up.

"I'll take that," I said as I held out my hand and Valerie handed me the blanket and picnic basket. I ran it all back to the car.

"All right," I said, slightly out of breath. "Let's go see about that boat." I grasped Valerie's hand, and we strolled over to the marina as the small waves rolled in to the shore. I felt the cool air drifting off the water as we approached the small shack.

I pulled the handle of the gray wooden door. There was an older, bald-headed man wearing round, wire-framed glasses and a dark blue shirt with tan suspenders sitting behind a small counter, reading the newspaper.

"Can I help you kids?" he asked.

"Are you Charlie?"

"I happen to be. What can I do for yas?"

"We were just talking to Hank and he told us to ask you about renting a boat," I replied.

"Oh yeah, he's my neighbor, and a good fella too. How long do you want to rent it for?"

I looked over at Valerie. "What, an hour or so?"

She shrugged her shoulders. "That sounds good."

She smiled. Excitement lit up her eyes.

"That will be seventy-five cents for the hour."

I reached into my front pocket and placed three quarters on the wooden counter. Charlie put the change into a wooden box that was sitting on a shelf behind him.

"Follow me." Charlie stepped out from behind the counter, and we trailed behind him. "I have two of the larger row boats left." He pointed to the two wooden row boats, each of which was tied to a post. "Let me just untie one, and you two can step into the boat over on the dock."

"Let's go over here," I said, and we stepped onto the wooden dock and walked out to the end. There were two dead fish floating among the seaweed by the shore. I caught a whiff of the decaying seaweed and rotting fish. I couldn't wait to head out on the water where the air was fresher.

"This is my first time on a boat," Valerie said excitedly.

"This is my first time rowing a boat... alone." I smiled.

"All right you two," Charlie called out. "I'll hold the boat steady so you can step in."

I climbed in carefully and held Valerie's hand as she stepped into the swaying boat. We both sat down across from each other. I gripped the oars and began to move the boat away from the dock.

"Thank you, Charlie!" Valerie looked up at him as she shielded the sun by resting her hand above her eyes.

"See you in an hour!" I pulled out my pocket watch. "See you at 3:30!"

I began to row out into the lake, enjoying the sound of the water as the waves gently rocked the boat.

"It's beautiful out here! I'm so glad that Hank mentioned it to us!" Valerie said as she gazed into the water.

"Me too!" Being out on the lake again on a sunny fall day brought back so many good memories. It allowed me to drift away to tucked-away places and experience them all over again. Maybe it was something to do with the water, the gentle waves breaking against the shoreline, the unique scent of the water and seaweed that worked its magic on me.

I rowed out to the center of the lake. I counted five other rowboats across the water. As I scanned the shoreline, I noticed a few scattered cottages. Some even had their own docks.

"Wouldn't it be nice to have a cottage here?" Valerie asked.

"I was just noticing all the cottages too. Yeah, it would be nice to wake up in the morning to the sound of the water. It's so peaceful here," I said as I stopped rowing and carefully stepped over to Valerie as the boat rocked and sat down next to her.

"What are you doing?" Valerie asked and began to giggle.

"Kissing you," I replied with a grin.

"You're the most romantic boy I know!" Valerie leaned over, and her tender lips pressed against mine.

I placed my hand on the back of her head, pulled out the pin that held her hair up, and set it on the bench. We continued to kiss. I kissed her harder as our mouths opened. My body started to heat up. I began to move off the seat and lay back toward the end of the boat. We threw our legs over the seat. As I kept kissing her, our breathing became heavier. I placed my hand on her soft breast. She began to breathe even more heavily.

"Maybe we shouldn't have come here today?" I whispered.

Valerie stopped kissing me and gave me a puzzled look. "What do you mean?"

"We would have had the whole house to ourselves all afternoon."

"Then what would we have done?"

"Hmmm... I don't know," I said and started to laugh before kissing her again. I unbuttoned her blouse to her waist. Then I slipped my hand inside and under her undergarment, gently massaged her supple breasts, and began gently stroking her nipple which turned from soft to erect.

She slightly arched her back and moaned quietly with pleasure. "That feels good," she whispered.

"You feel good," I said tenderly as I drew my hand out of her blouse, grasped her hand that was resting on my chest, and placed it on top of the zipper of my trousers. She began to rub my manhood. "Mmmm... That feels so good," I whispered.

"Good and hard," she said. "Maybe you're right. We should have gone to your house instead," Valerie said and started to giggle as she placed her two fingers, teasingly, on my zipper, zipping it slightly down, then back up. Then she unzipped it all the way and began to move her hand inside.

I heard voices. The voices seemed close. We sat up. There was a boat not far from us. There was a man, a woman, and a little girl in a rowboat just like the one we rented. They weren't close enough to be paying any attention to us, but they were rowing toward us.

"Well, we better stop. I sort of forgot we're not alone out here." I zipped up my trousers, grabbed Valerie's hand, and helped her to her seat. I then carefully moved back over to my seat and grabbed ahold of the oars. Valerie buttoned her blouse back up.

"So, do you think your mom's home yet?" Valerie asked.

"Now why do you ask that?" I stared at her with a playful grin. "I'm sure by the time we get back she will probably be home... unfortunately for us." I pulled out my pocket watch: 3:12. "Are your mom and dad home?"

"I'm sure they are. They're always home, unfortunately. Next time, we'll plan better," she said with a chuckle. "What time is it anyway?"

"It's almost quarter after three. By the time I row back in, it will be almost time to bring the boat back."

"We better start heading back then."

The family with the little girl rowed past us and waved as I started to row, and I saw that Charlie was standing on the shore. He walked out onto the dock as he waited for the family. When their boat was lined up with the dock, he picked up the little girl and set her on the dock. Then he held the mother's hand as she stepped out. Charlie held the boat for the father to step out. By then, I was ready to line the boat up with the dock.

"Let me move this boat, and then you can bring your boat in," Charlie called out as he held the rope, moved it to the shore, and tied it up. He walked back out onto the dock.

"Ready?" I asked.

"Bring it in!"

When we had the boat lined up next to the dock, he grabbed Valerie's hand and she stepped out of the boat.

"Did you kids have a good time out there?" Charlie asked.

"Yes, we had a really nice time!" I replied as I picked up Valerie's hairpin from the floor of the boat and then handed it to her.

"This is such a beautiful place," Valerie added.

"Sure is!" Charlie agreed.

I stepped out of the boat and grabbed Valerie's hand.

"Thank you, Charlie! I'm glad we took Hank's advice."

"I don't think I got your names earlier," Charlie said as we stepped down on to the shore.

"My name is Fritz, Fritz Reynolds. And this is Valerie Kessler."

"It's been nice meeting you both, and I hope to see ya here again."

"We'll be back again." I smiled at Valerie.

"We will definitely be back again," Valerie added.

As we walked toward the car, Valerie leaned over and gave me a kiss on the cheek. "Thank you. It was a good idea to come here today."

"Are you sure about that?" I looked at her slyly and placed my arm over her shoulder. "We could have just stayed at my house. I gather you'd be thanking me even more if we did that." I smiled and chuckled.

"You're probably right," she said and started to laugh. "But really, I'm glad you brought me here anyway."

We drove by the county home, crossed the intersection, and then headed down Linden Road around the bend past Florence Kingsley's old farm. Her farm now had a new family living in it, which gave it back its life.

"What's going on down there?" Valerie pointed.

"Where?"

"Nelson's house, with all the police cars!"

Then I saw what she was talking about. Suddenly, I felt sick. An ice-cold feeling landed in the pit of my stomach. "What the hell?" I said under my breath as fear gripped my spine with black claws.

Eighteen

I felt the heat of Valerie's eyes resting on me as I stared straight ahead in a dead gaze at all the black touring cars. It was as if the long, dark claws pierced my spine and paralyzed me. My heart began to pound. My bones began to shake.

"Are you going to stop?"

Valerie's question rolled around my brain as I tried to find the answer. *What the hell happened?*

"Stop! I want to see what's going on!" Valerie shrieked.

"Calm down; if we see someone outside, we'll stop." Just as the words nervously tumbled out of my mouth, a young officer stepped out of Nelson's front door. I pulled in front of the driveway, and we both stepped out of the car.

"Excuse me, Officer," I called out as he was about to open his car door. Then I realized that it was Deputy Ornsby, the officer who helped me over to the porch the night of Flo's murder.

Deputy Ornsby strolled over to my car, holding a small notepad.

"The Nelsons are neighbors of ours. I live just down the road." I pointed in the direction of my home. "I don't know if you remember me or not, but I'm the one you saved from passing out at Florence Kingsley's house. You helped me over to the porch."

Ornsby nodded. "I thought you looked familiar."

"Can you tell us what's going on?"

"Well." He paused for a moment and took a quick look back at the house. "While the Nelsons were at church this morning, someone broke into their house and set their bed on fire."

Valerie gasped. "That's awful!"

"Luckily, the perpetrator wasn't much of an arsonist, because he shut the bedroom door. The fire just smoldered in there; it never spread to the rest of the house."

"Are they okay?" Valerie asked with concern.

"Yeah, they're just really upset, and understandably so. I'm just glad that no one was hurt today."

"Will they be able to stay in their house tonight?" Valerie asked.

"Probably by Tuesday. They need to clean up the room and buy a new bed. They mentioned staying with their son for a few days."

"I appreciate you letting us know what happened," I said.

"No problem. There were a lot of folks here earlier, so most of the neighbors know what happened." Deputy Ornsby looked around, then turned back to us. "I better be on my way. I need to head back to the station."

"Any ideas on who set the fire?" I asked anxiously.

"No, not so far. But if you two hear of anything, or know of anyone who might have done this, would you please call the station?"

"I will. Thank you, officer," I replied.

We stepped back into the car and drove down the road. I pulled into Valerie's driveway and saw the front curtains move.

"I think your mom is waiting for you. I just saw her in the window."

"I know. I saw her, too."

"Valerie," Mertie called as she stepped out the front door and rushed over to my car.

Valerie didn't wait for me to open her car door.

"I just came out to tell you two what happened to the Nelsons today," Mertie said.

"We already know. We just finished talking to a sheriff's deputy who was leaving the house," Valerie said as she shut the car door.

Mertie stood there with her arms folded for a moment, scanning the surrounding houses. "I've been thinking. This *wasn't* some vagrant who got off the train looking to set someone's house on fire. Whoever did this *knows* most everyone 'round here goes to church Sunday mornings," she said with a huff as she shook her head and pressed her lips tightly together. "Since I heard about it, I've been trying to think of the ones who weren't there this morning, and I'm not coming up with anyone."

"Who would have a problem with the Nelsons?" Valerie asked.

"I don't know, but I'm really sickened by the whole thing." Mertie shook her head. "The thought of someone entering our house who didn't belong really bothers me."

"Maybe someone was mad at Marty and was being vengeful," Valerie said.

I shrugged my shoulders. "Could be. Maybe some-one didn't like a decision he made. As Justice of the Peace, not everybody's happy when they leave court."

"You could be right about that, Fritz. It does make sense. I'm sure the sheriff will investigate," Mertie said. "Well, I'm glad they didn't walk in and surprise whoever was in their bedroom. It may have been a *very different* story."

Valerie's eyes widened. She glanced over at me. "Yeah, it could've been," she said in a fearful voice.

Mertie looked over her shoulder at the door. "Well, I have supper on the stove, and your father is sleeping on the sofa, so be quiet when you come in." She turned away and headed toward the front porch.

"I better head home," I said, feeling uneasy about what happened.

"We know everyone who lives here," Valerie said with uncertainty. "Even if someone didn't like what Marty handed down... to break into their house and set their bed on fire? I don't understand."

"It looks like we don't know everyone as well as we might think."

"I'm really angry," Valerie said.

I nodded. "I know. And they'll probably get away with this too," I said, feeling a little deflated.

Any confidence I may have had in the authorities to solve a crime faded after Florence's murder. I could understand how the woman's murder on Harlow's farm was never solved. She was never identified. But Florence's murder was much different. Someone knew she'd go into her fruit cellar at the end of her day. Just like someone knew the Nelsons would be at church.

"Listen, I'd better go. I'll stop by Mrs. Adleman's when I get home from the farm tomorrow." I grabbed her hands, leaned in, and kissed her soft lips. "I love you," I whispered.

"I love you, too."

"Remember, make sure all the doors and windows are locked at Mrs. Adleman's. And don't forget your gun," I said, staring directly into her eyes.

"Don't worry; the gun will be by my side."

"Good!"

"I better go in and help my mother. She's probably wondering what's taking me so long."

I nodded and gave her another kiss. "Okay, see you tomorrow," I whispered.

When I arrived home, I unlocked the door, stepped

into the kitchen, and set the basket on the kitchen chair. The aroma of turkey soup filled the kitchen. My mother strolled in with a bright smile on her face.

"I was wondering when you'd be home. Did you and Valerie have a good time at the lake?"

"Yeah, it was really nice. We ended up renting a boat," I said as I unpacked the basket, setting the glasses in the sink and the small jug of cider into the icebox.

"How nice. That must have been fun." She paused and gestured to the chair. "Can you sit down? I have something I need to talk to you about."

By the beaming grin on her face, I gathered she didn't know about the fire at Nelson's. I didn't have it in me to tell her the bad news and dust any gloom onto her obvious joy.

"What is it, Mom?" I sat down at the table and she sat down across from me.

"Well, I was so excited to tell you. Now, I'm a little nervous." She paused for a moment. "All right, let me start by asking. How do you feel about Joseph?"

"I really like him."

"That's important to me. He really *is* a wonderful man." She anxiously rubbed her hands.

"He's always been really good to you. Why, Mom?" I asked, becoming a little impatient.

"Joseph asked me to be his wife today," my mother said as tears welled up in her eyes.

"He asked you to marry him?" I asked, a little surprised.

She nodded. "Yes." She pulled a handkerchief out of her apron pocket and dabbed her eyes.

"Did you say yes?"

"Yes, but I accepted his proposal on the condition that you will give us your blessing and accept him into our family."

"Yes, of course... of course, I will accept him into our family. Mom, that's so wonderful!" I gave her a tight hug as she began to sob, holding my arms close to her. "Why are you crying?"

"Well, I'm so happy, and I also don't want you to think that this means that I don't still love your father. I really thought that after your father died that I'd never marry again."

I sat back down and stared into her eyes. "I would never doubt that you still love Dad. But he wouldn't want you to spend your life alone. He'd want you to move on and be happy."

"The years have gone by so fast, and you've grown into a fine young man. In a few years, you'll be out on your own, married with your own family... And that would leave me here alone. I've come to realize that I don't want to grow old alone."

"You love Joseph, don't you?"

"Yes, I do love him. He is a good man. And he's from a good family; they've welcomed me like a daughter. And they are eager to meet you, their future grandson. I know you will grow to love them as I have. They are wonderful people."

"Did you two talk about when you'll have the wedding?"

"Late April or early May, when the weather is warmer. And it will give us time to plan."

"Did you tell Uncle John yet?"

"No, I wanted to talk to you first. I wanted your blessing before I told anyone else."

"Of course you have my blessing." I reached over and held her hand. "And I'm sure you have Dad's approval, too."

"I'm so lucky to have such a wonderful son." My mother stood up, gave me a kiss on the cheek, and dabbed her eyes. She stepped over to the counter, opened her purse, and pulled out a round silver ring box. She set it on the table and sat back down. "I told Joseph that I would wait for your approval before I would wear it." She opened the box, placed a diamond ring on her left ring finger, and set her hand down on the table.

"It's beautiful," I said. "I'm so happy for you, and for us." I smiled.

My mother reached over and grasped my hand. "Me too." She nodded. "Well, I'm sure you're hungry. Let me get you some soup." She tucked her handkerchief into her apron pocket, grabbed two bowls out of the cupboard, and filled them to the brim. She set both bowls on the table and sat back down.

I was so excited for my mom. The last time I saw her this happy was when my dad was alive. An image of her sitting on our sofa next to Uncle John the night my father died flashed in my mind. She was inconsolable. She kept asking, why? At that moment, I didn't think she'd ever stop crying. I remembered Uncle John's words: "We don't know those answers. Only God knows why. But I promise the pain will lessen over time." John's promise held true and it was good to see my mom enjoying life again.

I reached over and pulled two spoons out of the drawer behind me. "So, did you two talk about where you were going to live?" I shoved a big spoonful of soup into my mouth.

"A little bit. Joseph wants to live in Batavia." She glanced up at me with uncertainty.

"Do you want to move to Batavia?" I asked.

"Well, I thought about that a lot today. Batavia is only a few miles away. And I can always drive out here to visit," she said and then sipped from her spoon.

"What about the house?"

"Now, you have a decision to make. I already discussed this with Joseph. We can sell the house and both of us move to Batavia. Or you can live here because it is closer to the farm."

"I'll probably stay here most of the time. I don't want to leave Valerie."

"That's what I expected you to say. I'll go ahead and sign the house deed over to you when you turn eighteen."

There was a knock at the door. I turned.

"It's Helen." My mother pulled her ring off. "Don't say anything to her about the wedding, or everyone in Linden will know before the sun goes down," she said cheerfully. She dropped the ring into her purse and headed over to the door. "Hello, Helen, come in. We're in the middle of supper; would you like to join us? We're having turkey soup."

Helen stepped through the door. "No, no thank you. I stopped by twice earlier, but no one was home."

"Is everything all right?"

"No, it's not. I'm glad I stopped, because you must not have heard. Someone tried to set the Nelsons' house on fire today."

"What?" my mother said as she placed her hand over her mouth.

"Someone broke into their house, poured kerosene all over Marty and Emma's bed, and set fire to it."

"Are they all right?"

"Yes, they're fine," Helen replied.

My mother turned to me. "Did you know about this?"

I nodded. "Valerie and I found out on our way

home. I was going to tell you, but..." *You were too cheerful to hear any bad news. I couldn't bring myself to tell you.*

"Joseph and I drove in through Alexander, so we didn't drive by their house."

"I rushed right over there after Doty called and told me about the police cars in front of their house. Emma showed me the kerosene can. It was left right in their bedroom. It's the same can of kerosene that Martha sells at the store. And I already talked to Martha; she doesn't remember anyone buying any kerosene lately. So Merle must have sold it."

"Maybe he did, but doesn't everyone have a kerosene can in their house? They only sell one size at the store," I pointed out.

My mother glanced back at me. "You're probably right about that, honey." She turned to Helen. "We probably have the same can here."

"I don't know if we have one like that. But maybe we do. Travis would know better," Helen said. "Well, I just stopped by to let you know what happened. Where were you earlier?"

"Joseph and I had dinner with his parents."

"Did you have a nice time?"

"Yes, we had dinner at the Richmond Hotel."

Helen looked at me. "Did you go with them, too?"

"No, Valerie and I took a drive to Silver Lake instead."

"How nice. We haven't been there in years. Well,

it sounds like both of you had a wonderful afternoon," Helen said.

I finished my soup and placed my bowl into the sink. "I'm going to take a walk." Listening to Helen could be exhausting.

"All right, honey," my mother said as Helen sat down at the table. "Would you like some tea, Helen?" my mother asked.

"That sounds good, Ella. Thank you."

I stepped out the door and headed down the driveway with my hands in my pockets. I strolled down to the bridge and leaned over the railing to collect my thoughts. The streaming water below me relaxed me as I sorted through the events of the afternoon: thoughts of boating on Silver Lake, someone setting a fire in the Nelsons' bedroom, and my mother starting her new life with Joseph tumbled around in my head.

I pulled out my pocket watch: 4:40. I held it tightly as if I were squeezing my father's hand. I gazed past the line of rustling leaves over to the waterfall that was hitting the rocks below. It was as if a blanket knitted with tranquility wrapped itself around me and held me still. On the shelf of my tucked away memories, I noticed a dark violet vase filled with buttery daffodils.

Suddenly, I was taken back to my childhood. My father held my hand as we carefully stepped, stone by slippery stone, at the water's edge. In my other hand, I was holding a small bouquet of daffodils. I had picked them for my mother. I remembered holding them in my hand and climbing the steps up to our side door. The scent of daffodils brushed past my nose as if I were holding one close to my face. I recalled my father telling me that daffodils were the first sign of spring as life began again. When my mother opened the door, she picked me up, thanked me, and kissed me on the cheek.

I had to believe this was my dad's way of telling me he was giving us his blessing for our new beginning.

"Thank you, Dad," I whispered. "I love you." Grasping my tarnished gold watch, I smiled, and placed it back into my pocket.

Nineteen

Almost a week had passed. Amber and gold had begun to lick the leaves that were rustling around me, announcing autumn's arrival. Their shadows danced beneath my footsteps. Once the foliage rested, the sounds of the waterfall filled the air again. I stepped onto Mrs. Adleman's porch. The drapes moved. Valerie waved and smiled at me through the window, and then opened the front door.

"I thought I'd stop by before supper because I'm really tired. I didn't sleep well last night." I leaned in and kissed her.

"We have to be quiet out here; Mrs. Adleman just fell asleep." Valerie grabbed my hand and we sat down on the steps. She looked at me for a moment. "You do look tired. I can see the dark circles under your eyes."

"I haven't slept that well all week."

"I've been waking up at every noise too," Valerie said. "You said that you didn't eat supper yet?"

"No, I came right over. Helen and Martha were just left leaving my house. My mother had them over for tea this afternoon. She finally told them that she was getting married. They're really happy for her."

"Are you happy for her?"

I turned to Valerie and felt my eyebrows slightly

twist. "Yes, of course I am. Why would you ask that?"

"I don't know. Maybe deep inside, I thought it might bother you a little and... maybe that's why you haven't slept well all week."

"No, I think that has more to do with the fire over at the Nelsons'. It's just everything adding up."

"I know; I feel the same way. But I'm glad that it's not the wedding that's bothering you."

"No, it's hard to put into words. It's a big change, that's all. I really like Joseph, and I know he will take care of Mom." I glanced over at Valerie and grasped her warm hand. "But do I wish life hadn't turned out the way it has? Yeah, I'd rather have my father here." My eyes settled on Valerie's deep blue eyes for a moment. "It's like the sourest lemons sprinkled with a lot of sugar," I replied, almost tasting the drops of lemonade on my tongue.

"Bitter at first, but the sugar makes it better."

"I guess. Yeah, that would be the best way to put it." I nodded. "I remember when my mom first met Joseph; I'd catch her smiling to herself when she was cooking. It's been good to see her happy. That's really all that matters now."

"Well, I'm really happy for them!" Valerie smiled.

"So am I." I nodded and pressed my lips for a moment. "But I'm going to have to get used to living in the house alone. It's going to be so different. I'm used to having my supper ready for me every night." My eyes swayed over to Valerie.

"Is that a hint? You want me to cook for you?"

I grinned and gently moved my knees toward her. "It'll be good practice."

"Practice? Is that your strange way of proposing to me?"

"No, one proposal was enough for this week," I said and followed with a chuckle.

"You think you're funny, don't you?" Valerie said, then she pressed her lips slightly to one side.

"Yeah, I do!" I started to laugh. "And you have to admit... You think I'm funny too!"

She grinned, let go of my hand, stood up, and peeked in the window. "Still sleeping." She sat back down. "Okay, when your mom moves, I'll make you a plate at home and bring it with me. I'll give it to you when you stop by here. And for all my hard work, you're going to have to take me out to some place really nice. How about the Richmond Hotel?"

"That's fair! And thank you." I leaned over and kissed her again. "You'll make somebody a good wife someday."

"Yeah, you're funny all right!" She knocked my arm with the back of her hand.

The 5:10 train whistle blew. The sound of the freight cars droning over the tracks continued on and on. After a few minutes, the sound of the train faded away into the distance.

"Would you ever want to live somewhere else?" I asked.

"I don't know. Why?"

"I've been thinking about it lately. After all that has happened around here, I'm not so sure that I want to live here," I said in a somber tone. "I've known these people all my life, but I think there's someone living here that's not as neighborly as they pretend to be."

Valerie nodded. "Whoever set that fire lives here," she said with conviction.

"I'm also thinking that this might not be the best place for us to raise our children."

"So that was a proposal!" she said jokingly.

"Not the official one," I said gazing into her eyes. "But seriously, I think that's part of the reason I couldn't sleep most of the week. I don't know that I want to stay here. There are only a few people I know I can trust. And the rest... I question."

"I know what you mean. I get the sickest feeling when I think about Florence, and now the Nelsons." Her voice faded.

"We still have some time to decide... at least a couple of years," I said, forcing a smile and trying to change the mood.

"A couple of years? That long?" Valerie's eyes widened.

"Yeah, I want my mother to settle into her new

life. That'll give me time to save some more money for a house. She's planning on turning the house over to me, but I'm going to tell her that she probably won't need to."

Valerie smiled. "She won't, not if we're going to move."

I nodded.

"I better head back inside. I am supposed to be working. I have to heat up Mrs. Adleman's supper, and I'm sure she'll be waking up any time now."

"Okay; my supper is waiting for me too."

Just as I stood up, two black touring cars came around the bend. We watched them pass us, then drive over the bridge and up the hill.

"The police again?" Valerie cried. "What's going on now?"

"Listen, go inside and lock the door. I'm going to take a walk up the road and see where they're going. Maybe they're just passing through."

"Please come back and let me know!" Valerie pleaded.

"I will. Just lock all the doors." I leaned in and kissed her.

"I think two more years in this town is two years too long!" Valerie said in a panicked, higher-pitched tone.

I nodded. "You're probably right."

As I stepped off the porch and headed toward the

road, my chest tightened as if there were thick ropes trying to suffocate me. I began to gasp for air. My heart thrashed against my chest. I made it over to the bridge and leaned against the railing, thinking I might vomit or pass out. Feeling light headed, I didn't move. As I hung my head over the railing, saliva dripped off my lip into the water.

After a few minutes, the feeling began to fade. I wiped my mouth and stared out at the waterfall for a moment. Then I glanced up the hill at the Morgans' store. I could see the back ends of the two black touring cars parked in front.

What the hell is going on now? Finding my strength again, I walked up the hill. Merle was standing on the porch, talking to one of the officers. I watched the officer go inside the store. Merle waved and met me by the Depot.

"What's going on here?" I asked.

"Someone cut Martha's phone wires," Merle replied nervously.

"What? Cut them? Are you sure? Do you think it could've been from a squirrel or a raccoon?" I asked. "I've heard about them chewing through wires before."

"No, it was sliced clean, not gnawed. I saw it for myself, so Martha called the police from Helen's house."

I scanned the houses nearby with suspicion. "Someone *here* is sending us a message. Or he's getting his thrills by taunting us."

"Yeah, it's beginning to feel like that," Merle said in a deflated tone.

"I don't know... I don't know what to think anymore. Why would someone cut her phone wires?"

"I don't know, but I started thinking... Weren't Flo's phone wires cut too?" Merle asked.

An icy chill shot through my veins and landed deep in my gut. *Her wires were cut.* Suddenly, my heart began to pound. *I had forgotten about her phone wires being cut.* I nodded.

"Yeah, I think they were," I replied in a soft voice. "I don't like this at all!"

"Martha is really upset, and I can't blame her. I can't think of one person who would do this to her and Gerry. At least they didn't set the store on fire."

"...or kill anyone," I said under my breath, glancing over at the store for a moment. "You know, I'm really fed up with this shit! I was just talking to Valerie about moving the hell out of here."

"I know. It's disturbing. And you're not the first person to mention moving either." Merle turned to the voices that were coming from the store. Two officers stepped out the door and were talking on the porch.

"I have to go tell Valerie what happened. We saw the police cars go by, and I wanted to see where they were going."

Merle turned and headed back to the store. "Okay,

I'll see ya later."

"Yeah." I nodded and stepped over the railroad tracks. When I looked up, I saw Valerie standing in the middle of the road with her shotgun by her side. We met on the bridge.

"Mrs. Adleman woke up. I told her that you were going to be stopping by and that I was going outside for a few minutes. So what happened?"

"Someone cut the phone wires over at the Morgans'."

"What! Why would—?"

"I have no idea, other than someone finds it amusing," I replied, shaking my head with disgust. "And Merle reminded me that Flo's phone wires were also cut."

"That's really scary!" Valerie said.

I nodded. "I know."

"I think that I'm going to ask Junior to stay here tonight with me. He's working close by this week."

"That's a good idea. I'm sure he won't mind."

"I don't want to scare Mrs. Adleman, though," Valerie said.

"You have to tell her the truth. Just tell her that someone cut the phone wires at the Morgans' store and you'd feel better having your brother stay here tonight. It's understandable. She'll probably feel better, too," I assured her.

"I know. I'll call Junior in a little while. He's usually home around 6:30."

"It makes me feel better knowing he'll be staying with you."

"Maybe the whole week!"

"Even better!" I gave her a quick kiss. "I better go, I'm sure my mother is wondering where I am. I'll see you tomorrow."

"Okay. Try and rest if you can." She opened the front door and stepped inside.

I nodded. "I'll try."

I left the porch as Valerie closed the door and ambled up the road toward my house, sharing the road with scattered leaves and two squirrels who were chasing each other. I stood on my porch steps for a moment, angry and reeling from the loss of control that resonated inside of me. As I stared out into the hamlet, questions swirled through my head as the last hint of the sun faded away, and the shadows disap-peared—all but the one shadow who lived among us and in our nightmares.

Twenty

1924

The aroma of roasted turkey rushed me as I opened the door. I kicked off my snow covered boots and hung my wool coat on the hook. *That smells good!*

"Mom!"

"In here, honey," my mother replied from the parlor. "I didn't expect you home this early."

"We finished a little early today," I said from the doorway. My mother was standing on the wooden footstool in a silky, dusty rose colored wedding dress.

"Doesn't she look beautiful?" Helen smiled as she stepped out from behind her.

My mother turned around, her eyes sparkling with delight. She was beaming with joy.

Martha was on her knees, holding the hem of the dress. She pulled a pin from between her lips and placed it into the fabric. "Isn't your mother going to make a lovely bride?"

"Yes, Mom! You look beautiful!"

"So do you like it?" she asked anxiously.

"Yes! Very much!" I nodded.

"Your soon-to-be Grandmother Genevieve called me this morning and asked me if I wanted to shop for my dress. We found this one at C.L. Carr's. I thought this was such a lovely gown." My mother motioned with her hand from her hip to slightly down her leg. "The sales woman told us that the drop waist is the latest style in wedding dresses, and I thought the color was perfect for a second wedding."

It was starting to become a reality: shopping with Joseph's mother, soon to be her mother-in-law. My mother, a bride again: Joseph's new wife.

Martha stood up. "I took the dress up about three inches, Ella, so now it's about six inches above your ankle."

Helen circled my mother, examining the hem. "That looks good, Martha. Wedding dresses sure have changed. My wedding dress fell all the way to the floor... And we all wore tight corsets. We wouldn't dare show our legs," she said as she checked each pin.

"I wore a corset under my first dress, but with the drop waist, I don't need one. It's the new style—and much more comfortable, I might add," my mother said as she looked at herself in the hall tree mirror by the front door.

"Ella, why don't you step down and put on your shoes so we can see how it will look?" Martha reached out her hand.

"All right," my mother said as she stepped off the stool.

Martha turned to me. "Oh, before I forget to tell

you, Fritz: Cliff called today, and he's going to be per-
forming on a Rochester radio show!"

"Oh, yeah... When?"

"He didn't have the exact date, but he said that it
was going to be either at the end of February or sometime during the first week or two of March."

"That's great!"

"He was thrilled because there were only three
students selected from his class to perform on the
show."

"When you talk to him again, tell him I said congratulations."

"I'll do so," Martha said with a proud smile. "I'll
have the show on at the store for anyone who wants to
listen. It'll be a nice evening."

"I'll plan on being there," I said, feeling a little
envious of his talent.

Martha inspected the dress. She started at the
shoulders, down to the waist then down to the hem of
the dress, which hung above my mother's ankles and
white shoes. "All right, Ella: you can go upstairs and
take it off, but be careful of the pins."

"I'll be careful," my mother said as she held the
skirt away from her legs and headed toward the
stairs.

"Why don't I help you?" Helen suggested, and
followed my mother. "Then I can make sure the pins
don't fall out. I'm going to try to sew the hem tomor-

row."

"Thank you, Helen," my mother replied.

Martha began to place the scissors and unused pins back into my mother's sewing basket. "Fritz, your mother told me that you're not going to be moving in with her and Joseph after the wedding."

"Yeah, I'm going to stay here for a couple of years. It's closer to the farm and Valerie," I said as I placed another log in the fireplace and rubbed my cold, chapped hands together.

"That's good!" Martha said. "I'm glad that you'll still be around. But we're really going to miss your mother when she moves. I'm sure Helen and I will make a trip out to Batavia from time to time, and I'm sure she'll come to visit."

"Of course she'll visit. She'll probably come out here once a week." I glanced up at the ceiling, listening to my mother and Helen talking upstairs. "She sure looked beautiful in her dress. I'm really excited for her!"

"Yes, she did. She's a beautiful woman with a beautiful heart to match. And we're all excited for her too. Your father was such a good man, and I know how devastated you both were when he passed. Helen and I are so glad she found a good man to take care of her. She didn't want to grow old alone." Martha sat down on the sofa.

"It's the best thing that could have happened to

her."

"I agree." Martha nodded with a smile. "So what about you? When are you getting married?"

"Married?" I asked and began to laugh. "*That* won't be for a while." I sat down in the rocking chair next to the fireplace and prodded the logs with the iron rod. I paused for a moment and glanced up at the ceiling again, listening to my mother and Helen laughing.

"So are you thinking that you'll eventually move to Batavia then?"

I nodded. "I haven't really thought about it, but probably." I stared into the fire for a moment and then looked over at Martha. "After all that has happened, I'm not sure I trust anyone around here."

"Does Valerie want to move?" Martha asked.

I nodded. "Yeah, she wants to move now."

"Well, I certainly can understand why, Fritzy. We never did find out who cut our wires. Well, I'm glad that my children are grown and have lives of their own. And you're right, after all that has happened, I can't blame you for wanting to move. There were a few people talking about moving away right after what happened to Florence. But it seems everyone stayed put."

"We'll visit all the time. Valerie's parents and Junior are still here."

"Well, you and Valerie are young. At our age, we ain't going anywhere. I have a store to run." Martha's face looked as if she had drank a cup of vinegar. She shook her finger at me. "It's been our home for over thirty years. And we're not going to be chased away."

Mom and Helen were chatting and laughing as they came down the stairs. Helen was carrying my mother's dress over her shoulder.

"Ella, I should have this finished in the next couple of days," Helen said.

"That sounds good. And there's no hurry. I didn't even expect to find a dress today."

Martha rose up from the sofa. "Are you ready, Helen? I have to check on Mom and start supper."

"I need to start supper too. Travis will be home in about an hour," Helen replied as she headed toward the kitchen.

"Ella, that turkey smells wonderful!" Martha commented as she grabbed her coat off the kitchen chair.

"Yes, it does! Joseph found himself a good woman and a good cook," Helen said as she carefully placed my mother's dress over the kitchen chair.

"Thank you. Well, you know that I've always enjoyed cooking."

"Is he coming for supper tonight?" Helen asked as she slipped on her wool coat and then gently picked up my mother's wedding dress.

"Yes, he should be here within the hour."

"Good, because I'm hungry," I said.

Helen opened the door. "Have a good night."

"Thank you so much for all of your help with my dress today."

"It was our pleasure, Ella," Martha said as she waved.

"Yes, it was," Helen echoed. "Any time."

My mother turned to me. "I'm so grateful. After Genevieve brought me home, I called Martha and told her that I found a dress, but it needed to be hemmed, and they came right over. They've been here all afternoon. We had a really nice time. I'm going to miss them when I move." She opened the cupboard and placed three dishes on the table. "Joseph will be here soon. You better go upstairs and wash up."

"All right." I began to unbutton my shirt as I headed toward the stairs.

I heard a quick knock at the door, and then the door opened.

"You're early," my mother said with a bright smile spread across her face and a tinge of excitement in her voice.

With my foot on the first step of the stairs, I watched through the doorway. The setting sun's rays streamed through the branches of the bare trees, casting a warm romantic glow into the kitchen. As Joseph walked in, my mother threw her arms around his neck and kissed him. I was really happy for her. But it was also *more* than I wanted to see. Trying to forget the sight of my mother kissing, I headed up the stairs, feeling a little tarnished.

Twenty-One

"Mom!" I called out. Then, I threw my wool coat over the kitchen chair. There was no answer. The aroma of chicken and gravy filled the kitchen. I was starving. There were two small pots on the stove and a plate of biscuits on the counter with an empty plate sitting next to it.

I untied my icy boot laces, set my boots next to the door, and wandered over to the cellar door and opened it.

"Mom, you down there?" No answer. *Huh...*

I removed the lids off of the two pots. One was filled with steaming, moist shredded chicken, the other with simmering gravy. I broke off a piece of biscuit and dipped it into the gravy, then placed it in my mouth. *Mmm...that's good!* I set three small biscuits on my plate, grabbed a fork out of the drawer, and piled the shreds of chicken on top of the biscuits. Then I picked up the ladle and poured a heaping amount of gravy on top. I sat down at the table and began to eat. Then, I saw the note next to the salt and pepper.

Honey,

I tried to call you at the farm, but there was no answer. Joseph called and we have a 5:30 appointment to look at a house. After, we're having dinner with Joseph's parents. I should be home around 9:00.

I made chicken and biscuits for supper. The chicken and gravy are on the stove.

Don't forget, Cliff's radio show is tonight at 7:00. Martha invited everyone over to the store. Tell Martha I'm sorry for not being able to be there tonight, but let her know we will have the show on during supper.

Love you,

Mom

After I finished eating, I washed up, changed, and headed out. It had finally stopped snowing. I took a deep breath and filled my lungs with the brisk, fresh air mixed with the scent of burning firewood. I strolled down the hill among the slumbering trees that were resting in a soft blanket of fresh snow. The sun had just sunk behind the hills, allowing the darkness to show the sparkling Big Dipper across the sky. I pulled out my pocket watch: 6:10. *Just enough time to stop in and see Valerie.*

As I traipsed through the icy ruts in the road, I saw the light was on in Mrs. Adleman's window. I knocked at the door and waited a minute before Valerie opened it.

She signaled with her index finger for me to wait a minute. "Let me grab my coat." She shut the door for a moment, and then came out wearing her powder blue wool coat. "It's freezing out here!"

"I know."

"At least it stopped snowing."

"I just stopped for a minute. I'm on my way over to the store."

"For what?" She paused. "Oh, that's right: Cliff's on the radio tonight. I almost forgot about it. My dad and Uncle Matt are going too. What time does it start?"

"7:00."

"Is your mom going?"

"She was planning on it. But Joseph called, and her plans changed. She left me a note. They had a 5:30 appointment to go look at a house. Then they were going to have dinner with his parents."

"That's good. I can't wait to hear about it... Hold on a second." Valerie turned, opened the door, looked inside, and then shut the door behind her. "I just wanted to see if she was done eating. I'll ask Mrs. Adleman if she wants to listen to the show. I'm sure she will."

I grabbed her hand and gently pulled her over to the corner of the porch, away from the window. "You look cold." As we moved over, I gently moved a strand of hair away from her eyelash. I heard two gunshots. "Who the hell is shooting at this time of night?"

"It's probably my brother... Yesterday he said he was going to shoot those tomcats that had been fighting under his bedroom window the past couple of nights."

I walked over to railing of the porch and looked down the road. I could see Junior's small house. Sure enough, Valerie was right. It was Junior. He stepped onto his porch. It looked like he had something in his hand. I watched him walk through his front door.

"You're right. It looks like he took care of 'em. I just saw him go inside," I said as I walked back over to Valerie. "Here, let me warm you up." I leaned in and kissed her and kept kissing her as I rubbed my hands up and down her arms. "Did that help?" I whispered.

"Yeah; any more of that and I'll have to take off my coat," Valerie smiled and started to giggle.

"That's the idea," I whispered and kissed her again.

Valerie began to laugh as I brushed my lips against hers. She pulled away. "All right, mister, you need to behave yourself and move along to where you were going." She leaned in and our lips locked again.

"It's a little hard when you keep kissing me," I said and began to laugh. "All right, I better head over there. I'll stop back on my way home, so watch for me around 8:30 or so."

Valerie stepped toward the door and placed her hand on the door knob. "See you in a little while." She leaned forward and gave me a quick peck on the lips. "Love you."

"Love you, too." I smiled and then headed to Morgan's store.

I stamped my icy boots on the rug in the store's entryway.

"Hey, Fritz, I'm glad you could make it." Merle rose up from the stool behind the counter. "Where's your mother? I thought she said she was coming too."

"She was planning on it, but Joseph called, and they had to go look at a house. It must have come up suddenly," I said as I threw my coat over the back of Mrs. Harrison's rocking chair.

"Hey, Matt, is Senior coming?" I tossed my leg over the stool in front of the counter and set my cap down in front of me.

"He's supposed to be."

Matt pulled a ciggy out of his front pocket and held it up to his mouth. "Did you hear the gunshots on your way over?"

"Yeah, it was just Junior shooting at those pesky tomcats. Valerie said that they've been keeping him up at night," I replied.

Matt struck a match and lit his cigarette. The smoke curled above his head as he puffed away. "It's hard to believe one of our boys is about to perform on the radio. I bet Martha's proud!"

I heard footsteps on the porch and wondered who else was coming on such a cold night.

"She's very proud! She's been telling everyone that

has come in the store for the past month," Merle said as he strolled over to the window and then opened the door.

Martha walked in and stamped the snow off her boots onto the rug. "Hello, Fritzy. I thought you'd be here with your mom; is she coming?" she asked, gripping a handful of letters as the icy air blew in behind her. She wiped her boots as she pulled her scarf off and placed it on the counter.

"My mom left me a note that they had to go look at a house tonight. It must have come up suddenly. She wanted me to tell you that she's sorry she couldn't make it, but they'll be listening." I nodded as Merle set a glass of cider in front of me, and I sipped the cold sweet cider.

"Well, I hope they have some luck. I know they've already looked at a couple of them." Martha turned to Matt. "Is Ellie coming?"

"Nah, she's been in bed most of the day. I think she has a bit of the flu."

"That's too bad. I'll have to make her some soup tomorrow and bring it over," Martha kindly offered as she set the mail on the back counter next to her new wooden radio. A jazzy melody played from the radio that reminded me of my promise to Valerie about taking her to the Richmond Hotel.

"Thank you, I know she'll appreciate that," Matt replied with a grateful nod, a smile, and then a sip of his cider.

"Merle, before you lock up tonight, can you unload these crates in the back? Follow me, and I'll show you the ones I'm talking about."

Merle followed Martha to the back of the store as the 6:35 train whistle blew, rattling all the glasses on the shelves behind the counter. After a few minutes the sound of the train trailed off into the distance.

"Is my milk pail out there?" Martha asked from the back of the store.

My eyes scanned the back counter. Then I leaned over. The tin pail was on the floor. "Yeah, it's here. Do you want it?"

"I'll get it. I have to grab my scarf anyway," Martha replied as she strolled behind the counter, picked up the tin pail, and then wrapped her scarf around her head. "Well, I'll be back in a few minutes. If my mother happens to call down, tell her I ran over to Helen's for the milk."

I heard heavy steps coming up the porch, and the door swung open. Senior was standing at the door with a cheery smile.

"Where's everybody?" he asked, his eyebrows in a slight twist.

"Everett, Leon, and Felix should be here soon. But I'm not sure who else was planning on coming," Merle replied.

"It is really cold out there. I can't say I blame

them if they don't," I said.

"Have a seat. I'll pour you a glass of cider," Merle said as he grabbed a glass off the back shelf.

"Where's Ellie?" Senior asked as he sat down on the other side of his brother.

"She ain't feeling so well. What about Mertie: is she coming?"

"Nah, she's tired. Did you stop and see Valerie already, Fritz?" Senior asked.

"Yeah, I stopped in on my way here."

"Mrs. Adleman's son, Ted, called me earlier today. He told me that Valerie's doing a really good job for her."

"I'm sure she'll be glad to hear that," I replied.

"But I'm not sure how long it will last. That was the reason he called. He told me that he might be selling the house and moving his mother to Warsaw with him and his wife."

"Well, it was going to have to end sometime, I guess."

"Martha," Grandma Harrison called down from the top of the stairs.

Merle walked over to the doorway to the stairs. "She just left for Helen's to get the milk," Merle replied. "She shouldn't be too much longer." Merle turned to us. "What time did she leave, anyway?"

I shrugged my shoulders and pulled out my pocket watch again. "It was just a few minutes ago... I think it was around 6:40 or so; it was just after the 6:35 train."

"What time is it now?" Merle asked.

"It's about ten minutes to seven," I replied.

Merle turned to the stairs. "She should be back any minute."

"I just looked out my window and Helen's house is dark," Grandma said. "Well, when she gets back, tell her I need her."

"I'll tell her as soon as she walks in," Merle replied.

I heard Grandma Harrison's door close.

"On my way here, I left my pail on their back steps. The house was dark, so I didn't think anyone was home," Matt said. "So she's right."

"It can't be dark. I saw Travis walk by the store less than a half hour ago. Then I saw him cut over toward his house, so he's gotta be home." Merle fumbled with the radio dial. He looked over at me. "Fritz, do ya want to go next door with me to see what's keeping her? I don't want her to miss any of the show," he asked with a tinge of anxiousness.

"Sure, I'll go," I threw my cap on and grabbed my coat off the rocking chair.

"I'll go too," Matt said. "Travis might be wondering who left their pail on his porch."

The door swung open and Leon's father, Everett, walked in. A gust of blowing snow and frosty air filled the store again.

Merle looked over at Senior and then at Everett. "Do ya mind watching the store for a few?" he asked. "We're going to see what's keeping Martha next door. Maybe she lost track of the time."

"I don't think they're home. There ain't no lights on," Everett replied.

"That's strange," Merle said in a baffled tone. "Grandma said the same thing."

"I'll be here. I ain't going anywhere," Everett replied as he shrugged off his jacket and removed his hat, then tossed them on Grandma Harrison's rocking chair.

"Thanks." We headed out the back door, then up the slight hill. I heard Travis' cow bellowing not too far away.

I turned to Matt and Merle. "Huh. They're right: the house is dark."

Merle stepped onto the small back porch and knocked on the door. There was no answer. He placed his hand on the door knob and tried to turn it. "It's locked."

Matt and I stood on the icy back steps, not far from Matt's tin pail. We moved away from the porch. Merle tramped through the snow over to the fence and knelt down at the cow's udder.

He ran back. "She's bellowing because she ain't been milked yet," Merle said.

"Well, where the hell is Martha then, if Helen and Travis aren't home?" I asked, puzzled and frustrated.

Matt shook his head, perplexed. "That's strange."

"Doesn't Travis always milk her as soon as he gets home from work?" I asked.

"Yeah, he always does." Merle shook his head with a bewildered expression on his face. "Maybe he didn't go right home after I saw him walk by the store," Merle said as he scanned the nearby houses. "Martha already went to the post office, so she wouldn't have gone there."

I yanked my pocket watch out of my trousers and held it to catch the moonlight. 7:00. "The show is about to start."

I realized that we hadn't tried the front door, so we ran through the snow to the front of the house. I stepped onto their small, snow-covered front porch, and jiggled the door handle. "Locked!"

We tried to look into the window, but the drapes were closed. Merle followed me as Matt walked around to the other side of the house. We circled the house, peeking in every window. Oddly, all the drapes were closed.

"I smell smoke. Do you smell it?" Merle asked as he stepped through a snowdrift to reach the first floor bedroom window.

"Yeah, I do," I replied with uneasiness in my stomach.

Merle placed his hand on the glass. "It's hot," Merle yelled, and then looked up. He pointed at the smoke leaking from the roof.

"Help!" Merle yelled. I ran over to him and Matt, who were now both standing by the bedroom window.

"Go get Everett and Senior! And anyone else you can find!" Merle yelled in a panic. My spine began to prickle with fear. Matt turned and ran down the hill toward the store, yelling Everett's and Senior names.

Minutes later, Everett, Felix, Leon, and Senior came running up the hill. We ran over to the back door again. The only way in was to break the kitchen window and crawl through it.

Merle smashed the kitchen window, and Matt helped him quickly clear the glass out of the windowpane. "Helen!" he yelled. "Anyone home?"

I stood at the window. "Travis! Helen!"

No answer.

"Leon, you're slim enough to fit through the window," Merle said.

"I might be." Leon gave a quick, anxious glance at all of us before shaking off his coat and laying it on the windowpane.

Merle and Felix formed a step with their hands.

"On three," Merle said.

"One… two… three." We counted and shoved Leon through the opening, and he tumbled to the floor. I could hear the sound of the table and chairs moving across the wooden floor as he made his way through the dark kitchen. The light flicked on. Leon unlocked the back door and let us inside.

We walked into a gray smoky haze. My eyes began to burn, and I bent over coughing. As I hacked my lungs out, something red caught my eye.

"What the hell?" I asked as a sharp, frozen grip pierced my gut. It looked as if a bleeding deer had been dragged through the kitchen. My heart pounded, sending raw panic through my veins. Then, something with a dull shine on the floor caught my attention. It was bullet shell. And then I saw another one by the sink.

"I'm going to call the police," Everett said in an unsteady voice as he ran past me.

"That's a good idea," Felix replied.

"Helen! Travis! You here? Martha!" Merle yelled as he coughed on the smoke. He pulled out a hankie, and then covered his nose and mouth.

My eyes continued to water from the smoke. My heart thrashed against my chest. *What the hell happened?* I stared at the bloody path leading through the house to the bedroom. My body trembled. Black smoke was seeping from the bottom of the bedroom door. My coughing and hacking became too much, and I ran to the back door to breathe for a few minutes. After I caught my breath, I stepped back into the house.

Matt pointed out the back door. "Go grab the ladder out of the barn. I'm going upstairs to let the smoke out," he yelled in panic, and then began choking on the smoke.

"I'll grab some water!" Merle shouted.

People were beginning to gather around the back of the house. My watery eyes rested on Mertie's for a moment. Her eyes were full of distress and pooling with tears. I didn't see Valerie—and was glad.

I helped Matt set the ladder against the side of the house.

"Go help Merle!" I yelled to Senior, who was standing near the back door coughing. Leon was right behind him.

"Merle's filling buckets!" Leon yelled to me.

I held the ladder steady, and Matt climbed up to the second story window. He turned his head and smashed the window with his arm. A cloud of black smoke spilled out, choking him, as he took a few steps down the ladder. After the smoke thinned, he made his way back up the rungs.

"Tell Merle to hurry! I need some water, now!" Matt shouted down to me in a raspy voice.

I ran over to Irvin Packard, who ran the train depot. He was standing on the edge of the crowd surrounding the back door. "We need water! Fast! There's fire upstairs!"

Irvin and I ran into the kitchen. I could see into the parlor. The wall of black smoke was now a thin

gray haze. Everett and Leon were helping Merle fill
the buckets. Irvin grabbed two buckets full of water
that were sitting next to the sink. I grabbed the other
one, set it by the back door, ran in to the room where
Travis kept his firewood, and picked up another tin
bucket.

"What the…" I said under my breath. A set of false
teeth was lying near the stack of Travis' firewood. A
chill ran over my skin and landed in the deepest pit
of my stomach as the blood drained from my face. But
there was no time to think about that. I picked up the
tin pail and kept moving. I set it down near Merle, not
mentioning what I just saw.

"I need this filled!" I said. "Matt's on the ladder—
the fire's upstairs!"

"Take these." Merle shoved the one he just filled
toward me and pointed to the one on the floor, not
bothering to look over at me.

I ran out the back door with the two sloshing tin
pails of water. Irvin climbed up and handed them to
Matt. He tossed the water through the window, then
threw the pails down into the snow. We watched Matt
crawl in head first. A few seconds later, the sound of
shattered glass came from the other upstairs window
as Matt kicked it. Shards of glass stabbed the icy
snow like knives.

"Matt, come on! Get down here," I yelled as Irvin
jumped off the fifth rung of the ladder.

"It's out!" Matt yelled from the window. "I'm com‑ing down!"

 Matt and I ran back in to the kitchen. All of Tra‑vis's eight tin pails were filled with the water Merle had pumped.

Merle rushed over to the bedroom door, "Ready?" He grabbed the door handle. "Shit!" He shrieked and drove his hand into one of the buckets of water. "It's hot!" He waved his hand around in the water for a mo‑ment. "We're gonna have to kick it in!"

Senior and Merle stood in position, ready to bust down the door.

"On three," Everett yelled. "One... two... three!"

Senior and Merle kicked the door open, and a storm of thick, black smoke filled the two rooms. We stumbled through the kitchen and out the back door, coughing and choking. The crowd around the house had grown.

Minutes later, the smoke had turned into a thin haze, and we entered the house again. We stood at the bedroom door, trying to see what was on fire. The flames were shooting up in the center of the bedroom. We formed a line, and Irvin filled the empty buckets as Senior passed them back to him.

A few minutes later, the smoke began to fade and the flames fizzled out. Merle had found a flashlight, and we made our way into the bedroom. The pungent smell of burning hair hit me. I stood there, trembling and terrified. My eyes were burning and watering. I felt a hand on my shoulder. I turned around, shaking uncontrollably. It was Senior.

"God be with us," he whispered.

I nodded, trying to make out what it was that was heaped in a pile in the middle of the room. Merle aimed the dim flashlight around the room. We took a few more steps. The mattress was overturned and shoved against the far wall. In the middle of the floor, there was a pile of burnt rags and an overturned chair. Merle shined the light on the pile. I moved a little closer. I gasped in horror.

Twenty-Two

I stared in horror, my bones trembling.

"No, no, no," Merle shrieked.

On the floor lay three bodies covered with burnt linens. Martha's body was strewn on top. Her face was beaten and mutilated, her eyes swollen shut and forehead bashed in. Her skirt was above her waist as if she was dragged by her feet, and then thrown away like garbage.

I took a step closer.

Helen's body was off to the side, near the cot, set against the wall. Her glasses were still on her bloody face, her hair soaked in blood. The right side of her body was covered in burns. I saw Travis at the bottom of the pile. His upper body and face, charred. I could barely tell that it was him.

Sickened by the sight and smell of burnt hair and flesh, I broke down crying. The only one I could think of was my mother. *My God, how am I going to tell her?*

"My God!" I cried. "Who could do this?" I screamed.

"No, Jesus, no! It can't be." Senior's words seeped out under his breath as he stepped to the other side of Merle, who was sobbing while he kneeled on the floor near Martha's head.

"Why? Why? Who could? ...Who could do this to

them?" Merle cried.

I wiped my eyes, trying to keep it together, but the tears kept flowing. I reached over and placed my hand on Merle's shoulder. "Come on. There's nothing we can do." Out of the corner of my eye, I noticed a bloody adz handle a few feet from Martha's bare legs.

He looked up at me, shaking his head and trembling. "No, this couldn't have happened," he whispered. His face was covered in soot and tears, carved with devastation. He put his face in his hands and wept. He looked up at me again. "She just went for milk." His voice was weak. "How could this happen?"

I slowly pulled him up and guided him out of the bedroom and into the kitchen as Everett headed toward the bedroom, holding a kerosene lantern.

"Jesus Christ!" he shrieked. Moments later, he came back into the kitchen and set the lantern on the kitchen table. His face was pale and green. "They're dead! They're all dead," he said softly with disbelief as he pushed his hair back out of his face. Tears began to swell in his eyes, and he began to cry.

My chin quivered. My eyes burned. My stomach twisted and ached. I turned to Merle: "We're too late," I said softly. I grabbed his arm again. "Let's go. The police will be here soon. And we don't want to be in their way." I noticed the bullet hole in the wall by the sink as I guided him out the door behind Senior.

"They're dead. By God, they're dead," Senior said,

sobbing as he told the neighbors who were standing around the house. "Who the hell would do this? Who?" He cast his eyes over the crowd. Mertie ran to him and threw her arms around him, crying.

The shrieks and cries echoed through the night as the news traveled from mouth to ear.

"Martha!" It was the faint voice of Gerry Morgan off in the distance.

I grabbed Merle's arm. "Gerry's headed over here! We have to stop him!" I ran out the door and jumped off of the porch. "It's Gerry! We can't let him in here!" I said to Senior as Mertie started walking down the slight hill, toward the road.

Merle and I ran past Mertie and met Gerry at the side of the house.

"You ain't going in there," Merle said, holding his arm.

"Where is she? Where is she?" Gerry began to cry, struggling to pull away from Merle's grip.

"Gerry, you're not going into the house!" I demand-ed as I threw my arms around him from behind. His strength was overpowering. He was determined to go into the house.

"No!" Gerry yelled as he shook his arm loose from Merle and flung my arms off of him.

Senior ran up to him, stopped him and gripped Gerry's shoulders. "No, Gerry, you're not going in there. You're not," Senior sobbed.

I glanced up and saw Everett and Matt running toward us. Gerry was still trying to break loose from Senior. Everett ran up and grabbed Gerry by the coat lapels. "She's gone. They're all gone," Everett cried. "We ain't goin' to let you see her like that."

"How, how?" Gerry fell to the ground and pounded his fists into the snow.

"They were shot, and then whoever did this set the house on fire," Senior cried.

"I'll kill him! I swear to the day I die, I'll kill him!"

Tears fell down my face as I watched Gerry cry like I'd never seen a man cry. The night turned into a nightmare. As I watched Gerry try to pull himself together and stand up, I heard the sound of car engines. Three trooper cars pulled up to the side of the Wilsons' house.

I reached over and grasped Senior's arm to gain his attention. "I need to talk to you." Senior stepped over to me. "Valerie: she can't stay there alone. She's done staying there alone with Mrs. Adleman!" I said.

"That's where Mertie was headed. We don't want her staying there alone either. Mertie was going to call Ted and let him know what happened and that we can't have our daughter there alone with his mother. He'll have to figure out something else."

"I'm going over there right now."

"All right. I'm going to stay here with Gerry. I don't want him to get any ideas about going into the house."

"I'll let Mertie and Valerie know where you are," I said as I turned and trudged through the snow toward the road. I glanced back and saw five officers walking toward the back of the house.

Mrs. Adleman's door swung open before I set my foot on the first step. Valerie was standing at the door with tears streaming down her cheeks. I could hear Mertie's and Mrs. Adleman's voices in the kitchen. I stepped through the doorway and threw my arms around Valerie as she wept.

"How could this happen? How could this happen, again?" she asked.

"I don't know," I replied, feeling a warm tear fall down my cold cheek. "I don't know."

"I'm really scared!" she cried. "I've never been so scared."

"I know, I know. We all are."

She pulled away and wiped her eyes. "My mother said that my dad was with you when you found them."

I nodded and said nothing else.

"Was it bad?"

I nodded. "Yeah," I replied softly. "I can't... I can't talk about it."

"Okay. And I'm not sure I want to know."

"You don't," I whispered.

"Ted is on his way here to take his mom back to Warsaw with him. She's going to be staying there for a while. She's really scared, too."

"That's good. Your father will be here later; he is staying with Gerry for a while." I looked around the parlor. "Where's your gun?"

Valerie pointed to the fireplace. It was leaning against the mantel.

"Keep it close to you." I wiped away the tears that were streaming down my cheek. "I have to go."

"Where? Where're you going?" Valerie asked with panic.

I began to weep again. "To Batavia. I have... I have to go tell my mother... that, that... Martha, Helen, and Travis are all dead. That they were murdered! And I don't know how I'm going to tell her."

I began to sob uncontrollably for a few minutes. Valerie wrapped her arms around my body as my tears fell into her soft blonde hair. "My God, they were like family to her. How... how do I tell my mother that they're now all dead?" I asked as I tried to pull myself back together.

"I can't believe this is happening. I can't believe it happened again!" Valerie cried.

"I know... I know."

"Are you coming back tonight?"

"Yeah, but my mother isn't. I don't want her to come back here. I don't want my mother to come back here at all. She is just going to move out of here a little sooner than she planned, that's all."

"I can't live here anymore either!" Valerie cried. "Let's just get married and move away from here! No waiting."

"We will. But right now, I have to get to my mother before she leaves Batavia. I'll be back in a little while."

"You can stay with us tonight. I'll tell my mother."

"All right." I gave her a long hug.

"I love you," she whispered, "so much."

"I love you, too." I gave her a kiss and felt one of her tears fall onto my lip.

I ran into my house and up the stairs. I pulled my mother's small chest out of her closet and packed her clothes and toiletries, hoping I had everything that she needed for the next few days. I grabbed the shotgun that was sitting against the kitchen wall. I threw my mother's small chest and the shotgun in the backseat of the car and drove out of Linden.

Several cars passed me as I headed toward Route 63. My eyes swelled with tears. Flashes of Martha, Helen, and Travis lying there on the bedroom floor haunted my thoughts. Their bloody, charred bodies propped themselves on a shelf inside my head next to the two shattered skulls. Tears streamed down my cheeks as I searched for the words to tell my mother that her dearest friends were now dead.

Twenty-Three

I turned down Ellicott Avenue and pulled up in front of Joseph's parents' home. Thankfully, Joseph's touring car was still in the driveway. I grabbed the chest filled with my mother's clothes out of the backseat and walked briskly to the large, wooden front door. My heart thrashed against my chest. Tears welled up in my eyes. After my knuckles hit the cold wood, I stared at the door for a moment, crying, dreading the story I would have to tell.

I reached into my pocket and clutched my watch. I closed my eyes and whispered. "Dad, please help keep Mom strong. She's going to need all the strength she can get to help her through this." Suddenly, the door swung open.

Joseph's dark brown eyes widened with surprise. "Fritz! I thought I saw a car pull up. We weren't expecting you. We were just getting ready to leave." He gazed at me for a moment. "What, what's wrong?" He held the door open. "Come inside."

"No, not yet." I gestured for him to close the door as a warm tear ran down my cheek. "Please, come out here and close the door," I said as I wiped my tears with the back of my hand. I felt like I was going to vomit at any moment. The bile was creeping up my throat.

Joseph glanced over his shoulder. "All right." He stepped outside and pulled the door closed quietly behind him.

I stood there, trembling and feeling nauseous. "Where's my mom?"

"She's in the house, Fritz. Tell me what's wrong. You're obviously very upset."

"Yeah." I began to sob.

With concern carved into his face, he reached over and put his hand on my shoulder. "What is it, Fritz?" he asked gently. "What happened? Is it Valerie? Is she all right?"

I nodded. "It's Martha, Helen, and Travis. They're... they're... dead," I replied, overflowing with anguish.

"What?" Joseph asked, shocked, staring at me with disbelief for a moment as he brushed his fingers through his dark, greased-back hair. "Are you sure?"

I nodded. "Yes," I said, shivering.

"How?"

"They were murdered," I replied faintly as flashes of their corpses lying on the floor bombarded by mind.

"Did someone tell you?"

"No," I wept. "We found them." I wiped the tears streaming down my cold cheeks as I stood, trembling. "Merle, Matt, and I left the store to get Martha over at Helen's. Cliff's radio show was about start. All of the

Wilsons' doors and windows were locked. We smelled smoke, so we broke in… and… and… we found their bodies in the bedroom. They were shot. And there was a pile of burning linens on top of them."

"Someone shot them… and set them on fire?" Joseph asked.

I nodded. "We broke in through the back window."

"Jesus, this is awful." He leaned over the side of the porch and took a quick look in the window. "This is going to devastate your mother." His rosy face had turned almost white.

"I know. Along with everyone else in Linden."

"I haven't received a call or anything."

"It just happened. I packed some clothes for my mother and drove here as fast as I could. I don't want her to go back there. Three police cars were just pulling up to the house when I left."

"That was smart thinking. I don't want her to go back home." Joseph hesitated for a moment and took a deep breath. "All right, we have to go inside and tell her."

I nodded, wiped my eyes, and tried to compose myself. I turned toward the porch railing and spit out the sour bile that had made its way into my mouth. I saw it land, yellow and garish, next to the snow-covered bush.

"We can both tell her," Joseph said as he placed his hand on the gold handle and opened the door.

"Somehow." His voice faded.

I entered the foyer and set my mother's small chest to the right of the doorway so that she couldn't see it. I glanced up at the grand stairway that led to the second floor where the bedrooms were located—a bedroom that my mother would be sleeping in. My mother was sitting on the cream colored sofa next to the fireplace, talking to Joseph's mother and father.

"Fritzy?" My mother looked over at me. Her eyes were wide. "We weren't expecting you." She looked at me, puzzled. "We were just about to leave. Is something wrong? You look like you've been crying; your eyes are all swollen."

Joseph shook off his coat and set it on the back of the sofa. He walked over to my mother. "Here, let me take your coat for now."

"All right," she said softly. Mom stood up. Joseph helped her slip her coat off from behind, and then they both sat down.

Joseph's mother, a nicely dressed, white-haired woman, gestured to her husband, Dr. O'Hara, a tall white-haired man with a wide waist and wire framed glasses, to have a seat in the chair opposite the sofa to make room for me to sit down on the other sofa.

The phone rang. "Hold on." Joseph briskly walked into the kitchen to answer it. I tried to listen to what he was saying, but he was being too quiet. A couple minutes later, he came back into the room and nodded at me. I knew that the phone call confirmed what I had told him.

I could feel my bottom lip begin to quiver.

"Fritz, I can see you're upset; what is it?" Mom asked nervously.

"Something terrible has happened." I began to sob loudly.

"That call was one of the attorneys at the office," Joseph said as he sat back down next to my mother. He grasped her hands that were sitting on top of the knitted scarf that Helen had made her. "I... I don't know how to tell you this, but there's been another murder in Linden," he said gently.

My mother's eyes widened. "What?" she asked and began to fumble with her scarf. "Who was it?"

My tear-filled eyes met Joseph's for a moment as I was just about to say Martha's name, but I hesitated for a second.

Joseph gave me a quick glance and turned to my mother. "There was more than one this time," Joseph said calmly, still holding my mother's hands. "Ella, I'm so sorry to have to tell you this, but it was Martha, Helen, and Travis." His words fell from his lips like a black feather that painted the entire room with darkness.

I sobbed violently, thankful and relieved that Joseph had taken the reins and told her.

My mother sat there, stunned for a few moments.

"No, you must be mistaken. How could... how could... No, there must be some mistake. I just saw them at the store this morning. And we just listened to Cliff's show. Martha invited everyone to the store tonight."

I glanced over at Joseph's father, who was shaking his head. He seemed to be speechless.

"Maybe there's been some mistake," Joseph's mother said softly while standing at the back of the other chair.

I looked over at her. "I was there. We found them," I said softly.

Tears filled my mother's eyes, and she began to sob quietly. Her sob grew into an animalistic wail, as if someone was ripping her skin from her body. "No! Not them... Not them!" She fell into Joseph's arms, crying.

Watching her agony was too much to bear. But I had no words to ease her pain. My bones shook.

"How could someone hurt them?" she cried. "They're good people. They're good to everyone." She wept into Joseph's shoulder as he held her.

"I know, I know," Joseph whispered as she continued to sob.

After a little while, she pulled away and tried to gather herself. "I'm just sick for Gerry, and their boys, and Martha's mom."

"We stopped Gerry from going into the house. And Senior stayed with him, and I'm sure he'll help him tell Grandma, Cliff and Harrison."

She looked over at me. "Tell me what happened."

"Martha left the store just after 6:30 to get the milk. And it wasn't but fifteen to twenty minutes after she left that we headed over there to see what was keeping her. Merle didn't want her to miss any of the show. She was only gone a short time... I'm thinking that she must have walked in on whoever did this."

"So you think whoever did this was after Helen and Travis?"

"I don't know. It looks that way to me. If Martha didn't leave the store for the milk when she did, she'd still be alive."

Joseph's mother wiped a tear that was running down her face. She opened the drawer of the end table and pulled out two hankies, then walked over and sat on the other side of my mother. Mom turned to her, and they hugged. After a moment, my mother sniffled and wiped her nose.

"Ella, we want you to stay here tonight, and for as long as you'd like," Joseph's father said. "We're your family now. And we have plenty of room."

"Mom, I brought some of your clothes so that you could stay here. I didn't want you to go back home tonight."

"Thank you, honey."

"And Fritz, you're welcome to stay, too," Joseph's father said.

"We don't want you to stay there alone, either," Joseph said.

"Thank you for the offer, but I'm staying with the Kesslers tonight."

"We know how important Valerie is to you; you can bring her back here, too. We have four empty bedrooms upstairs. And we only use the two downstairs," Joseph's father said. "We can finally make some use of the empty bedrooms."

"Thank you. I'll keep that in mind."

The phone rang again.

"Excuse me," Joseph said as he stood up and headed to the kitchen to answer it. A few minutes later, he came back. "I have to go to Linden."

"Now?" Joseph's mother asked.

"I didn't expect that either. Ron is on his way there now, and he wants some assistance," Joseph said as he sat back down next to my mother and turned to her. "But I don't want to leave you."

"I'll be all right here with Fritz and your parents."

"Mom, I don't want to leave you either," I said. "But remember, I told you I was going to stay with the Kesslers tonight. Before I left, I told Valerie I'd be back. But I can call her and tell her I'm staying here."

"No, no... Yes, you did say that," my mother said. "And Valerie does need you. So, yes, it's okay. Stay with them tonight."

I nodded, "Yeah. Valerie's terrified."

"What about Mrs. Adleman?"

"Her son was coming to get her. Senior didn't want her staying there alone—and neither did I."

"No, you go stay with the Kesslers. You need to be with Valerie."

My mother began to sob again. "I can't believe that they're gone. I feel like when I go back home, they'll... they'll be there at the store drinking their tea, stopping by the house, walking to the post office." My mother tried to speak through her tears.

"It's going to take some time," Joseph whispered as he reached his arms out and held her.

A few minutes later, my mother pulled away from Joseph's shoulder, sniffling. "Listen, I know you have to go. I'll be all right here with your parents."

"Are you sure?"

"Yes. There's someone out there that needs to be caught and punished for this!" my mother said as her anger bled into the room. "I want Ron to find out who did this! He needs to!" she cried.

"We'll stay up with her," Dr. O'Hara said. "Go on, son."

"Yes, of course we will," his mother nodded as she rubbed my mother's back.

"All right." Joseph stood up, slipped on his coat, and then leaned over and kissed my mother.

My mother turned to me. "Fritzy, you go too. Valerie's waiting for you. And after you leave, I'm going to call John to tell him."

"Okay. Tell him that I do plan on being there in the morning. And are you sure that you want me to go?" I asked.

"Yes, I'm sure." She paused. "Where's your gun?"

"It's in the car."

"You're going to be keeping it with you, right?"

"Yes. And I'm sure we'll all have our guns clutched in our hands all night." I stepped over to my mother and gave her a long hug. I pulled away and looked into her swollen, bloodshot eyes. "I'm so sorry. It was just a few minutes. If only we left sooner..." My voice faded.

"No, no! What if you walked in on him? I'd hate to think..." She fell apart again.

I reached over and hugged her again. "No, there were three of us. I guarantee he wouldn't have made it out of the house breathing." I felt her nod into my shoulder as she cried.

After a couple more minutes, my mother gained her composure. She dabbed her eyes with the hankie and kissed my cheek. "I love you, honey."

"I love you, too." I turned and walked out the front door behind Joseph.

"It is going to take some time, but I think she'll be all right. She's strong," Joseph said as we walked down the porch steps.

"I hope so."

"I know. We'll just have to take it day by day." He

nodded.

As we stood on the sidewalk, I looked at him. "Thank you for telling her," I said. "When it came time, I froze."

Joseph placed his hand on my shoulder. "You've been through enough tonight. I thought it would be better for you if I broke the news to her."

With my lips pressed together, I nodded. "Yeah, you're right. Thank you."

Joseph pulled me close to him and gave me a hug. "We're going to get through this as a family. I will take care of both of you; I love you like my own son."

I nodded as tears pooled in my eyes. I was overcome with emotion as I realized how much I needed to hear those words. And I realized that I also loved him like a father. He deeply cared for us and loved us. It was the first time since my father died that I felt secure. I was no longer the only one protecting my mother. "That means a lot to me," I said as our arms fell to our sides, and I stepped back.

"I mean it. We will heal and move on." He patted me on the back. "Listen, I need to get going. I'll see you in a little while, all right?"

"Okay. Valerie is probably wondering where I am." I turned and began walking to my car. "Joseph," I called out as I opened my car door.

He turned back to look at me. "Yeah."

"They need to catch this madman!"

Twenty-Four

It was well after 10:30 when I arrived back in Linden. A hint of moonlight reflected off of the parked cars on both sides of the road. I parked my car on the far right of my driveway, next to Joseph's car. I grabbed my shotgun and traipsed through the icy snow. As I walked up Valerie's driveway, I saw Senior looking out the front window. The porch light switched on, and Senior opened the front door. His eyes were puffy and red.

"Come in, Fritzy," he said as he locked the door behind me. "I hate to ask, but how'd it go telling your mom?"

"It was awful. I've never seen her cry so hard; the word devastated is hardly enough to describe what she's feeling right now," I replied softly. "I'm just glad that I made it over there in time. They were about to leave. She's also going to be staying there for a few days."

"Good. She doesn't need to be here to see all of this."

"No, she doesn't," I said as I stamped off my icy boots and set my gun against the wall. "Did you see all the cars?"

"Sure did. There're sheriffs, troopers, and reporters all over this place. Keller is already here. He's been taking statements over at the store. Matt came to get me after he gave his statement 'bout an hour ago. I just got back about ten minutes ago."

"Hey, Fritzy," Junior said as he walked into the parlor from the kitchen, eating a piece of bread.

"Hey, Junior. You staying here tonight, too?"

"I might," he replied as he sat down on the sofa.

"Where were you when all this was happening?" I asked.

"I was in bed. I ain't heard a thing 'til Pa came and knocked at my door."

"Lucky for you." I glanced around the room and listened for any noise in the kitchen. "Where're Valerie and Mertie?"

"They're lying down in our bedroom. Valerie didn't want to sleep alone. I told them to stay in there, and that you and I would stay out here and keep watch," Senior said as he glanced over at Junior. "And Junior too, if he decides to stay."

I grabbed my shotgun again. "I'm going to head over to give my statement. Joseph must be over there helping Keller."

"I didn't see him, but he might be there now. Keller has a list of people he wants to talk to. After I talked to him, I got the feeling he ain't leaving here tonight until he talks to everyone."

As I headed up the hill, I made my way through

all the cars parked in front of Morgan's store. When I walked in, I could hardly move. The store was chokingly warm. The room was filled with people, few of whom I knew. By the looks, many of them were reporters, with their pencils and notepads in hand. Through the smoky haze, I saw Merle standing behind the counter. His eyes were bloodshot and puffed-up. He gave me a quick nod and signaled me over.

"What the hell? The news spread fast," I said.

"It sure did. There were less than five people in the store an hour ago. They're waiting for Keller to make a statement."

"I hope it's worth the wait," I said as I removed my cap and placed it on the counter.

"I hope so, too," Merle said. "Do you want a drink?"

"I'll take a cider—from the barrel if you got it," I said as I sat down on the stool, emotionally drained. Although the cider didn't taste the best, I knew it would help dull the pain.

I watched Merle stroll to the back of the store and come back with a full glass of cider. He set it on the counter in front of me. "This is on Gerry. I filled two jugs from the barrel in the cellar."

I lifted the glass and held it under my nose. The scent slightly burned the inside of my nose. I glanced through the smoke; no one was looking my way. The reporters were talking among themselves. I turned and took three big swigs. The glass was empty in less than two minutes.

"Thanks; how about another one?" I asked and shoved the glass toward him. The cider's warmth began to travel through my cold bones, relaxing my rattled nerves.

Merle picked up my glass and headed to the back of the store again. A minute later he walked back with a full glass and set it down in front of me. "So you drove into Batavia to tell your mom?"

"Yeah," I replied softly. My eyes began to swell with tears. I picked up my glass and drank half of it down. "I never saw my mother cry that hard. Not even when my father died."

Merle placed his hands on the counter and stared at me for a moment. "I'm sure she did, but you didn't see it." Merle poured himself a glass. "This is my third glass. It's helping me keep it together," he said, drinking half of it down and setting it on the counter.

"I just need to ask: how are Gerry and Grandma taking it?"

"They're devastated. Gerry has been upstairs with her since he came back to the store. Senior and I were up there with them for about an hour. Then he gave his statement and left. That's when all these reporters started arriving. Some of them drove in from Buffalo and Rochester."

I nodded. "What about Cliff and Harry?" I wiped

away the tear that trickled down my cheek.

"They're on their way here. They should be here soon."

"I just came down to give my statement. Where's Keller? "

"He's in the house. Joseph walked in the door about ten minutes ago, too." Merle pointed. "Keller is using the kitchen for an office."

"Did you already give your statement?"

"Yeah. I was one of the first."

"All right. Is anyone in there now?" I asked as I finished my cider and began to feel some of the tension leave my body.

"No, I don't think so. Irvin just walked out before you came in."

"Would you hold my gun?" I asked Merle.

"Yeah," he replied as I handed it to him. "I'll put it back here." He set it on the back counter.

"Thanks. Let me go do this then." I wiped my eyes and pulled myself together as I headed over to the door. I took a deep breath and knocked at the door. Moments later, the door swung open to an officer who was standing there.

"I'm here to give my statement," I said nervously.

"Your name?"

"Fritzelle Reynolds."

"He's on the list," a voice said from behind the officer.

The door opened wider, and there seated at the kitchen table was District Attorney Ronald Keller, along with two other officers in uniform and one in plain clothes. Off to the side was the stenographer.

"Mr. Reynolds." Keller reached out and shook my hand. "This is Deputy Ornsby, Captain Robbins, and Detective Dawson."

I nodded as I recalled meeting Deputy Ornsby the day Flo was found in her fruit cellar and seeing him again at the Nelsons' house the day of the fire. The stenographer glanced up at me for a moment, adjusted her round framed glasses, and looked down at her keys. I also remembered her from the John Doe Proceedings.

"We've met before, haven't we?" Keller gestured to the seat directly across from him.

I nodded anxiously and sat down. Joseph entered the room from the parlor. He gave me a quick nod as Keller handed him a file. Then he left the room again. A few seconds later, he walked past me and left out the same door I had just entered from.

I nodded. "Yes, sir. I worked for Miss Kingsley."

"Your mother is Ella?"

"Yes, sir, that is correct."

"All right, Mr. Reynolds. We want a detailed state‑ ment from you, starting with the afternoon of today, March 11th, the day of these horrible murders. This is so that we may attempt to find out all occurrences that happened in the village of Linden in order to discover who committed this crime."

"Yes, sir, I understand," I said as my nerves began to settle down from the cider.

"I will ask you a number of questions and I would like you to respond truthfully and accurately."

I nodded, "Yes, sir."

Keller flipped over the paper on his notepad and wrote something down. I could hear the muffled voices coming from the store as I waited for the questions to begin. It had been a while since I'd been in the Morgans' living quarters. Nothing had changed. I could see the photo of Grandma and Grandpa Harrison hanging on the wall by the window in the parlor. I couldn't help but think of Grandma Harrison. When she called down looking for Martha, she was probably being murdered at that moment. It all seemed like a nightmare.

"How old are you?"

"Seventeen years old."

"You live in Linden, NY?"

"Yes."

"How long have you lived here?"

"All my life."

"Where do you live?"

"On Linden Road."

"Where do you work?"

"I work for my Uncle John on our family farm in

Bergen."

"Are you single?"

"I have a girlfriend."

"Her name?"

"Valerie Kessler."

"Gordon Kessler, Senior's daughter?"

"Yes."

I glanced over at the stenographer, trying to re-member her name. Her fingers seemed to move swiftly over the keys. The tick, tick, tick filled the silence lingering between Keller's questions and my answers.

"Did you work on your uncle's farm this after-noon?"

"Yes," I replied as the warmth of the cider be-gan to paint a fog over the memory of the night. The sound of the tapping began to distract me. Suddenly, I remembered the stenographer's name was Francine, Francine Whittle.

As Keller's questions continued, I eventually told them all about how Martha left for milk and didn't come back, and pulled more of the night's details out of my clouded head. Again, like the John Doe Proceed-ing, Keller's focus was on Anton Mitchell and Junior Kessler. After they were finished with their questions and I told them all that I knew, Keller glanced at the officers and then at Detective Dawson. Dawson nodded.

"Mr. Reynolds, thank you for your time and the

account of your day's occurrences. If we need to ask you any more questions, we'll be contacting you."

"All right, I'll be available if you need me." I rose from my seat, walked back into the store, and closed the door behind me. Out of the corner of my eye, I saw Joseph walk into the store.

I sat back down at the stool and Joseph sat down next to me. "I was over at the Wilsons'. They just took the bodies to the coroner's office. It was much worse than I ever imagined."

I nodded as Merle walked over and set another glass of cider down on the counter in front of me. "For my mother's sake, please don't tell her what you saw." I picked up my glass.

Joseph shook his head. "I wasn't planning on telling her. I'm not even going to tell her that I was in the house."

I drank half my glass down and rested my eyes on Joseph. "Does Keller have any ideas of who did this? The only two he asked about were Anton Mitchell and Junior Kessler. After the John Doe Proceedings, I wasn't too surprised by it."

"I know. And neither one had any ill feelings for Helen or Travis that anyone would admit," Joseph said.

"Admit? Huh. There were no ill feelings with any of them. Also, I just saw Junior, and he didn't even know what had happened until Senior woke him up. I saw Junior go into his house just before I headed over to the store. He wasn't anywhere near the Wilsons' house."

Joseph shook his head in disgust. "I don't... I just don't know."

My eyes roamed the room as the smoke stung them. I tried to listen to the conversations, but didn't hear much. "Look at all these reporters. This story is going to be in all the papers."

"A triple homicide? It'll be a big news story!" Joseph nodded.

I glanced over at Joseph. "Yeah, my life feels like a news story," I said under my breath.

Joseph stared at me with a slight squint out of the corner of his eye.

"I guess we've all got a story, don't we?" I asked in a matter-of-fact tone, not expecting an answer. Then I drank down the rest of my cider and looked over at Joseph for a moment. "Some are just bloodier than others." I set my glass down for Merle to fill it again.

Twenty-Five

The layers of dark gray clouds hinted at another blanket of snow. The drive on the icy road from Bergen to Batavia seemed never ending. My eyelids felt like tiny lead weights bobbing on a scale.

For a moment, they shut.

Suddenly, the car shook as I drove over a small mound of ice in the center of the road. I caught myself swerving into the oncoming lane.

I felt sick to my stomach from all the cider I drank. But I didn't regret it. It helped deaden the grief and anger.

The overnight watch with Senior and a long day at the farm had caught up with me. It had been almost twenty-four hours since I had last seen my mother. Even though I was exhausted, and all I wanted to do was sleep, I was more concerned about her condition.

I pulled up in front of the house, stepped out of the car, and took a few deep breaths of the brisk air to clear my head. Feeling a little refreshed, I made my way to the front door and knocked. Moments later, the door swung open, and I was surprised to see Valerie standing there.

"What're you doing here? I mean, I'm glad to see

you, but I didn't expect—"

"It all happened so fast. Come inside and I'll tell you." Valerie rubbed her arms and closed the door behind me. As I shrugged my coat off and stamped the snow off my boots, bits of ice scattered onto the small black rug. I untied the laces and set my boots next to the foyer wall. Valerie grabbed my coat and hung it in the closet under the stairway.

I leaned in and gave her a quick kiss. "So tell me..." I grasped her hand and we wandered into the warm parlor. The house was so much more than our house. A large black and white tiled floor continued into the parlor. The burgundy area rug below encompassed the soft white Victorian sofa, the coffee table, and two high-backed upholstered chairs. We sat down on the sofa.

"Well, let me tell you: Ted called this morning to tell me that he is moving his mother in with him and his wife. He is going to sell his mother's house when all of the negative attention stops."

"That worked out. Your parents and I weren't going to let you stay there alone anyway."

"I know, they told me it was for the best. Okay, let me finish telling you... So, after we finished dinner, your mother called to check on us. My mom told your mom that I wasn't going to be working for Mrs. Adleman anymore. After my mother hung up the phone, she told me to pack all my clothes and that I have a new job. Then she drove me here to meet Joseph's parents. They told us that the last girl that had been working for them got married just after Christmas, and they'd been looking to hire another girl. Your mother let them know that I was available, so here I am!" Valerie smiled.

"All of this happened today?" I asked, overflowing with relief. "You know this was my mother's doing, right?"

Valerie nodded. "Yeah, I know. But I'm just grateful. So after we got here, Joseph's mother showed me around the house and my new room upstairs. Then my mom left to stay with my Aunt Rosie in Albion for a few days. Or maybe longer."

"I'm so relieved!" I said and yawned. "Then it looks like I'll be staying here, too." I leaned in, gave her a loving kiss, and just held her. The warmth of the fire soothed me. "Where's my mom?" I asked.

"She's upstairs, lying down. She didn't sleep much last night."

"I didn't either. Where's Joseph's parents?"

"They left for the market about an hour ago. They should be back soon." Valerie gazed around the room. "Isn't this a beautiful house?"

"It sure is!" I rested my hand on her knee as I looked into her tired eyes. "How did you sleep last night? I left this morning before sunrise."

"I slept a couple of hours." Valerie fixed her eyes

on mine. "You look tired! Your eyes look like they're going to bleed, they're so red. And you have dark circles under your eyes... You need to get some rest," she insisted.

"I know; I'm exhausted!" I leaned back against the arm of the sofa and placed my head on the velvet pillow. I closed my burning eyes for a few seconds to cool them. Forcing my eyelids to lift, I looked over at Valerie. "What was it like when you left there today?"

"It was quiet; too quiet. When my mom and I left, we drove out Chapman Road so we could see what was happening. The Wilsons' house is all boarded up, and there were a few cars parked outside the house."

"Reporters and police?"

"Well, they were there too. But we also saw a couple cars stop in front of the Wilsons' house and then drive away. I think they were just nosing around."

"I'm sure there'll be more of that."

"Especially after today's paper." Valerie swiftly walked over to the dining room table. "Read this."

I sat up, and she handed me the *Batavia Daily News* evening edition. The front headline read, *Linden Triple Slayer Eludes Net*. The subheads read, *Authorities are Determined Mysterious Linden Murderer Shall Not Escape Justice*. The next line read, *Investigation in Full Swing—Offer of $1,000 Reward*. And the next line, *Autopsy Findings – Two Die from Bullet Wounds – Third Clubbed to Death*.

I continued to read the article, and then set the

paper on the coffee table. I was drained and kept wishing it was all just a nightmare. All that I knew and loved—people and my home—were reduced to headlines and a list of facts. The screams, the tears, and the terror remained hidden behind the words.

"It's hard to believe, isn't it?" Valerie's voice became shaky as she sat back down next to me. A tear made its way down her cheek. "I feel so awful for the Morgans."

I reached over and held her hand. "I know; we all do."

"Your mom called Gerry today."

"She did?"

"Yeah."

"How're they doing?"

"They're doing the best that they can. Mr. Morgan is trying to stay strong for his sons and for Grandma. He's put up the thousand dollar reward. And he closed the store for now."

"He did?"

Valerie nodded. "Maybe a reward will help."

"Any word on when the funerals are going to be?"

"The Wilsons' are going to be on Friday and Martha's is going to be on Saturday."

I shook my head. "I'll have to let Uncle John know that I won't be there on Friday or Saturday. I'm not leaving my mom's side. It's going to be a really hard two days for her. He'll understand. He's really upset about all of this too."

I heard the door open in the kitchen and two sets of feet stomping. Minutes later, Mrs. O'Hara entered the dining room, untying the scarf around her head.

"Hello, Fritz. I'm glad that you're here. Did you meet our new house girl?" She gave me a smile, and then set her coat and scarf over the dining room chair.

"Yes, I did. Good choice." I smiled.

"We think so, too." She grinned. "Our future granddaughter-in-law needed a job, and we had an opening to fill."

Valerie glanced over at me with her mouth open and eyes wide.

"What did you tell her?" I whispered.

"I didn't tell her anything," she whispered back.

I nodded, pressing my lips together. "Mom," I whispered.

"We're going to make supper. We bought a smoked ham. You two visit until it's ready," Mrs. O'Hara said. "Where's Ella?"

"She's lying down upstairs," Valerie replied.

"I hope she's finally getting some rest. She really needs it." She walked toward the kitchen.

Valerie stood up. "Wait, shouldn't I be helping you with supper?"

Mrs. O' Hara turned back around. "No, no. You can start on Monday. For now, I just want you to get acquainted with our home... and your new home."

Valerie sat back down. "They're really nice people," she said quietly.

"They are." I nodded. "They've been so good to my
mom and me, and also now to you." I smiled.

The sound of creaking stairs came from the foyer.
My mother was slowly coming down the wooden stair-
case.

"Mom!"

"Hi, honey." Her soft voice drifted tenderly
through the air as she walked through the parlor
doorway.

Her eyes were red and puffy. Her hair was tou-
sled, and her skin was sallow. She walked over to the
back of the sofa, leaned over, and gave me a kiss on
the cheek.

"I came right from the farm. I wanted to see how
you were."

My mother walked past the fireplace over to one of
the high-backed chairs, moved the pillow to the side,
and sat down across from Valerie and me. "I was up
all night last night. I finally fell asleep for a couple
hours." She sat there quietly for a moment. "I will
miss them terribly." She began to weep a little.

"We'll get through this," I said, trying to reassure
her and be strong.

She nodded. "We have to," she whispered. "We
have to."

"What time is it?" my mother asked.

I yanked out my pocket watch. "It's almost 6:30."

"It's late. Joseph ought to be home soon." Mom wiped her teary eyes. "Is that the evening *Daily*?"

Valerie nodded. "Yes," she replied nervously.

My mother reached over to pick it up.

Like a striking snake, I reached over and slapped my hand on top of the paper. "Mom, you don't need to read it. You don't need to make it worse on yourself."

"Fritz," she raised her voice a bit. "Please; I understand what you are trying to do, and I appreciate it." She pulled the paper out from under my hand, and I pulled my hand away. "They were my dearest friends, and I am going to read the paper!"

"All right," I said, feeling overpowered, and then I watched her eyes as she read the front page.

"No arrests yet." The quiet words seeped out with sadness.

"No, not yet," Valerie said softly.

Mrs. O' Hara stepped out of the kitchen, wiping her hand with a towel. "Ella," she said caringly and strolled over to my mom. "Were you able to get some rest, dear?"

"A little," my mother replied.

Mrs. O'Hara leaned over the back of the sofa and gave Mom a hug. "I'm so glad. We're going to get through this. It is going to take some time, but we will get through it."

Mrs. O'Hara's concerned eyes held mine.

"We will... We'll get through it." I gave Mrs. O'Hara a slight nod.

"Are you hungry, Ella?"

"No, not really," Mom replied.

"Well, I want you to try to eat a little so you don't find yourself ill. Supper should be ready in about twenty minutes or so," Mrs. O'Hara said.

"Okay, I'll try," Mom said.

"That's good. We bought a nice ham, and it's in the oven," Mrs. O'Hara said and strolled toward the kitchen.

My mother set the newspaper back down on the coffee table. "I'm not really hungry."

"You have to eat, or you'll get weak and sick," Valerie insisted.

"My stomach has been aching all day," my mother whispered.

"Mom, just try to eat a little. Your stomach will feel better once you get some food in it."

A few minutes later, the aroma of hickory smoked ham began to fill the dining room and parlor.

I heard the back door open and more stomping on the floor, followed by the mutter of Joseph's voice. Valerie and my mother walked into the dining room. My mother opened the hutch, pulled out a stack of plates, and set them on the dining room table. Joseph shook off his coat. Valerie reached out and took Joseph's coat and grabbed Mrs. O'Hara's coat off the back of the dining room chair. Then Valerie hung them in the foyer closet. Joseph gave my mother a kiss and a long hug. My eyes met his, and he nodded.

Carrying his briefcase in one hand and loosening his bow tie in the other, he walked over to the sofa, then pulled his tie off. "How's your mom doing?" he asked in a quiet voice so that she didn't hear him.

"Okay, I guess."

"Let's go into the library so I can put this away and we can talk."

"Sure." I followed him.

Joseph shut the door behind us, and then set his briefcase on the large, sophisticated mahogany desk that sat in front of the wooden-paned window. My eyes circled the room, which was lined with shelves and shelves of books. Each shelf was filled with pages and pages written about medicine and law, and works of literature. I'd never seen so many books in one room. "Your mom doesn't need to hear any more of the details."

"She read the newspaper. I tried to stop her, but she read it anyway."

"Well, you can't stop her from reading the paper, but she doesn't need to hear us talk about it." Joseph walked over to the table that sat against the wall opposite the leather sofa. He picked up the cantor, poured a glass of golden-brown liquid, and then hand-ed it to me. "Here, you look like you could use a drink.

It's bourbon."

"I've never had it." I placed the drink under my nose. It had a sharp, spicy aroma and a little bit of caramel mixed with it. I took a sip and pressed my lips together. "It has a strong burn to it." After a minute, I took another few sips and began to enjoy the sweet flavor it left on my tongue. "How're you able to buy alcohol?"

"As you know, my father is a doctor; he has a special license to prescribe bourbon for medicinal purposes. I'm sure it tastes a lot better than that cider you drink." He nodded and gestured toward the sofa for me to sit.

With my glass in hand, I nodded in agreement. He was right, it did taste smooth. Then I lowered myself to the sofa. "Were you in Linden today?" I asked, and sipped more bourbon. After only a few sips, it began to pleasantly warm me from the inside out. I understood why Joseph's father prescribed it. It was the medicine I needed.

Joseph turned the russet colored leather chair that was sitting in front of the desk so that he faced toward me. "Part of the day, I was. Keller was still taking statements when I left."

"I read in the paper that the autopsies were already done?"

"Yeah, Keller had the reports this afternoon."

"Did you read them?"

He nodded. "Yeah, I read 'em," he answered, grim-ly.

"I'm only asking because I read in the paper that Helen and Travis were shot and Martha was beaten. I thought that they were all shot."

"No, Travis was shot in the neck, at least four or five times," Joseph said. "The coroner couldn't even determine exactly how many... I'm not sure I should be telling you all of this because it's not public record yet, but I trust you."

"You *can* trust me."

"I know I can." Joseph nodded. "Helen died from a single gunshot wound to the face. So, it's possible that, when Mrs. Morgan walked in on the perpetrator, he had run out of bullets, panicked, and beat her with the closest object he could find—the blood covered adz handle that was found in the bedroom." He sipped from his glass.

"You're not going to tell my mother any of this, are you? She doesn't need to know the details."

He shook his head. "Of course not." His voice was adamant.

"That's good. What was it like there today, with everyone in a panic?" I took another sip from my glass. Each tip of the glass was better than the last.

"Yeah, they want an arrest, and there's a lot of hysteria—and anger, of course. Captain Robbins is trying to ease their fears, and announced that he's putting a three-man outpost on horseback twenty-four hours a day there."

I pressed my lips together and nodded. "That's good to hear."

"At least it gives them a little relief... we hope, anyway." Joseph finished his glass and poured another one. "Let me know when you're ready."

I nodded. "I will."

"I got a question," Joseph said with a slight squint in his eyes as he leaned against the table that held the bourbon.

My eyes rested on his as I waited for the question to follow.

"Is Leon a big talker?"

I shrugged my shoulders, trying to figure out where he was going with that question. "I don't know that he's a big talker, but he doesn't know how to keep his mouth shut. So yeah, I guess you could say that. Why?"

"Well, he's been boasting about being the last one to see Travis alive."

"Honestly, I never gave it much thought as to who saw Travis last," I said. "I think it was Merle who saw him walk past the store after he got off the train. Maybe Leon saw Travis go into the house. The Chapmans live across the road from the Wilsons. And Leon is usually outside working around the same time Travis gets home from the railroad, so he probably did see him walk into his house."

Joseph took a deep breath and sipped on his drink. "Or maybe he was *in* the house when Travis got home."

Puzzled, I locked eyes with Joseph. "Leon? No, he might like to shoot his mouth off from time to time, but murder? Especially a triple murder," I said as I shook my head in disbelief. "Besides, he thinks a lot of Martha." I tipped on my bourbon a little more, disturbed by the thought.

"It's just one of the theories Keller and Dawson came up with, because his story doesn't match up with Merle's."

"What story?"

"Leon claims he stopped into the store around supper time, but Merle can't recall that he did," Joseph replied as he brought his drink to his lips for a moment, then took a sip. "And Keller and Dawson aren't ruling out that there was more than one perpetrator."

Felix? "I didn't see Leon or Felix until Everett ran over to Felix's and got them. Are they suspects?"

Joseph shook his head and finished his drink. "No, not in particular, but Keller isn't taking anyone off his list who wasn't at Morgan's store at this point... I was just curious. I don't know Leon like you do, so I thought I'd ask you."

I took a huge swig of my drink and finished it. "He

was also the first one in the Wilsons' house too. He probably thinks he's a big shot."

"Yeah, I got that feeling from him too," Joseph said. "Anyway, as I said, I don't really know him." Joseph grabbed the bottle and filled my glass again.

"Thanks," I said.

Joseph also filled his glass and sat back down. "Enough about Leon. I'm concerned about you. You look like hell."

"I'm really tired. I hardly slept last night, and I worked all day. I just need some sleep."

"I've been thinking—you've been through a lot for a kid your age."

"Yeah, I guess. Along with everyone else living there."

Joseph leaned back in his seat, took a deep breath, and sipped from his glass. Meanwhile, I poured more of the smoothness down my throat.

"I'm just glad that your mother wasn't there to see it."

"So am I."

Joseph took another swig from his glass. "I've been thinking about what you said last night."

"What'd I say?"

"Something about having a story, and how yours is a bloody one."

I nodded. "It's true." My chin began to quiver. It was as if the Black Hand followed me and waited to strike when I was nearby to show me the darkest side of evil. The lady in the woods wasn't enough... Evil had to bring Hell to my doorstep. I drank down the rest of the bourbon and set my glass on the table. "I can still see the blood," I whispered. "When I close my eyes, that's all I see. I see their crushed skulls and all the blood. I can even smell the burnt hair and flesh."

Joseph set his drink down, sat down next to me, and gave me a fatherly hug. I felt his strength and security wrapped around me.

"Those memories will fade. Like I said last night, we'll get through this. And you're safe here."

I shook my head, holding back my tears. "Safe? I don't know that I'll ever feel safe."

Joseph pulled away. His eyes were teary. "Listen to me: after all that has happened, there's no one there who feels safe. That's why they brought in the deputies. And now you're living here, ten miles away from all of it. And I promise that life is going to be better from here on. In time, those horrific memories will weaken, and fade away. I promise. And living here, in a new city and a new environment, is exactly what you and your mother need right now. There are a lot of opportunities out there. You could start a business, find another line of work, or even go to college. My family has the money and is willing to support you in whatever you'd like to do."

"But I work on our family farm."

"Yes, now you do. But if you'd like to pursue something else, I'm sure your Uncle John would be supportive."

"Maybe—he always talked about me taking over the farm someday, but maybe he never thought that I'd want to do anything else."

"And for now—when those memories creep back into your head, do your best to push them aside. That's why a new focus will be good for you. Leave the bad memories where they belong—in the past."

"Locked away in a trunk inside my head," I said softly.

"And throw away the key," Joseph said steadfastly. "For now, try to look ahead. What that madman did was horrendous, but don't give him any more than he has already taken. If you relive it every day, he's not only taken those lives, he's also taking yours. Just because you're breathing, does not mean you're living—not if the fiend has a hold on your mind."

I nodded, absorbing every powerful word. "No one has ever said any of this to me."

"You can't change the past, but you can choose whether you let it destroy you or make you stronger."

I nodded. *He was making a lot of sense.*

"If I'm going to be living here, what about the house?"

"Your mom can sell it or rent it out. Let's see what happens over the next couple of months."

Feeling a sense of relief, I nodded. "All right. And I'm so glad that Valerie's living here and working for your parents."

"Living here? Working for my parents? She is? I thought you just brought her for supper."

"Nope, she's your parents' new house girl," I replied. "I am sure it was my mother who suggested her for the job."

"Oh, I'm sure it was," Joseph said as he leaned back on the sofa, chuckling. Then he picked up his drink and took another sip. "All of you living here is all for the best."

I nodded. "I'm starting to see it that way." I mustered up a smile.

There was a knock at the door, and then it swung open. "We can eat," Dr. O'Hara said from where he was standing in the doorway.

"Do you want a drink, Dad?"

"Sure, I'll have one."

Joseph stood up and headed over to the table, poured another drink, and handed it to him.

Feeling drained, I stood up from the sofa. Talking to Joseph seemed to have calmed my shaky nerves. Or maybe it was the soothing, amber liquid that had just befriended me.

Twenty-Six

Shortly before 2:00, we parked our car a little ways down Chapman Road to attend the second service within two days, which bled together into a blur mixed with fear, grief, and shock. We made our way past the Wilsons' boarded-up house and through the melting snow, heading toward the Morgans' living quarters. The sun was shining brightly on our faces, which were drenched in sorrow. The sound of a horse's neigh was heard off in the distance. I glanced up the road and saw an officer, a Gray Rider, not far from my house, sauntering down the hill and over the bridge toward us. Uncle John steadied himself with his cane through the ice and snow as Joseph and my mother walked arm-in-arm beside him. I could tell Uncle John's arthritis was giving him a lot of pain by the expression on his face. This had been the first time he'd been to Linden in a while. But he felt that he needed to pay his respects to Martha. I kept an eye on him in case he fell as Valerie and I followed closely behind, absent of any conversation. The silence spoke for all of us.

The crowd moved slowly through the back door. I wondered how they would be able to accommodate so many people. Martha was well known in Linden and had customers from at least two counties. We entered through the back door; the kitchen was filled with people. Irvin Packard and his wife nodded, their eyes filled with sadness. The house was noticeably warm, and lacked fresh air.

As the line moved into the parlor, I saw that the far wall was overflowing with flowers that surrounded both sides of the steel gray casket, which was open for public view. After a few minutes, the line to the casket lessened. Out of concern, my eyes were fixed on my mother as she stood in front of us. She wiped her tears and placed her hand on Martha's.

"I'm going to miss you," she cried. Joseph placed his arm around her and rubbed her upper arm. "May you rest in peace, my dear friend." She spoke softly through her tears. She then placed her hands in prayer for a few moments and turned away from the casket.

After Uncle John gave his condolences to the family, it was our turn. Valerie and I stood there, staring at Martha's body. The image of her lying on the floor of the Wilsons' bedroom, bloody and beaten, flashed in my head. My heart began to race. I took a deep breath. I began to feel like I was going to vomit. I took another deep breath.

Valerie turned to me. "She looks better than I expected," she whispered.

I nodded. "They fixed her up good."

Martha's face had been repaired, and she looked as if she was sleeping peacefully. We both said a small prayer and turned away. My mother was hugging Gerry Morgan, who was standing in the front row next to Grandma Harrison. Next to her stood Cliff, Harrison, and his wife.

I approached Gerry, and I saw the pain and anguish in his eyes. "I'm sorry," I whispered.

Gerry put his arms around me and gave me a hug. "Merle told me how you tried to save them," he whispered. "Thank you."

"We tried," I said softly. "We thought we were walking into a fire." I stopped there, saying no more.

He nodded. "I know, son, I know."

Then, I walked up to Grandma Harrison. I gave her a long hug. "I'm so sorry," I whispered. "We all loved her."

"We were all blessed to have her," Grandma cried. "She was a good daughter, and a good mother, and so good to everyone who knew her," she wept.

I saw Cliff's red puffy eyes. There were tears running down his cheeks. "Thank you for coming, Fritz."

"We're all going to miss your mom. We all loved her," I said with grief.

Cliff reached out and gave me a hug. "I don't understand why this happened," he whispered. "My mom was such a kind woman."

I nodded. "I know."

Harrison, with tear-soaked eyes, reached out and shook my hand. "Thank you for coming."

"I'm sorry about your mother," I said gently.

"Thank you. Our family appreciates all the support we've received." He gestured to the woman who was standing next to him. "I don't know if you remember my wife, Claire."

"Yes, we've met a couple of times." I nodded.

Harrison turned to his wife. "This is Fritz, Ella's son. Our mothers were close friends."

Claire reached out her hand to shake mine. "Yes, I remember meeting you. Thank you for coming," she said softly.

After we said our condolences to all of the family, I scanned the room for open seats. As I looked around the room, I saw Leon walk up to the open casket alone. He turned around and glanced over his shoulder as if he was looking to see who was watching him, but he didn't see that my eyes were bolted on him. His face was pale, and he looked anxious. As I watched him, my pulse quickened as I thought about what Joseph and I had talked about in his office. There was something about his behavior that disturbed me.

The words "the last one to see Travis alive" lingered with me for a while. The more I thought about what Leon was telling people, the more it began to bother me, and it made me a little suspicious because he was *not* at the store that night—and he was supposed to be. At that moment, Senior stood up and gestured for us to come over to him and Mertie at the back of the room. There were three seats, one for my mother and the others for Valerie and Uncle John. Joseph and I let them sit down, and we stood against the back wall. I watched Leon turn around and head back to his seat. When all was quiet, Pastor Daly began to speak.

My eyes moved throughout the parlor, noticing that Merle was leaning against the side wall, taking note of the Chapmans sitting two rows behind the Morgans as Leon sat down next to his brother Felix. I didn't see Felix's wife in the room. Anton and his wife were to the left of us, along with all of our neighbors. Then I noticed District Attorney Keller, Detective Dawson, and three men in plain clothing who were still official in appearance standing near the kitchen doorway.

I couldn't take my eyes off Leon. He sat there and kept running his fingers through his hair. As I stared at him, a sick feeling began to grow in the pit of my stomach. Then he whispered something to his brother. Felix shook his head and stared straight ahead. I glanced over at Keller and Dawson to see if they were looking at Leon, but they weren't looking at anyone in particular.

Senior turned back to me. "Have you seen Junior?"

I leaned over to Senior without taking my eyes off of Leon. "No, I don't see him. But I'm not surprised."

Valerie turned to her father. "Dad, you know he doesn't attend funerals," she whispered adamantly.

I turned to Joseph for a moment. "They'll probably try to arrest him this time," I said. Then I glanced over at Leon and Felix, wondering exactly where they were on the night of March 11th at 6:30.

Joseph pressed his lips and nodded. "Keller is serious about solving this case, so it would have been in Junior's best interest to attend his neighbor's funeral."

Pastor Daly performed the second service, once again, without a mention of the horrific event that brought us all together. As Daly ended the service with a prayer, I gazed at the bowed faces around the room. Leon was not bowing his head, and his eyes halted on mine as he noticed me staring at him. I couldn't help but glare at him. He quickly looked away. The prayer ended, and everyone began to stand up. My eyes followed Leon as he stood and made his way through the people rather quickly.

Valerie rose from her seat and stepped toward me. My heart began to pound as I watched Leon swiftly walk out the door.

Joseph looked over at me. "Your mother wants to stop at the house on the way out to pick up a few more things."

"Okay, I'll catch up with you outside," I said and grasped Valerie's hand for a moment. "I *need* to talk to Leon for a minute." Then I ran out the door and saw Leon standing across the road in front of the Mill smoking a cigarette.

"Hey, Leon," I said as I traipsed through the melting snow toward him.

Leon gave me a slight nod as he dragged on his cigarette. "What's going on?" he asked as the smoke seeped out the corner of his mouth and disappeared into the cold air.

"You looked like you were in a hurry to get out of there." I shoved my cold hands in my front pockets.

He dragged on his cigarette and stared at me out of the corner of his eye. "I was... Why?"

Thinking fast, I replied: "I just wanted to tell you that we're moving to Batavia."

"I heard." Leon flung his cigarette onto the ground. The orange tip sizzled for a second on the pile of muddy snow and then turned black.

The air between us became uncomfortably silent.

"That's probably a good idea for you and your family," Leon said calmly, without making eye contact with me, and then shoved his hands in his front pockets.

I nodded. "Yeah, with all that's happened..."

Leon stared directly into my eyes. "Yeah, they make it easy to get away with murder 'round here...

don't they? And Martha's death was just... just unlucky."

"And what the hell do you mean by *that*?" I could
feel the heat of my blood rush through my body and
up to my face.

He stood there staring at me with his eyes widened and his mouth slightly opened as if he'd said too
much.

"Did you have something to do with this?" I blurted out, raising my rigid voice. My chest tightened.
"Did *you* and *Felix* have something to do with their
murders?"

Leon nodded his head with a bold stare. "I've
already been questioned, Fritz... I was over at my
brother's house before the fire," he replied in a steady,
calm tone. "I helped him kill the skunk in his hen
house."

I felt the fire raging through my veins. The word
kill rang loud in my ears. It was as if he was giving
me a metaphor or something. "What did you do?" I
yelled as flashes of Travis, Helen, Martha, and Flo's
dead bodies flooded my mind. The next thing I knew,
we were on the ground, and I was on top of his chest,
socking him across the face over and over again.

"Get off of me," Leon yelled as he tried to push me
off. His face was covered in blood.

Then I felt two strong arms pull me off of him.

"Stop it, Fritz! Stop it!" Joseph shouted as he

pulled me away from him. Blood was pouring out of
Leon's nose, and his bottom lip was cut. He slowly
pushed himself up from the ground. His trousers were
soaked. Small chunks of ice were stuck to his trousers
and coat.

"Are you all right, Leon?" Joseph asked.

Leon reached up and wiped his nose. "What the
hell is wrong with you, Fritz?" He shook his head,
gave Joseph a quick look and a slight nod, and then
walked away.

Out of breath, my eyes fastened on Joseph's. "That
son of a bitch did it. I know it! It was him and his
brother."

Joseph stared into my eyes. "How do you know
that?"

"Fritz," Valerie cried out.

I turned and saw Valerie and my mother standing
at the edge of the road. Valerie was crying. My mother was staring at me with questions in her tear-filled
eyes. Uncle John had disappointment etched on his
face as he shook his head.

"That's what my gut is telling me, and... He just
told me that he was over at his brother's house helping him kill—"

"Kill what?" Joseph asked, staring into my eyes.

"A skunk in the hen house, but that's not what he
meant!" I replied. "It was the *way* he said it," I said,
clenching my teeth. "I *know* what he meant. And I *know*

what he was trying to say." I took a deep breath and looked down at my bloody hands.

Joseph shook his head with disapproval. Then he glanced back at my mother, Valerie, and Uncle John. "We'll be right there."

I walked over to the step of the Mill and picked up a wad of snow and cleaned off my hand, which was starting to hurt.

"It takes more than a gut feeling and the way someone answers a question to convict someone of murder, Frtiz," Joseph said, and then he shoved his hands into his long, dark coat pockets.

"Yeah, I'm sure it does," I said heatedly as we started to head toward my mother and Valerie. "But he was also the *last* one to see Travis alive. He's telling everyone that to taunt us... He was taunting me! And he's taunting the authorities! Don't you see that? Doesn't Keller see that?"

Joseph stopped, his eyes fastened on mine. "In a criminal case you need evidence that will hold up in court. Keller can't act on his theories and win the case without proof! That's how the justice system works, Fritz!"

I just stood there staring at him, feeling the fire pump through my veins. "They're going to get away with it," I said under my breath.

"I don't know what else to tell you," Joseph said, calmly.

We walked in silence for a moment. Then Joseph turned to me. "How's your hand?'

I fanned out my fingers and made a fist. "It's a little sore, but worth it."

"What are you going to say to them? They saw the whole thing."

I shrugged my shoulders. "Valerie and my mom know how Leon is. I'll just tell them he had it coming."

As we approached my mother, Valerie, and Uncle John, I glanced over at the Morgans' porch. Leon was cleaned up and standing by the door talking to Felix. I locked my eyes on Leon, waiting for him to look over at me. I could feel the fury burning in my blood. Felix caught my stare and nudged Leon. He gave me a quick look and turned away.

I knew that was the last time I'd see either of them—by choice.

Before Uncle John left to go back to the farm, he warned me not to let other people get the best of me. Then he gave me a hug and stepped into his car. He always gave me great advice.

On our way to the house, I thought about what Uncle John said, and I wavered between guilt and satisfaction for socking Leon. What bothered me the most was that they had to see it. I explained to Valerie and my mother that Leon had it coming for a while, and he said something that didn't set well with me, which

was nothing new to them. They were just glad that
I wasn't hurt. My mother believed that all that had
happened over the past few days was just too much
for me, and I took it out on Leon. She just wondered if
Leon was okay. I assured her that I saw him talking
to his brother when we were leaving, and he didn't
look like he was in too much pain, which made me
wish Joseph wasn't there to pull me off of him.

As soon as I stepped into our cold kitchen, I started a fire inside the wood stove. My mother and Joseph
headed straight to her bedroom to pack. I placed the
remainder of my modest belongings into a small crate,
and set it on the floor next to my father's shotguns
that I brought up from the basement. I then sat down
at the kitchen table, tired and drained.

Valerie followed me in from the parlor, carrying
my mother's sewing basket, and set it on the counter.
From behind, she put her hand on my shoulder. "I was
really scared when I saw you on the ground socking
Leon. What did he say, anyway?"

I reached over and placed my sore hand on top
of hers as she leaned over, wrapped her arms around
me, and kissed my cheek.

"He told me that when the fire started at the
Wilsons' he was over at his brother's house, and I just
started socking him. I knew he was lying. And I think
he wanted me to know."

"Do you really think—" Valerie sat down across

from me and reached for my hand.

"Yeah, I can't explain it, but yeah, I think he had something to do with it. I know he never liked the Wilsons and neither did Felix. And he said that Martha was just *unlucky*. What the hell was that supposed to mean?"

"I don't know... But that doesn't mean he killed them," Valerie said. "I've known them all of my life, and I don't believe—"

"Well someone we know killed them and Flo! It is someone here, and Leon heard what Anton said!" I could feel the heat inside me start to flare up.

"What did Joseph say? You told him what he said, didn't you?"

I nodded. "People don't get convicted on gut feelings."

Valerie took a deep breath. We sat there in silence for a minute. I could hear my mother and Joseph walking around upstairs.

"Maybe," I said. "I don't know... I was watching him standing by Martha's casket too. I know him, and he was *not* himself. It all added up in my mind."

"Try not to read too much into all of it. Aren't we all on edge?"

I stared at the table and nodded. "Yeah, I guess," I replied quietly. *Was I reading too much into Leon's behavior?* Deep down, I didn't think so. I knew exactly what he was telling me.

"So much loss, all at once—even this house."

I looked around the kitchen. "I'll miss it here. It's all just so sad."

"Do you want to stay?"

"No, not with an arrest record of zero out of five!" I said as I imagined Leon and Felix walking toward a police car, handcuffed. "I guess we're lucky to have another place to stay."

"I know what you mean by sad. But we have a lot of great memories to take with us."

I nodded. "We do."

"We're going to be city folks!" Valerie said with a little excitement, changing the subject.

"We'll have to find a new waterfall."

"Yes, we will." Valerie grinned.

I smiled with the realization that, after all that I had been through, a new start was exactly what I needed. I thought back to one of my conversations with Joseph. The idea of attending college began to interest me. I imagined myself blowing the dust off the shelves and the books inside my head and pulling them out.

Suddenly, I saw an image of a man wearing a bow-tie and glasses holding the last book I read, *The Great Quest* by Charles Hawes. He set the book down on his podium, fumbled with some papers, and looked up at me. "Let's talk about the book, shall we."

Twenty-Seven

"Fritz!"

I slowly opened my eyes. Then I saw the small light on my desk was still on.

"Fritz!" Joseph called.

"Yeah," I answered in a raspy voice while reaching into the front pocket of my trousers. I yanked out my pocket watch and waited for my eyes to focus. It read 6:40, and I realized that I must have dozed off for a few minutes. I sat up, rubbed my eyes, and shuffled over to my bedroom doorway.

"Did you just wake up?" Joseph asked from the bottom of the stairs. I noticed that he was holding the newspaper.

"Yeah, I must've nodded off."

"Valerie and your mom are in the kitchen making supper. My parents just left to have dinner with some friends of theirs. Why don't you come down?" Joseph gestured with the folded newspaper. "I have something you'll want to read," he said in a steady, eager tone.

The stillness of his words set off a panic in my head. My heart rate began to speed up. *What? What happened now?* I ran down the stairs, followed Joseph into the office, and closed the door.

"Do you want a drink?" Joseph asked as he set the newspaper in front of the bottle and poured a glass of bourbon. Then he handed me a glass that was filled halfway.

"For some reason, I think I'm going to need one." My hand began to shake as I reached for the glass. "Tell me what happened."

"Here, sit down, and I'll tell you. No one got hurt or anything, so you can relax."

A little more at ease, I sat down on the sofa. "Well, that's good." I brought the glass to my lips and sipped down the friendly amber liquid.

Joseph picked up the paper sitting next to the bottle and sipped his drink as he glanced down at the newspaper. Then he swung the leather chair around to face me, sat down, set his glass on the table, and fixed his eyes on mine.

"Someone's lying about the gun they own." He picked up his drink and held it near his lips. "The ballistic comparisons were completed from the triple homicide. So, anyone owning a .32 was checked for a match, and no matches were made."

"What're you talking about?"

"Here, read." Joseph handed me the *Daily News.*

My veins turned to ice as I read the headline. *"Firing of a Bullet through Train Window Adds to Linden Terror."* The subhead read, *"Shooting may have been another Fiendish Act of the Murderer."* Feeling flustered with my blood pumping harder, I read the article and set the paper on the table. I took two large gulps of my drink, finished it, and handed the glass back to Joseph. My empty stomach sent the bourbon directly to my veins. Minutes later, the amber liquid did its job; it numbed me.

"Another?" he asked, rising from his seat.

I nodded.

"Here." He filled my glass, handed it to me, and then sat back down. He picked up the paper and began to read aloud. "The captain thought that it was possible, or even very likely, that it was the murderer that shot at the train, and that the fiend did it to embarrass the officials and continue to scare the residents of Linden."

"I guess he accomplished it!" I snapped.

Joseph nodded. "That he did." He set the paper down on the table between us.

I sat there for a moment and looked over at Joseph. "That's exactly something Leon would do! And he owns a lot of guns!" I took a drink from my glass. "It's a game to Leon, and he's winning."

"Don't worry; *he* won't be winning for long." Joseph finished his drink and filled his glass again.

"You're assuming the officials will catch *him*," I said as I began to follow Joseph's lead by not using Leon's name because I was guessing that would turn my theory into a fact.

"Fritz, I'm just trying to stay positive."

"I'm trying to stay positive, too. And the more days that go by, the more positive I am that *he or they* won't be caught." I took another sip from my glass. My thoughts made their way through my lips more easily with each drink.

Joseph had a blank expression on his face. He seemed at a loss for words, probably because he knew that I was right.

"*He* was sending us all a message—*he* can do whatever he wants and get away with it," I said.

"Well, as soon as the troopers received the call, they headed right to Belknap Crossing. They probably missed him by a few minutes." Joseph sat back down and loosened his bow tie. "It's too bad that they didn't find anything." He pulled his bow tie off and reached over and placed it on the desk behind him.

He picked up the newspaper again and read. "It happened at about 7:30, so it was just getting dark. A few of the people on the train said that they saw a dark figure step from behind the huge signboard along the tracks. They saw the flashes from the gunfire. One woman sitting at the back of the train mentioned seeing the figure running toward Linden into the trees, not far from the bridge."

Leaning back on the sofa with the glass in my hand, I closed my eyes for a moment and saw a shadow by the bridge, a fiend that tormented and killed for amusement—and that *figure* looked just like Leon. I opened my eyes as the bourbon melted away the images of the shattered skulls, the charred bodies, and the shadow.

Twenty-Eight
1985

The warm, moist breeze brushed past me and gently swayed the wooden blinds that were hanging on the side of the porch as my granddaughter, Jenna, pulled into our driveway. Noise blasted from her 1978 burnt orange and white topped Thunderbird.

The sound stopped, and she smiled, waved, and stepped out of her car. She was wearing frayed blue jean shorts and a tight, black T-shirt with the word "Scorpions" written in metallic silver across the front. Her long blonde hair caught the breeze as she walked up the front sidewalk.

"What's that racket coming from your car?" I asked, shaking my head with distaste.

"Racket, what racket?" she asked, and then began to laugh as she ascended the porch steps. "That's the Scorpions, Grandpa. That was my favorite song, 'The Zoo.'" She shook her head with a grin. "I just saw them in concert." She pulled on the side of her shirt. "I bought this shirt there."

I nodded. "Never heard of 'em," I said. "So is that what you kids call music these days?"

"Yep! It is," she replied with a lively grin, and sat

down on the white wicker chair to the right of me.

"You shouldn't drive with your music blaring like that; you won't be able to hear an ambulance or fire truck coming."

Jenna smiled. "I only turned it up for that song."

"Song? I didn't hear any singing."

"Oh, Grandpa," she sighed. "Where's Grandma?"

"She's in the house making cookies," I said, look-ing over at her pretty face and sparkling blue eyes. I noticed how much she was beginning to resemble my daughter, Christine, and Valerie when they were younger. "You know, you're looking more like your mother every day."

Jenna laughed a little. "I've heard that a lot late-ly."

"So, are you all done with college?"

"Yep, I handed in my last paper today. I'm all done!" she replied happily.

"So then, you're all done with GCC now?"

She nodded. "Yep!"

"Well, congratulations!" I nodded. "That's a big accomplishment. You should be proud of yourself." I knew that I had said it before, but it deserved to be repeated.

"It does feel good to be done," she said with a grin.

"Your mom told me that you're not transferring anywhere?"

"Not yet. I'm going to take a year off and just work

at La Ponta's until I can decide what I want to major in."

"That's probably a smart idea." I nodded. "So what brings you over here on this nice afternoon?"

"I came over here to talk to you."

I gazed at her for a moment with curiosity. "Oh, yeah, about what?"

"When I handed in my last paper for my American Lit course, I ended up talking to my professor for a while. She started telling me about the research she's doing for a novel that she's going to write."

"Oh, yeah?"

"Yeah, it sounded really interesting, and I thought you may remember the news stories when you were young."

"I might have... So what's her novel about?"

"The Linden Murders," she replied with enthusiasm.

I sat there speechless for a moment, frozen as an icy chill hit the center of my stomach. It was not the reply I was expecting.

"She was telling me that they were never solved," Jenna continued.

Feeling a bit taken aback, the images began to flash in my head. The dust-covered trunk—filled with all that needed to be forgotten, pushed back to the deepest part of my mind—slid forward.

"I can't believe that I've lived in Batavia all my

life and never heard anything about them until today." She fixed her attentive eyes on me as if I had more to add to the story. "Where's Linden, anyway?"

"It's near Bethany—not far from the Genesee County Park... Your grandmother and I grew up in that area," I replied, wondering where this conversation was going and how far I was willing to take it. Valerie and I had agreed to leave what had happened buried in the past. It was too painful for us to talk about, especially for me. After moving to Batavia, we'd married and had three children: Marianne, Jimmy, and then Christine. After our wedding, we never talked about the murders again.

I turned to my inquisitive granddaughter, who was wide-eyed and attentive. "Jenna, you have to remember that was back in the twenties. Most of the people involved have been gone for years, so I'm not surprised that you never heard about it. I'm sure you're not the only one."

"Yeah, I sorta figured that. It was a long time ago... But my professor knows a lot. She told me that there were five murders, and one of them was a triple murder—how *totally* awful!"

I nodded as the image of the three charred, bloody bodies on the bedroom floor flashed in my head. I placed my hand on the arm of the wicker chair and uneasily adjusted my position.

"So, I figured that you'd probably remember hearing about them."

"What's your professor's name?"

"Professor Hollenbeck. She's really nice."

"She must be new. I don't remember anyone by that name working in the department."

"Grandpa," Jenna said gently with a slight grin. "I'm sure there're several new professors working in the department since you retired. You retired ten years ago."

The screen door opened. Valerie walked out, wearing her house dress and floral apron, which was covered in flour. "Jenna," Valerie's eyes brightened. "I didn't know you were out here. This is a nice surprise."

"Hi, Grandma!"

She strolled over to Jenna; she leaned over to hug her, and then kissed her cheek. "You're just in time. I'm baking some chocolate chip cookies. The first batch will be done in about ten minutes; you can take some home with you."

"Thank you! I've always loved your chocolate chip cookies."

"Would you like something to drink, Jenna? Lemonade or ice tea?"

"I'll have a glass of lemonade with lots of ice, please," Jenna replied.

"Fritz?"

"I'll get my own drink." I stood up from my seat.

"I'll be right back," I said to Jenna and stepped into the house.

Valerie headed into the kitchen. I headed over to my desk. My hand began to tremble as I opened the drawer and grabbed my bottle of bourbon that was lying next to my tarnished pocket watch that had died decades ago. *I never expected to be having this conversation with my granddaughter.* Beads of sweat began to form on my forehead as I prepared myself. I heard Valerie turn the faucet on as I wandered over to the hutch in the dining room and reached for a rock glass that was sitting on the bottom shelf. Trying to stay out of her view, I set the glass on the dining room table and poured the clear, dark amber liquid into my glass.

With my glass in hand, I quietly placed the bourbon back into the drawer. I took a sip and set my glass down next to my electric typewriter before opening up the bottom desk drawer and lifting the lid of my wooden box. The one I found in my attic before I moved to Batavia in 1924.

I stared at my cherished fox trap for a moment; my last birthday present from my father. Luckily, I was able to retrieve it from the woods after the snow melted back in 1924, after my mother and I moved in with Joseph's parents. I had to drink a few glasses of bourbon before I could enter those woods again. I dug around for a little while and finally found it. It was rusted and buried in the brush, still sitting next to the rock I hid behind. Quietly, I shut the box, pushed it to the back of the drawer, and grabbed the manuscript that was lying beneath it, the one I had spent years laboring over and had long since tried to forget. As I picked up my glass, I held the draft of my novel in my hand. *Today or never...* Sipping my drink, I headed back outside. I opened the door and saw Jenna sitting patiently. Feeling my heart racing, I set my manuscript down on the small table and set my glass down next to it.

Valerie opened the door. "Freshly squeezed," she said cheerfully as she handed Jenna a glass of lemonade that was filled to the top with ice, as per her request. "I'll be right back with the cookies." She turned and her eyes locked on my glass of bourbon. Then she gave me a heated look.

"Where did that come from?" Her tone was serious.

I shook my head. "Not a word," I said quietly.

She looked over at Jenna. "If you don't mind me asking, what are you two talking about, anyway?" she asked curtly.

"The Linden Murders," Jenna replied with eagerness and innocence.

Valerie nodded slightly with her eyes fixed on mine. "Fritz, can I see you for a minute? Inside?"

I took a sip of my drink and set it back down. "I'll be right back, Jenna. Sit tight."

As I stepped inside the house, Valerie shut the door and looked directly into my eyes. "You told me that after you finished your manuscript there would be no more drinking. I'm not going to put up with it again! Do you understand, Fritz?" Her eyes were angered and moist. "I've had enough."

I took a deep breath and shook my head, thinking of what to say.

"After living through all the pain, I never understood why you wanted to relive it."

"I had to!' I said, slightly raising my voice while trying not to let Jenna hear me. "You'll never understand." And I knew she never would. "I had to relive those horrific memories to deal with them, sort through them, and finally put them to rest on paper. It was my way of metaphorically removing them from my head. And it has helped me. It has helped me a lot."

"Really? It has helped you?" Valerie asked in a loud whisper. "I don't know how drinking yourself into a stupor and sitting in front of your typewriter, crying at times, has helped you!" She stared at me with reddened, pain-filled eyes. "It makes no sense!" She leaned over and looked out the front window. "Can't you talk to Jenna about it without the drinking?"

I stared directly into her eyes. "No!" I grabbed the doorknob and opened the door. "It's the only way I'll get through the conversation."

With her arms folded and shaking her head in disgust, I stepped out the door and looked over at Jenna, who was patiently waiting.

"What did Grandma want?"

"Nothing that you need to concern yourself with," I replied and sat back down.

"So do you remember anything about the murders?"

I nodded. "Yeah, I remember them."

"How old were you back then?"

I thought for a moment. "How old are you now?"

"I'll be twenty this fall."

"I was a little younger than you. They happened over a period of a few years."

"It must have been a huge news story around here."

"It was." I nodded as I grabbed my drink and took another sip. Jenna was eagerly listening to every word. "My stepfather actually worked as an attorney in the Genesee County District Attorney's office. He worked for Keller: District Attorney Keller was his name. He was in charge of the case."

"Your stepdad worked there?" Jenna's eyes widened. "So you must know a lot about the murders then."

"Well, he wasn't the attorney on the case. He was fairly new when the murders happened. Keller was a seasoned attorney; he handled the big cases."

"Did he ever talk with you about the murders?"

"We had some conversations, but they were main-ly about what was in the newspaper."

"So the murders have gone unsolved all these years?"

I nodded as the screen door opened. "Here you go." Valerie set the plate on top of my manuscript. The aroma of the moist chocolate chip cookies filled the warm air and hovered next to me. She gave me a quick check with her narrowed eyes as I held my drink.

"Thank you, Grandma." Jenna sipped her lemon-ade and grabbed a cookie off the plate.

I brought the glass to my lips and nipped on the bourbon.

"So they were never solved?" she asked again.

I shook my head and swallowed. "No, they weren't. And people were upset, scared, and angry."

"I would be, too." Jenna bit into the cookie, leaving a trace of warm chocolate on her top lip. "So did they have any suspects?"

"Yeah; they ended up putting your grandmother's step-brother, Junior, who you may remember us talking about on occasion, in jail for a couple of weeks, but then they had to let him out because the officials didn't have any evidence to hold him on."

I glanced over at Jenna. Her eyes were wide. "I had no idea," she whispered.

I nodded. "I know you didn't." I sipped my drink. "People liked to single him out because he kept to himself. Also, he didn't attend any of the victims' funerals. So they thought they had their man—but they didn't."

"At least they let him out. Once in a while you hear about innocent people spending years in prison."

"Then there was a confession. It was all over the newspapers and the radio that a man confessed to the murders."

"Someone confessed? Really?"

"He was one of the professional confessors. The officials had to actually convince him that he didn't do it. He wasn't even in the same city when the murders were committed."

"I never heard of someone confessing to a murder that they didn't commit."

"Oh yeah, there're people out there missing a few marbles up there." I pointed to my head and took another swig of bourbon.

"More like missing a whole jar full of marbles," Jenna said and started to laugh before taking another bite of her cookie.

"And years later there were the suicides," I said softly as my thoughts began to flow more fluidly from the smooth bourbon. After I said it, my last memory of Leon and Felix standing on the Morgans' store porch flashed in my mind.

"Suicides?" Jenna's eyes widened.

I nodded and held two fingers up. "And they were brothers: the Chapman brothers, Leon and Felix... And Leon was once a friend of mine. Well, they were both friends of mine, but Felix was older, and I didn't see him as much as I did Leon."

"That's terrible! Did they do it at the same time?"

"No, several years apart. In the mid-1930s, Leon Chapman shot himself. He was young... I think he was in his thirties when he died."

"Do you think he had anything to do with the murders?"

I pressed my lips together and nodded. "My gut feeling was that they did... As it turned out, Leon bragged about being the last person to see Travis Wilson alive on the night of the triple murder. But what makes it even more suspicious was that his older brother, Felix, also shot himself. That happened in the 1970s—forty years later. It leaves me with even more suspicion about them."

"Did they leave notes confessing to anything?"

I shook my head, "No. I think Leon left a note as to who would get his money. But that's it." I finished my drink and set it on the table. "There was some talk about them. The Chapman family didn't like Helen Wilson because she was a busybody. She was one of the victims of the triple murder—Travis Wilson's wife. Travis was also one of the victims. The other victim was Martha Morgan. The officials figured that she walked in on the murderer or murderers."

"I wonder if my professor knows any of this. She showed me a stack of files that she had—copies of the newspaper articles, court transcripts, a bunch of stuff—and she also said that she had photos from the murder scenes."

"Did you read any of it, or look at the photos?" I asked.

"No, I didn't even think to ask. She must have had between fifteen and twenty files stacked on her desk. I'll just wait to read her book."

"I would imagine there is a lot to go through."

The screen door opened again. "Can I get either one of you a refill?"

I picked up my glass and nodded. "I'll take another. It's in the top right desk drawer."

Valerie came over to me. I felt the heat from her stare as she grabbed my glass.

"I'm all set, Grandma. Thank you anyway. Your cookies are *totally* awesome!"

"Thank you, Jenna. So, was your grandfather able to tell you anything interesting?" Her eyes rested on me as she spoke.

"Yes: he told me about the false confession and the brothers that committed suicide."

Valerie turned to Jenna. "The reporters kept the news story going for years. People connected to the case would end up in the newspaper on occasion. The reporters would always make connections to the murders with the officials involved every chance they could for the readers because it was such a big news story. And it was a constant reminder to everyone. But over the years, the news stories slowly stopped."

"I can't believe that I never heard anything about the murders. My mother never mentioned it. Did you ever talk about it with my mom?"

Valerie turned to me. "I don't recall the kids ever asking about it. Do you, Fritz?"

I shook my head. "No, I don't either."

"And it's not a pleasant subject, so it wasn't something we would have brought up. My timer will be going off any minute. I better get back in there." Valerie looked at me. "Another? Are you sure?"

I nodded, pressing my lips together. I lifted up the plate of cookies so that I could pick up my manuscript from underneath, and then handed it to Jenna.

"What's this?"

"It's my manuscript."

"I was wondering what you brought out here." Jenna looked down at the front page. "*Shadow by the Bridge*," she read in a whisper.

As she flipped through the manuscript, I was taken back to Linden. I could hear the sounds of the tranquil waterfall layered with the rustling of the leaves. The moon hung in the sky, streaming its rays down the hill and across the bridge. A dark figure stepped out of the trees and headed toward the bridge. I looked hard to see who it was: Leon, Felix, or Anton? Maybe it was all of them, or maybe there was a slight chance that it wasn't any of them, but someone who I have never suspected.

Valerie reluctantly handed me my glass of bourbon. I took a couple of sips. Sip by sip, the painful memories began to liquefy and drift away—once again.

<u>Sources and Suggestions for Further Reading</u>

Brown, William. *The Linden Murders: Unsolved!* New
York: Hodgins Printing Co., Inc.1984. Print

"Firing of a Bullet Through Train Window Adds to
Linden Terror." *The Daily News* 21 March 1924:
2. Print

"Kimball Murder Inquiry Exonerates Some Persons;
Search Being Continued." *The Daily News* 25
October 1922: 1. Print

Kurek, Albert S. *The Troopers Are Coming: New York State
Troopers 1917-1943*. New York: Rooftop
Publishing; 1st edition, 2007. Print

"Linden Triple Slayer Eludes Net." *The Daily News* 12
March 1924: 1. Print

The People of the State of New York v. John Doe. Court
transcript, Genesee Country History
Department, Batavia, N.Y.

"Witness in Linden Death Probe Dies of Self-Inflicted
Wound Coroner Defers Verdict in Case." *The
Daily News* 1 June 1936: 1. Print

During the years 1917 and 1924, a series of murders known as the Linden murders occurred in the vicinity of Linden, New York. The gruesome killings brought fear and panic to the western New York area. The news of the homicides appeared in the headlines of the Batavia Daily News as well as making the national news circuit. However, the news was not able to convey the deep effects that the murders had on the people who called Linden their home.

On November 12, 1917, a woman was killed in a small wooded area of Frank and Grace Hunt's farm. Witnesses living along Route 63 in Batavia, New York described seeing a couple walk past their house arguing shortly before 11:00 AM that day. Approximately thirty-minutes later, the man was seen running alone toward Batavia.

A few days later, Frank Hunt was out gathering firewood on his farm and found the woman's body lying in what appeared to be a shallow grave. Her face was destroyed.

During the investigation, it was determined that several witnesses at the Lehigh Train Station in Batavia saw the couple. It was never determined where the couple traveled from.

Investigators made every attempt to identify the woman through two showings at the H.E. Turner Funeral Home along with items found at the crime scene believed to belong to the victim. The authorities also received several letters about missing relatives. However, the letters failed to help investigators determine the woman's identity. After all of the attempts to identify her, the woman known as "Ruth" was buried in the

Batavia Cemetery.

In the late afternoon of October 17, 1922 in the hamlet of Linden, seventy-three-year-old Francine (Franc) Kimball's body was found in her fruit cellar by the authorities. Earlier that day, Franc's neighbors noticed that she wasn't outside tending to her small farm as she always did and discovered that no one had seen her since 5:30 PM the day before, so they searched her property and proceeded to enter her locked home. Her neighbors discovered that her home had not been disturbed. With no sign of Franc Kimball, they attempted to make a call only to learn that her phone wires had been severed. Alarmed by the finding, the New York State Police were called.

During the investigation, the residents of Linden were questioned, vagrants who were seen within a ten-mile radius of the hamlet were arrested and charged with vagrancy. The closest possible motive was a comment made by Andrew Michaels after he found out that Franc Kimball told the dry agents that he was making and selling hard cider. He said: "Someone ought to kill old lady Kimball." District Attorney Kelly interviewed the residents and then held a John Doe Proceeding to determine who murdered Franc Kimball. It appeared that the two most likely suspects Gideon Kettle Junior, who worked for Franc on occasion, and Andrew Michaels both had alibis leaving the murder unsolved.

Seventeen months after the brutal murder of Francine Kimball, on the evening of March 11, 1924, three more residents of Linden were killed in a triple homicide. The owner of the Morse General Store, fifty-one-year-old Mabel Morse, her close friends and neighbors, fifty-six-year-old Hattie Whaley and her husband, sixty-five-year-old Thomas Whaley were found in a pile covered with kerosene soaked rags, rugs, and paper smoldering in the first-floor bedroom of the Whaley home. The autopsies determined that Thomas Whaley was shot several times, Hattie Whaley died from one gunshot to the face just below her eye, and Mabel Morse died as a result of being beaten with an adz handle.

The authorities proceeded with their investigation and theories of a motive. Some believed that the motivation for the killings was the result of a robbery. While others believed that there was a crazed killer who traveled the railroad killing at will. The local residents were interviewed and then interviewed again. In the end, the investigation did not result in any solid leads. However, law enforcement was convinced that the perpetrator of the crimes was a local resident who knew the habits of their neighbors in the close-knit community.

In telling the story of the Linden murders, I've taken the liberty to tell the account through my fictional character, Fritz Reynolds. Other fictional characters include Ella Reynolds, Uncle John, Joseph O'Hara, Dr. O'Hara, and Genevie O'Hara. All of the other characters are based on the residents who lived in Linden during that time period.

Through my research of the court documents, voices and personalities of those interviewed as well as the opinions given of each other became somewhat apparent. Hattie Whaley was known as the town's gossip. Gideon Kettle Junior had the reputation for being socially awkward. Andrew Michaels had a poor reputation due to his trouble with the law for petty crimes and cursing at his neighbors. I used the information to develop their characters.

I made the decision to change the names of the residents of Linden because in essence, they are a work of fiction. Other than the fragments of information that I was able to gather about Hattie Whaley, Gideon Kettle Junior, and Andrew Michaels, they are fictionalized characters who were created in the image of who I thought they might have been and not who they actually were in real life.

Over the years, I have read a number of court documents and newspaper articles. I also viewed several disturbing photographs of the crime scenes. I could only imagine the deep sense of loss and the terror that the residents of this close-knit community felt. Beyond the court documents, the headlines, and photographs, there was a story to tell… It was their story…

Suzanne Zewan
October 2017

Acknowledgements

I would like to express my sincere appreciation to the many people who traveled with me through my book writing journey; to all those who gave their support, conversed, read drafts, offered comments, assisted in the editing, proofreading, and the design of my novel.

I would like to thank my publisher, Mark Pogodzinski, who believed in my book and guided me through each step of the process. I would also like to thank my editors, Lore McSpadden, Sarah Paige, and Valerie Dimino for their input and expertise.

I would like to thank Roslyn Fishbaugh for your never ending encouragement and support from my initial idea to write this story. I carried your words: "You have to write this story" with me down each path, detour, and dead end until I reached this destination. And because fate stepped in, I would like to thank DJ Smith for reminding me that "Writers write" when I lost my way for a period of time.

I would like to thank Susan Conklin, the Genesee County Historian and Judy Stiles, the Genesee County Research Assistant for all of their assistance with the files and providing copies of court documents, photos, and newspaper articles.

I would like to thank one of my dearest friends, Laura Lewis for her never-ending support and for reading each chapter as I wrote them.

Thank you to my review team: Robbi Hess, Catherine Pelino-Curry, Judith Sobresky, and Jaime Brade for their interest in my novel and for reading my initial proof with a keen eye.

Last but not least: thank you to those who have been with me over the course of the years and whose names I have failed to mention.

Above all, I want to thank my husband, Bill and my son, Trevor, and the rest of my family, who traveled this voyage with me—even though the destination was uncertain.

About the Author

Suzanne Zewan is coordinator at Genesee Valley Educational Partnership and is an adjunct professor at Buffalo State College. She has a M.A. in English and Creative Writing and a M.S.Ed. in Career and Technical Education. Other publications include a poem in Jigsaw (2014), a short story and two poems in Jigsaw (2016), and a short story in Amaranth Review (2016).

www.ingramcontent.com/pod-product-compliance
Lightning Source LLC
Chambersburg PA
CBHW072322280626
47159CB00027B/256